LOVING
THE HAWKE

LANA WILLIAMS

AUTHOR'S NOTE

Thank you for reading LOVING THE HAWKE, the first full length story in The Seven Curses of London series. If you haven't yet read the Earl of Warenton's story, who is mentioned in this book, I invite you to read TRUSTING THE WOLFE, the novella that begins the series.

The Seven Curses of London was written by James Greenwood and published in 1869. Much like Lettie, I found the information in the book both fascinating and horrifying. The conditions in London at the time were appalling. Luckily, authors like Greenwood and Josephine Butler did their best to shed light on the problems though solving them took decades and continues to be battled today, as they are in many cities throughout the world. History has a funny way of repeating itself sometimes, don't you think?

The first chapter in Greenwood's book focuses on neglected children. I look forward to exploring the other chapters of the Seven Curses with you in the upcoming books in this series. Can you guess whose story is next?

Happy Reading!

Lana

ACKNOWLEDGMENTS

Much credit for this story goes to my critique partners, Michelle Major, Lani Joramo, and Robin Nolet. Thank you for your amazing suggestions. And another thank you to my beta readers, Linda Benning, Sarah Billing, and Lauren Billing. Your feedback is priceless!

Reviews help authors tremendously and also help other readers find books, so please consider leaving a review. They are much appreciated, and I read them all.

More historical romances are coming your way!

CHAPTER ONE

"It is a startling fact that, in England and Wales alone, at the present time, the number of children under the age of sixteen, dependent more or less on the parochial authorities for maintenance, amounts to three hundred and fifty thousand."
~*The Seven Curses of London, I. Neglected Children*
By James Greenwood, 1869

London, England, June 1870

Letitia Fairchild's stomach fluttered with nerves as she walked toward Blackfriars Bridge, wondering if she was truly capable of completing her mission. The bridge's polished red granite pillars and ornamental stone parapets were attractive, and the view of St. Paul's Cathedral was magnificent, as promised. But that was not what had brought her to this rather undesirable part of central London just before noon on a mild June day.

To her surprise, being here was a much different experience than reading about it. Warehouses and factories lined the River Thames to the south while a mix of homes, shops, and additional warehouses stood on the north.

She couldn't help but place her gloved hand over her

nose. The stench emanating from the river would be far worse in another month when the warm weather ripened the smell of sewage, industrial waste, and factory smoke, creating an even stronger fetor. The streets were dirty here, and the people passing by weren't the type with whom she normally bumped elbows. These men and women made their living working hard and had never attended The Derby or ridden on Rotten Row. Their clothing was simple and worn, their faces pale and tired. The general desperation and dreariness of the neighborhood took her aback.

She felt as out of place here as she did in the many ballrooms of which she'd graced the walls during her five Seasons. Seasons that had begun with hope but quickly faded to embarrassment, now leaving her resigned to spinsterhood. Mostly.

Yet she forced herself to march forward, uncertainty plaguing her every step. Today was the day she'd finally have a purpose, a reason for her existence beyond caring for her four younger sisters.

She'd planned this outing carefully. Midday was surely the safest time to be in the area. A few people walked across the bridge but none she sought. She wished she'd brought her pin watch though she'd decided against doing so to avoid catching the attention of unsavory characters. Her maid and footman waited with the carriage several streets from here, where they thought she browsed in a bookstore. The plain cloak she wore covered her modest but fashionable gown.

As a sudden throng of young girls crossed the bridge, rushing directly toward her, she realized the time for luncheon had arrived. Based on her research, they were between the ages of ten and thirteen, though many appeared much younger. Lettie searched for a target to approach but had no idea how to choose. A few of the girls passing by caught her gaze but quickly glanced away as though to avoid her. She frowned. How could she make them see she was here to help? With four younger sisters, she thought she knew girls well, yet none of these were acting as she'd expected. Perhaps it would be best if she approached a younger one who might be less guarded.

"Excuse me," she said, giving a friendly smile to one with a thin face and a long braid down her back.

"Leave off," the girl said with a snarl.

"Oh." Lettie froze, shocked at the response.

Now she stood directly in the path of the girls and many jostled her as they hurried past on their way to eat a 'meager luncheon' prior to returning to their 'jobs in factories or slop-shops', according to the book she'd studied. Lettie wasn't clear what exactly a slop-shop was. The name sounded less than appealing, but that was of little consequence. Surely one or two of these girls would welcome the chance for a different life.

Lettie pursed her lips, still determined to complete her objective of finding one of London's 'neglected children' to aid. She glanced about and selected another girl to approach.

"Excuse me," she tried again, half-expecting another abrupt response.

Instead, the girl paused, her brown gaze searching Lettie's face. "What is it? Are ye lost?"

The odd question gave her pause. Did she look as out of place as she felt? It seemed she couldn't mask her ineptitude here any better than she could at a ball. "No. I—I've come to offer my assistance." She wasn't quite certain what else to say. The conversation had never progressed this far in her mind.

"With what?" The girl's eyes narrowed with suspicion.

"Whatever you might need. Do you consider yourself a 'neglected child'?"

"A what?" The girl drew back a step, her body stiffening as caution filled her pale, thin face.

Lettie tried again, growing more uncertain by the moment. "Can I help you in some way?"

"What are ye about?" Two older girls paused to hear what Lettie was saying. "Why are ye botherin' little Alice?"

"I'm terribly sorry. I'm saying this all wrong." Lettie searched for a way to offer help without insulting or frightening the girl. "I'm here to offer an apprenticeship to one or two of you. My dressmaker is in need of two young women who are hard working, honest individuals interested in making a better life for themselves."

"A dressmaker?" one of the older girls asked. "Ha. Is she one of those la-de-da women who pretends to have a Frenchie accent?" She held out her hand, little finger lifted and pursed her lips to exaggerate her cheekbones.

The other girl snorted with laughter. "That's a good one. I heard tell those sort of dressmakers will work yer fingers to the bone."

The confidence of these girls as well as their camaraderie sent a pang of envy through Lettie. Neither of those attributes had ever been within her reach. She'd served more as a mother than a friend to her sisters, and somehow, the chance to make friends of her own had slipped by.

The younger girl, Alice, ignored her companions and studied Lettie closely. "Are ye fer real askin' or just fishin' for girls to sell?"

"What?" Lettie blinked rapidly, shocked the girl would think such a thing. "No, of course not. I am trying to find a child to help. One who is being forced to work in a factory against her will."

"Yeah, sure ye are. We're all workin' against our will, ain't we?" The blonde girl tugged on Alice's sleeve. "I wouldn't be trustin' her as far as I could toss her."

"Me neither." The other one agreed. "Ye know what the Widow Marcel says."

The two older girls looked at each other and said in unison, "If'n it sounds too good to be true, it likely is."

Alice scowled in disappointment. "I suppose ye're right. Though I ain't bad with a needle and thread." A far off look came into her eyes, as if she could see herself living a different life than the one she had.

Lettie recognized that look. She'd seen in it the mirror more times than she could count. It urged her on, making her even more determined to convince Alice she could have a better life. This was her chance to make a difference, and she wasn't about to let it slip through her fingers. "Alice, I'm speaking the truth." Lettie smiled at the girl as she reached out to smooth the collar of her smocked dress. "I have a valid opportunity. Allow me to explain."

Nathaniel Hawke, unwillingly retired captain of Her Majesty's Royal Navy, couldn't believe his eyes. Considering all he'd witnessed during the Indian Rebellion, the Second Opium War and his military service afterward, that was a considerable feat.

Yet no matter how hard he stared at the cloaked figure speaking with several girls near the end of the bridge, it didn't change what was happening. A well-to-do woman was accosting several young girls who'd crossed the bridge, leaving their factory jobs for a quick meal before returning to work. She was about to ruin an entire week's worth of reconnaissance.

He'd positioned himself in the deep doorway of a shop several doors down from the bridge entrance. His attire was something his butler had reluctantly procured for him when he'd decided upon this mission a week ago. The roughly woven, tweed jacket had seen better days as had the brown trousers, but they served the purpose of allowing him to better blend into the street. He'd hoped to identify the men said to be luring girls from their factory jobs with the promise of higher and easier wages as a house maid, only to put them on ships to be sold as slaves and prostitutes in faraway lands or to serve in London brothels.

Instead, a lady, by the fitted cut of her cloak, was drawing far too much attention by attempting to speak to the young women crossing the bridge. What on earth was she about? If one of the men he was trying to find observed her, she would be in grave danger. She might very well find herself on board a ship alongside the girls to whom she was speaking.

Nathaniel waited several precious moments, hoping the woman would proceed on her way. But no. She continued to speak earnestly with the girls. Several more stopped to listen to the conversation.

That was the last straw. The crazed woman was ruining his chances of identifying the men running this operation, which would allow him to save the girls. Now he'd have to take the risk of revealing himself in order to force her to move along before something terrible occurred.

As he stepped out of the doorway, cane in hand, he once again cursed the damaged leg that caused him to limp. It was the reason he'd been driven from his previous life where he'd made a difference. Its constant ache was an unwelcome reminder that he could no longer protect his men, that he was no longer needed.

He thrust aside the dark thoughts as he tried to decide how to play this particular mission. He'd been forced to disguise himself on various operations during his military career, so while this was nothing new to him, he didn't care to do draw attention to himself in a place he wanted to return to. *Blast the woman.*

Out of the corner of his eye, Nathaniel caught sight of a man strolling toward the bridge. With his bowler hat and better-than-most attire, he might very well be one of those Nathaniel had been watching for. *Double blast.*

Nathaniel had nearly reached the woman. Her face was hidden by a fawn-colored bonnet with a ridiculous bow on the side of it. He took an immediate dislike to the ugly thing.

"Excuse me," he said, with a slight bow to the group. "May I have a word with ye, miss?" He did his best to disguise his accent, not wanting to display his Cambridge education.

The woman turned in surprise as the side of her bonnet had blocked his approach. For some reason, he was stunned by how attractive she was. Large hazel eyes framed by dark blonde lashes and brows regarded him suspiciously. Her alabaster complexion was flawless with the exception of a tiny dent in her chin. "No, thank you." Her tone was polite but firm before she turned back to the girls.

"Beggin' yer pardon, but I must insist." Her refusal made it difficult to hide his irritation. His position as an officer for so many years meant no one refused his orders. At least until now.

She glanced at him again, brow furrowed. Then she looked back at her audience. "Do any of you know this man?"

"No," they all agreed as they stared at Nathaniel. They seemed to be waiting to see what might happen next.

"There's no loiterin' in this area," he persisted. "Ye need to be movin' along." He gestured with his hand, hoping the girls would continue on their way so he might have a moment with the woman to explain the danger in which she'd placed herself.

The older girls tugged on the younger one's sleeve. "Come along with ye, Alice. This don't concern us."

"Wait," the woman said, sparing a moment to glare yet again at Nathaniel. "If you're truly interested, here's the card of the shop I mentioned."

Alice reached out a cautious hand to take it, staring at it as though it might contain a hidden message. "I don't know..."

"Think upon it. That's all—"

Nathaniel snatched the card from the girl's hand to read it. *Madame Daphne. Seamstress.* "What is it ye're askin' these girls to do?" he asked, allowing suspicion to color his tone.

"None of your business. Please continue on your way." The woman seized the card from him then made a shooing motion. As if that would have any effect on him.

"Ye're causin' trouble for these poor girls," he said and turned to glare at them, hoping it would work better on them than it had on the woman. "Why don't ye leave them in peace?"

"We must be goin'." The girls eased back, pulling Alice with them, but not before she took the card from the lady once more.

"Wait. Please," the woman bid them. "I only want to help."

With one last glance over their shoulders, the girls hurried down the street as though anxious to put more distance between themselves and the woman.

Nathaniel breathed a sigh of relief. Now he need only get her to do the same. Perhaps his vigil wouldn't be wasted after all. He couldn't lose this chance to identify the men involved in the terrible scheme. "If you would—"

"How dare you." The anger in the woman's tone surprised him as did the passion that flared in her eyes. But it didn't sway him from his purpose.

He leaned close, intending to intimidate her, dropping his East End accent. "Do you have any notion of the danger you're in at this very moment?"

Her eyes widened in disbelief. Whether it was at the change in his intonation or his words, he didn't know. Nor did it matter. She opened her mouth, most likely to defend herself, but he was in no mood to listen.

"This is not the place for you." He glanced at the overly large bow on the side of her bonnet, uncertain why the damned thing irritated him so. "You would be better served on Regent Street." He took her elbow, intending to turn her in that general direction, but to no avail.

"Who are you to think you have any right to speak to

me so? I will not be dragged about by—"

Movement from the side of his vision caught Nathaniel's attention. The man he'd noted earlier drew nearer, a scowl twisting his lips that concerned Nathaniel. "We are about to be approached by an undesirable character," Nathaniel whispered. "I would suggest you do as I say and walk quickly."

The woman's gaze landed on the approaching man, and Nathaniel's meaning seemed to sink in. Apparently she didn't care for the look of him either, for she stopped fighting Nathaniel's attempt to move her and complied.

"Thank you," Nathaniel whispered as he escorted her, doing his best to modify his limp to more of a glide, not wanting her to notice it. "I have no desire to brawl on the street today."

"Who is he? Why was he approaching us?" she asked, sparing a glance over her shoulder, but it appeared her bonnet prevented her from seeing anything.

"I believe our presence is interfering with his business." He could feel the weight of her gaze as he glanced around warily for any additional associates the man might have lurking about.

"Who are you?"

"I'll explain once you're safely away." He walked with purpose, hoping not to draw more notice.

"I'm not going anywhere with you." The stubbornness in her voice irritated him though she had yet to wrest her elbow from him.

He didn't want her to stop now that they were nearly out of danger. "I promise to enlighten you once we're out of sight of the man who is following us. Don't look," he ordered when she started to turn back.

Perhaps she'd cooperate if he shifted her thoughts toward another topic. "Where is your carriage?"

She sighed. "A short distance from here."

He took a misstep. "You came here unaccompanied?"

"My maid and footman aren't far." At his questioning

look, she named the bookstore where they waited.

"That is a fair distance from here." And his leg already ached like a bad tooth. He'd spent another restless night walking more than he should've. No doubt that added to the stiffness in his thigh. Why had this woman ventured all this way by herself?

"Who are you? And this time, I expect an answer." She gave him a stern look, and for a moment, he wondered if she was a governess or the like.

"Nathaniel Hawke." He decided against sharing more. After all, his brother was an earl and had no idea of Nathaniel's activities. He'd prefer to keep it that way. He well knew Tristan wouldn't approve.

"Well, Mr. Hawke, please advise why you felt the need to interrupt my conversation with those girls."

"First, tell me what your purpose here is." He was curious at the very least. And her answer would help guide him as to how much, if anything, he told her of his own mission. It had started several months ago and come at the perfect time, prying him out of the spiral of hopelessness gripping him after his forced retirement. The sense of purpose that now filled him was a reason to rise each morning and beat back the despair his empty and pointless future had threatened.

"I intended to aid one of London's many neglected children."

"By giving them the card of your dressmaker?"

"I understand factory jobs are less than desirable. Giving them money seemed too great a risk." Something in her tone implied she'd given the matter considerable thought.

"Sometimes it takes more than money to truly make a difference." He said the words quietly, wondering if she understood that. So few of the well-to-do did. His brother, for example.

They turned the corner of another street, and he paused to look back. There was no sight of the man who'd been following them. But that didn't mean they were out of harm's way.

He glanced in the opposite direction, spying his carriage. At his nod, it pulled toward them. "May I offer you a ride to your carriage?"

"No, thank you."

"I'm afraid I must insist." He'd be damned if he'd risk her returning to the bridge where harm might befall her.

"You've ruined enough of my day already. I shall return of my own accord."

"I can't allow that," he said, taking her elbow to make certain she didn't attempt an escape. "I'll escort you. For your safety."

At last she looked up at him fully, her bonnet now serving to frame her heart-shaped face. That tiny dent in her chin appealed to him in the oddest way, as did her large eyes and long lashes. Eyes that were hazel. Or rather green. No, definitely hazel. Except for the inner ring of green. Perhaps hazel with gold flecks and a green ring would better describe—

He stopped short. What on earth was he doing? Since when did a captain in Her Majesty's Royal Navy wax on about a woman's eyes?

When they studied him with curiosity like she expected him to...well, he didn't know what she expected. Nor did he care to find out.

Those full lips the color of a deep pink rose that begged to be kissed couldn't be explored either.

"What is your name?" he asked gruffly. He shouldn't have asked yet found himself holding his breath, awaiting her answer.

"I—" She dropped her gaze for a moment, the sweep of her lashes doing odd things to his chest. Those lashes lifted, and he was struck anew by her amazing eyes. "I shan't tell you."

Once again, she'd refused him. After commanding so many men over the years, he was used to being obeyed instantly. Yet he had no hold over this woman, nor could he force her to do anything.

He shook his head. It was best she didn't tell him. He'd rather not have a name to put to her arresting face. After all, he would never see her again.

"Please accept my offer to drive you to your carriage." That was as close to a request as he could manage. "These streets are perilous. Even in the middle of the day."

He couldn't help but wonder if he'd correctly guessed that she'd thought herself safe here at this time, for she opened those lush lips as though to argue, only to firmly close them again. He studied her brows, trying to guess what color her hair might be. No hint of it was visible beneath the ugly bonnet.

"How do I know you're safe?"

Her quiet question took him aback. In truth, he wasn't. Far from it. It was good that she'd inadvertently reminded him of that.

"I'm a better alternative than walking these streets alone." That he could say with complete honesty. "I give you my word as a gentleman."

She pondered his response then nodded. "Very well." With a wary glance at his footman, she stepped up into the carriage as Nathaniel held open the door.

He advised his driver of their destination then took a seat beside her as she adjusted her skirts on the bench seat. It was such a feminine gesture, that adjusting of her skirts. After spending the majority of his time with men the past decade, the simple movements of women fascinated him. Her hands, encased in gloves that had the unfortunate aspect of matching her bonnet, were quite graceful in their movements as she drew her dark brown cloak over her fawn gown.

He didn't realize that was such a popular color in fashion these days. He preferred the brighter, more vivid colors he'd encountered in his travels, especially in India.

Damn. What on earth was the matter with him? Why

had he even looked twice at her clothes? He could only blame his behavior on the lack of women in his life for so many years. They were foreign creatures to him. Though many men in his position had mistresses, he'd avoided such commitments, unwilling to allow himself such an indulgence. Nor had he been overly tempted by a woman to bother. He pulled his thoughts back to the problem at hand.

"Don't return to this area," he warned. "There are far too many undesirable characters lurking about."

She looked up at him as the carriage eased forward, the horses' hooves clopping along the street. "Yet those girls walk there every day unaccompanied."

"True, but they are more capable of defending themselves than you."

"What were you doing at the bridge?"

"Merely admiring the architecture of it. The five wrought iron arches are quite impressive. The ends of the bridge resemble pulpits just as I was told." He glanced out the window, hoping they'd nearly reached their destination.

"Liar." The word was said without any heated inflection. Just a mere statement of fact.

He couldn't help but turn to look at her, shocked she'd say such a thing. The dim interior of the enclosed carriage created a cozy, private atmosphere that made him think of inappropriate things. Like how she might feel in his arms. How her lips might taste beneath his. What she might look like without the damned bonnet.

"I don't know what you mean," he said, forcing himself to look once more out the window, confused why this woman was such a temptation to him.

"Your accent doesn't match your clothes. I don't understand what a man like you would be doing near the bridge."

"I fear it is a rather long, boring story, and we have nearly arrived at our destination." He smiled to ease his rather terse explanation. "Do not return to that area under any circumstances."

"You have no say over me, Mr. Hawke."

"What would your father say if he knew where you had spent the luncheon hour?"

She gasped. "Are you threatening me?"

"No. I am trying to keep you safe."

"You don't know my name. Besides, I am old enough to see to my own safety."

"And you obviously are quite good at it, since you are now riding in a carriage with a stranger un-chaperoned. Do you have any idea what happens to nice ladies such as yourself in situations like this?" He leaned closer, hoping his presence was enough to frighten her into avoiding such trips in the future.

Her chin went up a notch as she met his gaze. With his next indrawn breath, her sweet scent that held a hint of orchids filled his senses. He'd grown fond of their heady fragrance during his time in India. Why couldn't she have smelled of roses or something normal like other English misses?

"Nothing untoward ever happens to me." She said the words with the utmost confidence. Yet they held an underlying hint of something he couldn't identify. Was it regret?

His gaze dropped to her lips. He could tell the moment awareness of the danger she was in struck her, for she gave a tiny gasp. The pulse just visible at the base of her throat sped. His gaze caught on the dent in her chin before he stared into her eyes once more, telling himself he needed to back away before doing something *he'd* regret.

But those hazel-green eyes with specks of gold left him no choice. There was a question in their depths. He recognized it as he had one too.

"Damn," he muttered then took her mouth with his. Any idea of intimidating her fell away the moment his lips met hers. A surge of desire took him under, and he slipped his tongue into her mouth, swirling in its depths.

His entire body quivered at the spicy flavor of her. She tasted as good as she smelled, with a hint of cloves and cinnamon. Then her tongue hesitantly moved against his as though she was unfamiliar with doing so, and he nearly groaned. He tilted his head to deepen the kiss.

Her gloved hand fluttered up to the side of his face, whether to push him away or draw him closer, he didn't know.

The knock on the carriage door had him jerking back.

"We're blockin' traffic," his footman called out.

Nathaniel shook his head in an attempt to clear it. The woman appeared as startled as he. Indeed, she should be after that potent kiss. He quickly opened the door and exited to assist her in alighting right outside the bookstore she'd named, as promised.

Her hand trembled in his as she stepped down to the street. Rather than please him, as it had been his initial intent to frighten her, it angered him. Now that he'd been successful in scaring her, regret filled him. Somewhere deep inside, he'd wanted her to enjoy that kiss as much as he had.

"Do not venture there again," he said then cleared his suddenly dry throat. "It's far too dangerous. Do I make myself clear?"

"Perfectly," she answered as she looked up at him.

He stared hard at her. Surely that couldn't be delight in the depths of her eyes or a hint of a smile on those luscious lips. Not when her hand shook so. She pulled it from his grasp.

"Good day, Mr. Hawke." She turned and walked into the bookstore without a backward glance.

He stood staring after her for a long moment.

"Where to next, Captain?" the driver asked.

"Home. I've had enough adventure this day." He stepped up into the carriage, rubbing his thigh even as he welcomed its pain, anything to quell his yearning to go after her.

He blamed his rash behavior on orchids. That was the only possible explanation for his outlandish conduct.

CHAPTER TWO

"It is scarcely less startling to learn that annually more than a hundred thousand criminals emerge at the doors of various prisons, that, for short time or long time, have been their homes; and with no more substantial advice than "to take care that they don't make their appearance there again," are turned adrift once more to face the world, unkind as when they last stole from it."

~ The Seven Curses of London

"Lettie? Are you unwell?" Her mother frowned as Lettie sorted through the array of gowns her sister, Rose, had decided against wearing that evening. "I've asked you to fetch the blue ribbon from Violet's room three times now."

"I'm sorry, Mother. I'll go find it." Lettie felt her cheeks heat at her mother's chiding tone, but her thoughts had been in a whirlwind since the events of the afternoon.

She abandoned the pile of gowns and took her leave, closing the door behind her, anxious to escape the stares of Rose and her mother. Her behavior had no doubt been odd since her return from her outing despite her attempts to calm herself.

With a deep breath, she leaned against the door and put

a hand to her lips. They still felt tender after the ardent kiss she'd shared with Mr. Hawke. The sensation of his lips against hers lingered, sending her spiraling from giddiness to guilt and back again. Guilt because she'd kissed a stranger. Giddiness at the result.

She'd had no idea a simple kiss could be so passionate. That it could rouse so many emotions in so short of a time. She would've sworn such an experience was limited to the pages of a gothic novel, not real life.

But now she knew it to be true. She smiled at the thought, and the giddiness returned.

Mr. Hawke was handsome, tall, broad-shouldered— everything a man should be. But it was his blue eyes that had thoroughly captured her attention. Their depths contained secrets that tugged at her. They were cobalt, much like the Bristol blue glass vase her mother had purchased at the Great Exhibition and proudly displayed in the drawing room. His eyes were positively arresting in his sun-darkened face and were framed by nearly black brows and ridiculously long lashes.

His dark hair was clipped short but the front was long enough to fall over his forehead with a hint of a wave. His sideburns emphasized the strength of his face. There could be no doubt that he was a man of action, capable of carrying out anything to which he set his mind. The very memory of his powerful presence set a flurry of butterflies loose in her stomach.

His confident air had made her think twice before refusing to do as he bid. While his ordering her about had been rather annoying, something about him made her tingle. Or perhaps it was everything about him. And that was a completely new experience for her.

She sighed in disappointment as she realized there was no chance of her ever seeing him again unless she dared to venture to Blackfriars Bridge once more.

Though she and her sisters had discussed the possibility at length, none of them had ever been kissed. This was

Lettie's fifth Season and, with no offers, she, along with the rest of her family, had determined she was quite on the shelf.

As the eldest of four sisters, she'd expected to be the first to marry, but her initial Season had been a disaster. She always seemed to be a step behind other girls her age, from her gowns, to which parties she attended, to whom she spoke with. The competition for attention was fierce, but Lettie hadn't wanted to be noticed anyway. Not as self-conscious as she felt.

Her mother had been little help. She meant well but as Lettie was her first daughter to make her debut, several mistakes had been made. Lettie had neither the ability nor the determination to overcome them. Shortly into her first Season, she'd been labeled a wallflower and nothing seemed to change it.

She told herself she relished the idea of the freedom spinsterhood offered. Granted, what was most appealing about it was the absence of caring for her sisters. She loved them dearly, but once in a great while she dreamed of caring only for herself. Of having what *she* wanted matter.

Another benefit would be that she'd no longer adorn the walls of the various ballrooms through which they traversed. She detested the pitying glances that came her way from other ladies when she stood near the mothers, aunts and grandmothers. It seemed she did not fit in with the debutantes of the Season nor with the mothers and chaperones. The uncomfortable feeling of not belonging she encountered at every ball made her long for a change. Surely becoming a spinster in full would grant her that.

Then why did this small voice of doubt continue to plague her?

With a shake of her head, she fetched the ribbon from Violet's room, found the long white gloves Dalia searched for as well as the slippers Violet wanted that had somehow found their way into Holly's room. Such was the normal pandemonium of preparing for an important ball, sending Lettie and the maids scrambling for lost items while soothing nerves.

Each of her sisters was a beauty in her own way, much like their mother with light blonde hair, blue eyes, and peaches and cream complexions. Lettie took after their father with his dark blond hair, pale skin, and hazel eyes. She was a bit like the ugly duckling compared to her sisters, she supposed, though there was no promise of a swan in her future.

When the disarray calmed, allowing her to dress, little time remained before they needed to leave. Then again, what would be the point of asking the maid to do something different with her hair? Not when the gown she'd be wearing was once again a dull shade that did nothing for her coloring. The pale shades that were all the rage and required for debutantes looked lovely on her sisters but did nothing for her. However, her mother insisted pastels and the like were the only colors suitable for an unmarried lady, regardless of how many Seasons she'd seen.

She rushed to dress in a pale yellow satin gown with her maid's assistance and hurried down the stairs, only to realize none of her sisters had yet come down.

With a sigh, she entered the drawing room, a smile warming her heart as she saw her father in his evening attire, a squat crystal glass with a splash of whisky dangling from his fingers. Though quite tall, his portly figure had expanded each year until now there was half again as much of him. Lettie adored him.

"There's my lovely Letitia," he declared with a smile when she entered the room. "How are you this evening? Ready to dance the night away?"

"How was your day, Father?" She crossed the room to kiss his cheek. She didn't bother to respond to his comment. Sometimes he seemed to forget she was the wallflower of his daughters.

"Excellent. Do you think tonight will be the night?" he asked, a twinkle in his hazel eyes.

"That Rose will receive an offer?" She pondered the question at his nod. "Don't tell Mother or Rose, but I don't think the duke is ready to propose. He's only danced with her three times. That hardly seems enough time to—"

"Is the landau waiting?" her mother interrupted as she glided into the room. "We will be late if there is any traffic."

"Yes, it's outside. Are the girls ready? I thought we'd follow them in the carriage." Her father seemed to have forgotten his question. Or perhaps he didn't care for Lettie's answer.

She loved her family but sometimes wondered what it might have been like to be an only child. She had dim memories of a time when she had been the center of attention. When her parents had showered her in love. But with the birth of each daughter, that attention had been spread between them all with less and less for Lettie. Her mother had been quite overwhelmed by the girls, and Lettie had been a natural helper, wanting to please her mother.

Somewhere along the line, Lettie had become more of a governess and less of an eldest daughter. Even her name was different than her sisters. Her mother hadn't decided on a flower theme for her daughters' names until Rose had been born three years after Lettie.

All of her sisters, except Holly, the youngest, would be attending the Fretwell's ball. Lettie only wished she could remain home with Holly. An evening with her would be far more fun.

The landau was so full with gowns and bustles, they could barely budge. Luckily it was a short ride to the ball. Their mother and father arrived behind them.

As they started up the stairs of Lord and Lady Fretwell's home in Mayfair, Lettie fell back to walk alongside her father and mother.

"Father, I wanted to ask..." she hesitated, debating the wisdom of her question, especially in front of her mother.

"What is it?" he asked.

"I've come across a book on which I'd like your opinion."

"Another story on the poor, is it?" he asked with a brow raised, just visible beneath the brim of his top hat. "What is the name of it?"

"The Seven Curses of London."

"That sounds like one of those penny dreadful novels," her mother commented. "Why do you insist on reading such depressing stories? Rose has a lovely book of poetry I'm certain she'd share with you."

She'd had this discussion with her mother more often than she cared to recount. While she quite enjoyed poetry and novels, now that she'd read *The Seven Curses of London*, she felt compelled to take action. The idleness of the rich seemed wasteful to her. If she wasn't going to marry and have a family of her own, she could at least have a purpose, a cause that mattered. One that would make a difference in someone's life.

Yet she didn't take Mr. Hawke's warning lightly. Parts of London were certainly dangerous, but she wanted to help. How to take care for her safety but still make a difference was a challenge.

Her father enjoyed discussing social journalism articles with her. He even donated money to several causes she'd brought to his attention. But that was the extent of his interest thus far. Maybe, just maybe, this new book would compel him to do more. Or at the very least, help her do more.

"I look forward to it," he said. "We'll discuss it at breakfast, shall we?"

"Thank you, Father," she said with a smile. They often had the breakfast room to themselves as the rest of the family preferred to rise later. Lettie enjoyed those moments.

Drawing a deep breath, she braced herself for what would no doubt be a long evening. She stepped away from her father to draw closer to Rose, searching her sister's visage to make certain all was perfect. Her sister had caught the duke's eye two weeks ago, much to their mother's delight. Luckily, Rose confessed to having a growing affection for him as well.

"How do I look?" she whispered nervously to Lettie as they neared the entrance, her dark eyes shining bright.

"Lovely." She squeezed her sister's gloved hand to reassure her.

Rose's blonde hair, creamy skin and even features caught everyone's notice. She was truly beautiful and had a sweet, outgoing nature that drew men like moths to a flame. Her blush-colored silk gown showed off her slim figure to great advantage while maintaining modesty with a high neckline. With her innate elegance, she would make the perfect duchess if the duke decided to offer.

Lettie eased back to trail behind her family as they greeted their hosts. A servant came forward to take their cloaks and, all too soon, they entered the ballroom. The cream and gold décor was elegant. Double-tiered crystal chandeliers cast candlelight about the room. Potted palms graced the columns, lending a suggestion of privacy to several alcoves. Music from a string quartet filled the air from the top of the ballroom.

More people were here than Lettie had anticipated. She preferred larger balls, for it was easier to avoid those young ladies with rapier tongues, especially Lady Samantha Brown, who had become a thorn in Lettie's side this Season. She and her friends seemed to enjoy taunting her. Somehow, Lettie had become a frequent target of theirs.

Her family descended the stairs into the ballroom, spreading out to find friends. Her sisters had many, but Lettie's few friends had married. The limited balls they attended were spent with other couples after briefly greeting Lettie. Since then, she'd been so busy tending her sisters she hadn't made the effort to make additional friends. Now that her sisters were older and needed her

LANA WILLIAMS

less, it was too late.

Lettie decided a cup of lemonade was in order. At least then she'd have something to do with her hands before joining the chaperones. She liked watching the couples on the dance floor, the colors of the ladies' gowns in sharp contrast to the men's dark suits. Dancing was something she rarely did though she enjoyed it.

She eased along the side of the ballroom, nodding at a few ladies she knew until at last arriving at the refreshment table. The lemonade was cool and tart.

"Well, if it isn't Lettuce." The nasal tone of Lady Samantha's voice had Lettie clinching her jaw in response.

How could she have missed seeing her? She must've come up behind her.

Two other young girls who accompanied Lady Samantha tittered at her jest. Lettie did not. The first time Samantha had said it, Lettie had smiled politely. But no more. She didn't appreciate any of her comments. Samantha had a sharp tongue and, while Lettie knew she used it in order to feel better about herself, that certainly didn't make it easier to bear.

"How are you this evening, Lettuce?" Lady Samantha said again when she didn't garner a response from Lettie.

Lettie sighed, deciding she'd best respond in some manner with the hope that Lady Samantha would go on her way and find another target. "If you are speaking to me, my name is Letitia." She didn't suggest the woman call her by her nickname. That was reserved for family and friends, and Samantha was neither of those.

"Letitia? How...lovely." The pause combined with her tone suggested it was anything but. "What an old-fashioned name. But how is it that all your sisters have such lovely floral names, but you have Lettuce? Or was it Latrine?"

Lettie knew it reflected poorly on her that Lady Samantha's words still bothered her so much. But it was a barb that struck true. She did feel separate from the rest of her sisters, her name being one of the many ways.

If only she had some clever response that would quiet the woman. But alas, clever comebacks were not in her repertoire.

"I'm surprised you're not dancing. Two of your sisters are already. Don't you know how? You poor thing." The fake look of sympathy on Samantha's face had Lettie struggling for a stinging retort.

Her sudden desire for retaliation took her aback.

One of the ladies with Samantha whom Lettie had never met stepped forward and looked her up and down, her gaze lingering on the oversized bow on the side of Lettie's gown. "With a name like Fairchild, it seems like you should be one. The family trait somehow skipped you, didn't it?"

Lettie felt heat stain her cheeks. She didn't have the energy or defenses needed to fling insults with any of these women. And she had yet to understand what she'd ever done to earn their derision.

"Miss Fairchild. How lovely to see you this evening."

The deep timber of a man's voice sent shivers down her back. There was something oddly familiar about the voice. Surely any man speaking to her had somehow mistaken her for one of her sisters. She turned slowly to face him.

The cobalt blue eyes that had distracted her all day now held her gaze with a steady regard.

Mr. Hawke.

In evening attire.

In the same ballroom as she.

And looking even more handsome than he had earlier in the day. Her heart pounded, the memory of their kiss filling her senses.

Oh my.

Nathaniel did not for the life of him understand what was going on here. He'd overheard the conversation behind him, the voice he'd been trying to forget capturing his full attention, forcing him to turn to see if the determined lady from earlier in the day truly stood nearby.

Why was it that each time he came across this woman, she was in an impossible situation and in need of rescue?

Yet he could feel only gratitude at the chance encounter as he now knew her name. Miss Fairchild. Letitia. It was perfect. Different. Exotic. Just like her.

He studied her hair, which provided the perfect frame for her strong features. Warm honey. Not blonde. Not brunette, but the most interesting combination in between. His fingers twitched as he found himself longing to touch it.

Another odd bow graced her attire, this one at her waist. Why she insisted on wearing those things escaped him. Nor did he care for the dull yellow color of her gown. It hid rather than enhanced her curves.

Her hazel-green eyes stared up at him in amazement.

At the very least, his arrival had stopped the ridiculous comments from the ladies surrounding her. He tore his gaze from hers for a moment to glance at them.

With much effort, he forced what he hoped was a charming smile to his lips. "I apologize for interrupting," he said as he glanced at Miss Fairchild, "but I believe you promised me this dance."

The ladies blinked up at him, their expressions clearly showing their surprise.

That only annoyed him more. Why Miss Fairchild hadn't simply walked away was beyond him. She had no need to subject herself to their hateful comments. Where was the spirit she'd so readily exhibited earlier today? This woman appeared to be a mere shadow of that one.

He shifted, turning his back on the women as he offered his arm to Miss Fairchild. "Shall we?"

She took his arm hesitantly, as though she wasn't quite sure what he was about. Neither was he, but he refused to stand by and listen to the petty comments from the silly females any longer.

As he started toward the dance floor, he realized his mistake. He'd rescued her from one awkward situation only to place her in another. His leg would make dancing embarrassing for both of them if not impossible. The ache in his thigh rarely permitted him to forget his injury but his desire to rescue her had prevented him from thinking this through.

He slowed his pace as they neared the dance floor, prepared to make his excuses and set her free. A terrible feeling of inadequacy spilled through him, so familiar from his childhood and most unwelcome. He hated it with a passion. "I apologize, but I cannot dance with you."

She came to a stop beside him, the brilliant light in her eyes fading. "Of course not. I didn't truly expect you would." Yet he could clearly see the words were a lie.

Then it dawned on him that she didn't understand why he couldn't dance with her. "I injured my leg some time ago, and it causes me to limp."

"Oh." She glanced down at his legs. "I noticed that earlier today but thought it was part of your disguise."

"Please accept my apology."

She glanced over her shoulder at the group of ladies from whom they'd walked away, her shoulders sagging. "'Tis of no consequence. Truly."

He followed her gaze and saw how closely those ladies watched them. With a silent oath, he knew he had to do something. He couldn't allow her to become an even bigger target for their arrows. "Perhaps if we cross to the other side of the floor, it won't be quite so noticeable."

Miss Fairchild didn't budge. "Nonsense. Walking farther might tire your leg even more."

"We must at least pretend to dance or those ladies will not cease their taunts." He offered her his arm, tucking her hand into the crook of his elbow, and they continued on.

"If you'd consider allowing me to aid you," she whispered as she drew to a halt. "We could attempt smaller steps. I believe we'd manage well enough."

Now at the edge of the dance floor, she turned to face him, placing her hand on his shoulder.

Left with no choice, he took her hand in his and held it shoulder height, placing his other hand on her waist. Nerves tingled along his body. He hadn't attempted to dance since his return, nor had he done so during his time in the service.

But the practice he'd received in his youth had been firmly ingrained and his foot automatically moved to the side. Miss Fairchild modified her steps to match his and within a few beats of the music, they danced together quite well.

His nervousness faded as the music filled his senses. Or perhaps it was she who did so. He held her gaze, her amazing eyes riveting him. Now he knew both her name and the color of her hair, both an unexpected gift.

As she twirled in his arms, her spicy scent caught him once again, causing him to inhale deeper to experience it more fully. He tamped down the desire filling him, reminding himself they were in the middle of a ballroom surrounded by people.

Her gaze caught his as she turned in his arms, the light in their depths shining brightly once again. The extra pain the movements brought him were more than worth it.

"May I ask what brings you to the Fretwell's this evening, Mr. Hawke?"

He felt a twinge of guilt at her use of his surname rather than his rank. But he decided against explaining it for now. "I am here to keep my brother from leaving."

"Oh?"

"My mother insists it is past time for him to marry but he disagrees. He apparently escapes ballrooms at the earliest opportunity." His mother had become convinced that his brother, Tristan, needed to take a wife this Season. She'd made it sound as if Nathaniel was her last hope to convince her oldest son to marry and start a family.

Nathaniel's task this evening was to make certain his brother danced with at least three eligible debutantes. Thus far, he had failed.

In many ways, he hoped his brother would marry soon, for that would make it even less important that he had no intention of doing so. A family life was not for him. He'd been far better suited for the military. But now that he'd found a purpose since his forced retirement, he hoped to make a new life for himself.

His brother was very much like their late father. They shared the same name, the same looks, the same gruff manner. He did not yet know if Tristan had also taken on their father's beliefs. He sincerely hoped not. Their father had been a difficult man, expecting far too much of his sons and his wife. It seemed they disappointed him constantly. Especially Nathaniel.

Tristan had been acting oddly since his return. Then again, Nathaniel had been gone for some time and wasn't certain what might be going on in his brother's mind. He'd never been close to his brother. Their father had seen to that.

Despite all his years away in the military and his father's death three years ago, Nathaniel still felt his father's shadow over many things he did. He had yet to discover a way to remove it. Perhaps one day, he would speak to his brother about that. But not until he'd determined if Tristan had truly turned into their father.

He turned a bit too quickly as the dance continued, taking a misstep before catching himself. Miss Fairchild continued to glide smoothly as though nothing untoward had occurred. His admiration of her increased a notch. He'd had the impression of her stubbornness before, but after seeing her at the mercy of those terrible ladies, his sympathies had been aroused. Perhaps she was rather like him—more willing to stand up for others than herself.

Now he had one more reason to admire her.

She smiled up at him as the music drew to a close. "That was lovely. Thank you."

"I am the one who should be thanking you." He led her from the dance floor. "Tell me why you were at Blackfriars Bridge earlier."

She glanced around worriedly.

"Ahh," he said as he realized the reason for her sudden concern. She didn't want anyone to know where she'd been. He gestured toward a nearby garden door. "Perhaps you'd like to speak in private for a moment."

With a nod, she walked with him through the door to the darkness outside. The garden was lit only by the glow from the ballroom windows. No one was in sight, much to his relief. To ensure they had privacy, he drew her to a place in the shadows at the edge of the garden.

"I find myself quite curious as to your answer," he admitted. Her presence there didn't make sense even after he'd had several hours to ponder it.

"I recently became aware of the many young girls who have no choice but to work in factories or slop-shops, and how difficult their lives are." She held his gaze, the dim light from the windows glittering in her eyes. "I would like to help in some way."

Nathaniel nearly smiled. "If only other members of the *ton* felt as you did, London would be a different place."

"I don't understand why more people don't become involved." She studied him more closely. "How did you come to be at Blackfriars?"

"I recently returned to England after living abroad for several years. I was taken aback by the changes in London. It seems the gap between those with and those without has widened considerably."

"Assistance must be given to help the poor. But how?" The passion that lit Miss Fairchild's face should've been reserved for something other than the poor, but he appreciated it all the same.

He pulled his wayward thoughts back to her question. "There is no easy solution. Understanding the problem is the first step."

He marveled they had this in common—the need to make a difference. Surely few ladies her age shared her view. "But you must realize how dangerous it is to venture into those areas."

She raised her chin. "One must take certain risks in order to make progress towards one's goal."

He lifted a finger to tap the hint of a dimple in her chin. He'd been wanting to do that since he first saw her. "Only those risks which one truly understands."

Her eyes widened at his touch even as her lips parted ever so slightly. "I believe I understand the risks."

Awareness curled through him. It was almost as if she no longer spoke of trips to Blackfriars Bridge. He couldn't resist testing the water. "Have you ventured there before?"

"No. I have not. But I would like to. With the proper escort, of course."

Good Christ. She couldn't possibly be saying what he thought she was saying. Yet he found himself easing nearer to take her gloved hand in his. "One must be equally careful when selecting one's escort."

"Excellent point." Her gaze dropped to his mouth.

He could hardly breathe. What on earth was she about? Longing to taste her again overcame commonsense. He captured her lips with his.

The tiny moan that escaped her lips echoed his own. He released her hand to draw her into his arms, the feel of her against him heating him in places he hadn't realized were so cold.

Her hand touched his cheek, then his shoulder, resting there for a moment as they kissed. Her tongue danced with his, unloosening a tightness deep inside him.

The odd sensation had him pulling back to stare at her, perplexed at his reaction. She threatened to unleash emotions he'd carefully buried and hoped were dead. That was not worth a kiss, nor even a night of passion. Those feelings needed to stay buried, never to surface again.

His sanity depended on it.

"Forgive me," he said as he drew back. "I had no right to take such liberties."

The stunned look on her face gave him pause. Was it because of the kiss or his withdrawal?

He clenched his teeth, reminding himself it didn't matter. She was not for him. He had no intention of marrying, and a lady's sole purpose was to find a husband. Far more important missions were in his future than indulging in a heated kiss.

The neglected children of London needed him. And he had no intention of letting them down.

"You must stay away from Blackfriars Bridge. It's no place for a lady."

"But I—"

"No. Stay away." Did she understand that he meant himself as well?

He stepped back, noting how the shadows cast her gown into a deep shade of amber that caused her skin to glow with warmth. She would make someone a wonderful wife some day. But not him.

With a deep breath and an attempt to firm his resolve, he turned away and left through the garden, unwilling to wade through the ballroom. His brother would have to mind his own affairs this evening. Nathaniel had other things to tend to.

Chapter Three

"...winter and summer, within the limits of our vast and wealthy city of London, there wander, destitute of proper guardianship, food, clothing, or employment, a hundred thousand boys and girls in fair training for the treadmill and the oakum shed, and finally for Portland and the convict's mark."

~ *The Seven Curses of London*

Lettie strode into the dining room the next morning, hoping she hadn't missed her father before he left for the day. In her hand was the book that had given her the sense of purpose she'd been searching for. If she could make him understand how important it was to her, maybe he'd be willing to help her determine a way to make a difference.

She breathed a sigh of relief as she caught sight of him, sitting at the head of the table, his face partially covered by the newspaper he read.

"Good morning, Father."

"Morning, dear," he mumbled as his gaze continued to peruse the paper.

No doubt some article in the financial section had caught his interest. That made up the majority of what he read. It only made sense that a man who managed significant funds in shipping ventures would do so. She only wished to shift his attention briefly.

She set *The Seven Curses of London* beside his nearly empty plate and helped herself to the sideboard. She wasn't very hungry this morning. A small helping of eggs as well as sausage and toast were all she took.

"Did you enjoy yourself last night?" he asked, his gaze still on the paper.

"Yes. Yes, I did." For once she could answer in the affirmative without lying. Her time with Mr. Hawke had been truly delightful. She didn't pretend to understand how he'd come to be at the ball, but she certainly appreciated his rescuing her. While his presence the previous day had been an interruption, last night had been most welcome.

She nearly smiled at the memory of Lady Samantha's shocked expression. Granted, such an event might never happen again. But that was all the more reason Lettie intended to enjoy it.

She couldn't help but wonder how he'd injured his leg. The injury must've occurred recently as he didn't yet seem completely accustomed to the lack of mobility. The look of chagrin on his face when he'd thought he couldn't dance had tugged at her heart. She'd been in awkward situations too many times to count. It had been her pleasure to ease his embarrassment, to assist someone else for a change.

While not the most graceful dance she'd had, it had been one of the best. There was something about how he looked into her eyes that made her think he could truly see her. Past the pale gowns and other trappings to her essence.

She reminded herself that was nothing but nonsense. He didn't know anything about her. But that hadn't changed the way she felt when he looked at her, all tingles and butterflies.

His kiss had once again surprised and delighted her. She knew any additional time spent in his presence would be dangerous. He made her long for things that were not in her future. Things she no longer dared hope for. Yes, he was dangerous in more ways than one.

Which brought her back to her purpose this morning—to find someone to help her as she didn't think she could do it alone.

"Father?" she interrupted, knowing he'd need to leave soon. She wanted the chance to speak with him before her mother came down.

He looked up at her blankly. "Oh, hello, dear. Did you enjoy your evening?"

She frowned at the repeated question. "Yes, I did. Did you?"

"As Rose does not yet have an offer, it wasn't as pleasant as it could've been. I hope the duke hurries along."

Lettie held her tongue. She'd already offered her opinion on the matter. For Rose's sake, she too, hoped the duke proposed soon, but more time would give both of them a chance to grow to know each other better before marriage. Hasty weddings were often regretted ones.

"What's this?" her father asked as he caught sight of the book she'd placed near his plate.

"That is the book I mentioned to you last night. I was hoping you might glance through it so we could discuss it. At least the first chapter on neglected children." Surely he'd understand the urgency she felt to do something if he looked at that part. The facts the author shared were appalling.

"Ah, yes." He opened it, flipping through pages. "Another account of the terrible vices industry and technology have forced upon our good city."

"Actually, it is a carefully researched book which outlines seven different areas that require improvement. Such improvements would help everyone, not just the poor."

He smiled at her. "I appreciate you seeing the bigger picture. Where would we be without individuals such as yourself to bring these atrocities to our attention?"

"Thank you, Father," she said, pleased he appreciated her efforts. "I was hoping you might assist me in determining where I could best offer help."

"I've always found it rather remarkable how similar you are to my sister. She, too, feels the need to take action when she reads such things."

"We've corresponded often on similar topics." Aunt Agatha was one of the reasons Lettie had determined spinsterhood wouldn't be quite as disappointing and lonely as it sounded. She tried not to dwell on how the choice had slowly crept out of her hands now that she'd begun her fifth Season with no offer.

"It's unfortunate she's decided to remain at her cottage this Season," he added. "I always enjoy her visits with us."

Lettie had her suspicions on why her aunt decided against coming to London and also why her once weekly correspondence had dwindled to an occasional letter once or twice a month. She didn't think her father would appreciate hearing it, so she kept her silence. After all, she had no facts to substantiate her belief that her spinster aunt now had a man in her life, that she was indulging in an affair of some sort.

"You ladies with no families of your own have too much time on your hands and so create ways to make the rest of us feel obligated to take action." Though he said it with a smile and meant no harm, she couldn't help but take offense.

"If each of us did a small part to solve the problems, they wouldn't be problems any longer."

He rose from his seat and tossed aside his napkin, inadvertently covering the book. "True, but business must take a priority over social causes. You're old enough to realize that."

Lettie didn't argue. After all, she wanted his guidance in this matter. Irritating him by debating the subject would not aid her cause. In her heart, she felt they were equally important. All people deserved the basics of food and shelter.

He came to kiss her cheek. "I must be off. I will see you this evening."

"Don't forget the book, Father," she reminded him as he moved toward the doorway.

"Of course." He veered back to the table to retrieve it. "I look forward to discussing it with you."

"As do I." Lettie heard the sound of her mother's voice in answer to her father's. The girls wouldn't be far behind her. Hopefully Rose wouldn't be in low spirits at the lack of a proposal from the duke.

Her mother entered the dining room several minutes later, her rose-colored morning gown the height of fashion.

"You're not eating too much, are you, Lettie? We must all watch our figures."

"No, Mother." She pushed aside her plate, leaving most of her breakfast untouched. While she knew her mother meant well, it seemed like she mentioned it to Lettie more often than to her sisters. Her curves suggested a plumpness that was only emphasized by the gowns with ruffles and lace and bows her mother insisted she wear.

"I passed your father in the hall. He showed me the book you gave him." Her mother completed her selection from the sideboard and took a seat near Lettie at the table.

Lettie nearly groaned. She could already hear the lecture. "Oh?"

"I don't understand your insistence on dwelling on what is wrong with London. There are many attractive things and people here."

"Of course, there are. But those people and things don't need our help."

"Why not focus on the positive? The seedier parts of

London are not places for ladies such as us." Her mother's gaze held hers.

"I don't want to live there, Mother. I only want to help those who do."

"Why?" There was such bewilderment in her question that Lettie felt compelled to answer honestly.

"I want to have a purpose."

"You have a purpose. You are a Fairchild with many responsibilities."

"I want a purpose of my own. I want to make a difference."

"You make a difference every day. Your sisters and I..."

Hurt filled her as her mother continued. How she wished she could make someone understand. Being needed by her family didn't bring her joy. Not anymore. In all honesty, she felt used, as if she were an unpaid governess. If she weren't here to do as her family requested, a maid could easily fulfill the tasks. How sad was that?

It meant she didn't make a difference in anyone's life. Oh, she knew her sisters loved her. And she loved them, just as she loved her parents. But how to explain all this to her mother in words she could understand?

"Mother, I want to help someone outside the family. There are many people only a few miles away in desperate circumstances. If I could help even one of them, it might change their lives for the better."

"Nonsense, Lettie. You are needed here. With us." Her mother reached out and patted her hand, then proceeded with her breakfast.

Lettie rose. The conversation was obviously over. Trying to make her mother understand how she felt was impossible.

"Wait," her mother said and gestured for Lettie to sit before she'd had the chance to step away from the table. "There is one more thing I wanted to speak with you about."

Lettie sat, a sense of foreboding filling her.

"I couldn't help but notice the gentleman you danced with last evening."

"Yes?" Lettie didn't offer his name. She well knew her mother would latch onto it like a cat with a mouse, inquiring among her friends as to who he was and all the other details she deemed important.

"No one seemed to know his identity."

"Oh?" Was the only response she offered, feigning a sudden interest in arranging the silverware next to her plate.

Her mother sighed at her lack of an answer. "At the very least, I must remind you how important it is for all of us to behave above reproach. Rose might receive an offer any day from the duke. The slightest question about our family—such as you venturing into the garden with a strange man—could easily deny Rose her dream of becoming a duchess."

Guilt flooded Lettie as she thought of the kiss she'd shared with Mr. Hawke. It was impossible to keep the heat out of her cheeks. Of course, she wanted Rose to receive an offer. But was it so wrong to want a little something for herself as well? It seemed terribly unfair to think that one kiss—or rather two—could possibly result in denying Rose her duke.

But Lettie knew it to be true. Had the wrong person seen her, she and Mr. Hawke might've found themselves the subject of gossip or worse. Lettie had no intention of ruining her own reputation let alone her family's.

Did that mean she needed to keep her distance from Mr. Hawke? Or even worse, did she need to curtail her attempts to find a way to serve a purpose? Where did that leave her?

Hoping her father would show interest in her desire to take action, she supposed.

"Mother, I have no intention of doing anything that could harm Rose's chance with the duke. Please know that." She rose. "Now if you'll excuse me, I need a book from Father's library."

"I'm counting on you, Lettie," her mother's words followed her out the door.

Aren't you always? Her mother had been depending on her since Rose was born. The tasks may have changed over the years, but the fact remained the same. Her mother needed her. Perhaps not quite in the way Lettie would prefer, but she supposed being needed was better than being ignored.

She entered her father's study, intent on finding additional information on Whitechapel. The more she learned about that area, the better. His massive desk sat near the windows. The drapes had been drawn back to let in the morning light. A glint of something shiny on his desk caught her eye.

Her heart sank as she drew near. The black cover with ornate gold edging and gold title was very familiar. *The Seven Curses of London* lay on her father's desk. Perhaps he'd simply forgotten it in his rush out the door. But somehow she doubted it.

She picked up the book, running her fingers along the gold filigree decorating the cover, swallowing back the disappointment that filled her. Why was it so difficult for her parents to understand she wanted to make a difference? If she were married and starting a family of her own, she might have something else on her mind. But she wasn't. With all her heart, she wanted to have a purpose. Maybe even save someone's life or, at the very least, make it better.

With a sigh, she tucked the volume under her arm. It appeared that achieving her goal was up to her and her alone. That didn't change her mind one bit. She was still determined to find a way to help.

Nathaniel perused the newspaper as he finished his breakfast.

"More coffee, Captain?" Dibbles asked.

Part butler, part valet, Dibbles had insisted on moving in with Nathaniel upon his return to London. He'd been Nathaniel's servant since Nathaniel had been a boy.

"Please," Nathaniel answered. The dark, aromatic brew was a special blend that he had brought with him from his travels and enjoyed each morning. Luckily, Dibbles had found a specialty store that had been willing to order it for Nathaniel.

"Might I ask what is on your agenda today?" Dibbles inquired, his posture perfectly straight, his black suit impeccable.

Dibbles had taken to requesting Nathaniel's schedule when he'd learned where Nathaniel's wanderings took him. He insisted part of his duties involved Nathaniel's safety, and he couldn't ensure his safety without knowing his whereabouts. Though Dibbles had made his disapproval clear, Nathaniel maintained he should be able to walk in his own city without fear.

Dibbles disagreed.

The older man had served in Tristan's household the many years Nathaniel had been away. But he'd insisted he wasn't needed there and had left without a backward glance upon Nathaniel's return.

"I am seeing my brother later this morning. After that, I am watching a workhouse."

"Which one?"

"I only have one brother. I believe you know him." Nathaniel couldn't resist continually attempting to draw a smile from the older man. He gave the cliché of stodgy butler far too much credibility.

"I was referring to the workhouse," Dibbles replied without cracking a smile. "Which workhouse?"

"The Whitechapel Workhouse."

"Shall I accompany you?"

"No need. I will venture there on my own." At Dibbles' disapproving frown, he couldn't help but add, "I don't intend to seek out trouble. I only want to observe for a time."

"Yes, well, I've noted your observations often involve action, even if you don't intend it."

Nathaniel felt compelled to defend himself. "If the situation warrants closer observation."

Dibbles held up a finger. "I believe based on previous conversations our definitions of 'observation' also differ."

Nathaniel scowled. He was accustomed to action. Observation was a newly learned skill he had yet to master. Yet it seemed that at times, if he waited, the opportunity to learn more might very well slip away. "I have come to believe there is a tie between the disappearances of the young women working in the factory and those who live in that particular workhouse."

Dibbles nodded. "Be that as it may, my primary focus is your safety, Captain."

"I hardly think it matters if something untoward were to—"

"It matters to me."

An unfamiliar warmth filled him at the older man's quiet statement, making him uncomfortable. Warm, but uncomfortable. "Thank you, Dibbles. I will keep that in mind and try to be more careful."

The butler raised a brow, causing Nathaniel to sigh. "I believe our definitions of 'careful' also differ."

He'd only been home a few days when he'd encountered an extremely unpleasant fellow in the East End in the early morning hours. The man insisted on taking the money Nathaniel had on his person. He hadn't taken kindly to that. A scuffle ensued, leaving Nathaniel with a slice along his ribs.

Despite his lame leg, he'd come out the winner of the altercation. He wasn't certain if it was the cut that had displeased Dibbles, or the clothing he'd had to repair.

In any event, that had begun his investigation as to what was happening in the poorer areas of the city.

Then had come the rescue of several girls from a ship owned by his friend, Marcus de Wolfe, Earl of Warenton, back in February. The girls were being lured into taking positions as maids in Brussels, only to be sold as prostitutes instead. Although at first what he'd witnessed appeared random, he'd soon realized several of the same men had been in the vicinity in many of the cases.

Warenton has sent him a book, *The Seven Curses of London*, that shared schemes similar to the one they'd uncovered. He couldn't help but believe Warenton hoped he'd attempt to do something about them.

From what little he could garner from a policeman he'd befriended, young girls were disappearing from the streets at an alarming rate. Those were only the ones reported missing. Far more disappeared with no one the wiser. If a girl had no next of kin to worry over her whereabouts, she wouldn't be missed.

Nathaniel had been appalled at the idea of girls from his own country, one he'd defended on several fronts, being sold into slavery or as prostitutes. Putting an end to such terrible occurrences was what now forced him to rise each morning.

Those girls mattered. Whether they or anyone else agreed was yet to be determined. But they mattered. He refused to examine the reasons behind his need to make that clear.

"Dibbles, you know I take every precaution when I venture out."

"I believe that our definitions of—"

He raised his hand. "I hear your message." He closed his eyes for a moment. Lord knew what trouble he might find himself in if it weren't for the knowledge that Dibbles would chase him into hell if he didn't return home at a reasonable hour.

Christ, it was like living with his mother all over again. Though Dibbles was far worse. Of that he had no doubt.

"I will be home for supper."

"Will you be attending another ball this evening?"

"I sincerely hope not." Though he had to admit the previous evening had not been as bad as he'd expected. Miss Letitia Fairchild had been an unexpected delight to his evening.

There was certainly more to the lady than he'd anticipated from their brief encounter at Blackfriars Bridge. To discover she was a member of the *ton* was interesting. Few bothered themselves with the issues of the poor beyond giving money to one charitable cause or another. Not that money wasn't required to right wrongs, but it was only part of what was needed.

Why Miss Fairchild was the target of the negative comments from those other ladies was beyond him. She was different from others her age. Of that he had no doubt. He had been surprised how she'd seemed almost resigned to the way she was treated by the ladies. Especially after her stubborn behavior during his first encounter with her. She'd seemed more than comfortable standing up for herself then. What had happened in her past to make her think, even for a moment, that it was acceptable for those women to berate her in that fashion?

He shook his head. Enough problems filled his schedule. Miss Fairchild was not his concern. She had a family and was not in need of further assistance from him. He ignored the small seed of doubt at the thought. After all, he'd already rescued her twice. The odds of encountering her again were slim.

And if he valued his peace of mind, he needed to keep his distance. He'd kissed her as though he were some randy youth who could not contain his passion. Yet even the thought of her stirred him. He couldn't pinpoint what it was that made her so special, but she deserved someone in her life who could help her understand how unique she was.

That was not him.

He set aside the paper and rose from the table. "I had best pay a visit to Tristan before Mother accuses me of abandoning our family."

"Did he find an appropriate lady to dance with as agreed upon?"

"I am not certain. Hence my visit with him this morning."

Dibbles frowned. "Didn't you see him at the ball last night?"

"Yes, but I was interrupted in my quest and ended up leaving earlier than planned." Which was proof that Miss Fairchild was a distraction he did not need.

He wisely avoided meeting Dibbles' gaze. Heaven only knew what the man might read into his expression. The disadvantage of having had him as a servant since he was a boy was that Dibbles knew him better than he knew himself.

"I will return as per my schedule," Nathaniel said and took his leave.

The brief drive to his brother's gave him time to ponder Tristan's odd behavior. At least he thought it odd. After the many years Nathaniel had spent away, he didn't know his brother at all anymore.

That hadn't stopped their mother from insisting he nudge Tristan into selecting a debutante to marry.

However, Tristan seemed reluctant to do his duty as the Earl of Adair. If Nathaniel didn't know better, he'd think Tristan wouldn't marry if it was left to him. Something was amiss there, but he had doubts of his ability to discover what it was. Tristan was as likely to confide in him as the Thames was to run clear.

Upon arriving at the elegant townhome on Park Lane, Nathaniel was announced and shown into Tristan's study. He couldn't help but look around as he entered, struck by how little it had changed since the room had been their father's domain.

"Good morning, brother," Tristan greeted him from behind his desk. "To what do I owe the honor of this unannounced visit?"

"I came to inquire as to how your evening went last night."

Nathaniel studied his brother from across the expanse of the desk. It was truly amazing how much he looked like their father with his grey eyes and black hair.

"Have I sprouted horns?" Tristan asked, brow raised.

"I was just realizing how very much like Father you are."

"So I've been told many times. Remarkable, isn't it?" The tight smile Tristan offered him made Nathaniel wonder what he was thinking.

"Did you manage to find three debutantes to dance with last night?" Nathaniel reminded himself of the task at hand.

"No. Only one caught my eye. And dancing with only one before leaving would've caused a fuss, would it not?"

"True," Nathaniel admitted. The expectations for unmarried heirs were different than second sons. "Is there no lady who has caught your fancy?"

"None that can be found in the ballroom." His expression was one Nathaniel didn't find appealing in the least.

"No need to share those details." If his brother kept a mistress, he didn't want to know about it.

"You do realize I don't need a nanny despite what Mother says?"

"Indeed." Nathaniel supposed he'd hoped the ridiculous request from their Mother would draw him and Tristan closer together. A crazed notion, he knew. His brother had no interest in him.

He should've taken his leave, based on the lack of warmth emanating from his brother, yet something kept him seated. He tried again. "What duties fill your day?"

"Nothing extraordinary. You?"

Nathaniel hesitated, wondering if he should bother sharing his investigation.

He chided himself for even considering it. Sharing anything would only bring his brother's derision. He'd learned that lesson many times in his youth. Why was he tempted to do so now? Nathaniel's current project was nothing he would've ever shared with his sire. His father would never have approved, therefore he had to assume Tristan wouldn't either since he was so much like their father.

Besides, Tristan was the elder. Surely any attempt to have a closer relationship should come from him.

"Nothing overly exciting for me either." He eased forward in his chair, preparing to leave.

"How's the leg?"

Tristan's question caught him by surprise. "Still stiff. I am beginning to doubt it will ever return to normal."

"It could be far worse. You could've returned home without it."

"I will bear that in mind." He opened his mouth, nearly telling him about the sleepless nights. About where his ramblings had taken him. What he'd seen. And most of all, how much his damned leg hurt. "I hope my efforts to keep it strong haven't worsened it."

"I'm sure there is a balance there, hmmm? Don't want to push beyond your limitations, but only up against them."

Nathaniel stared at Tristan, seeing his brother in a different light. Their father never would've said anything of the kind. He needed to remember that Tristan was his own man, and just because he looked like their father didn't mean he was. It made Nathaniel want to try harder with him, to forge some sort of a bond.

"I suppose I have yet to determine where that line is."

"It's important to listen to both your mind and your body."

Nathaniel nodded. "Are you attending the ball tomorrow night?"

Tristan scowled. "Are you asking so you can report to Mother?"

"No. I am merely curious. I don't suppose there is any urgency for you to marry, despite what Mother says."

"I don't think so either. Convincing her the world will not come to an end if I don't marry this Season is another matter entirely." Tristan shifted in his seat. "What of you? Surely it would ease Mother's mind if you were to find a wife."

"Marriage is not in my future."

"Why?" Tristan seemed genuinely surprised at his response.

Nathaniel searched for an excuse—at least one he was willing to admit. He didn't think himself worthy of a wife for numerous reasons. But the main one had to do with their father. His words had been burned into his mind throughout Nathaniel's childhood. He couldn't deny them anymore than he could deny breathing. They'd caused a wound far deeper than the one in his leg. Luckily, no one could see it.

"Long story." Nathaniel rose. "Perhaps one day, I'll share it with you."

He bid his brother an abrupt goodbye and left before he did something ridiculous, like tell Tristan more.

CHAPTER FOUR

"When death snatches father away from the table scarcely big enough to accommodate the little flock that cluster about it—snatches him away in the lusty prime of life, and without warning, or, worse still, flings him on a bed of sickness, the remedies for which devour the few pounds thriftily laid aside for such an emergency, and, after all, are of no avail, what other asylum but the workhouse offers itself to mother and children?"

~ The Seven Curses of London

The Whitechapel Workhouse was just off Charles Street. From Lettie's research over the past two days, she knew it had been built in the shape of the letter H, with females housed in the north end and males in the south. Which made sense until one considered how difficult it would be for a family who'd been forced to move into the workhouse. Living separately during times of financial hardship would only add to a family's stress, in Lettie's opinion.

The red-brick building before her was five-stories tall. The central wing was only two stories in height and held the entrance hall, meeting rooms, and offices.

Lettie waited across the street late that afternoon. Once

49

again, she'd left her carriage with her footman and maid a few streets away. They would only draw notice, and that was something she was trying her best to avoid.

After much thought, she'd decided against requesting a meeting with the medical officer in charge of the workhouse. She had limited resources to offer and didn't want to take up the medical officer's time or attract his attention. Her sister's pending proposal was forefront in her mind, which made discretion key.

Thanks to a chance comment she'd overheard from one of their footman whose second cousin worked here, Lettie had managed to set up this meeting with the hope of gaining information. Lettie was to meet her outside when the woman finished her shift. She had money in her purse to pay the woman for her time and trouble. Until she knew more, she wasn't certain how she could help. That was her goal this day—to gather information.

The author of the book had noted that providing for children who ended up in a workhouse through no fault of their own was part of Christian charity. Lettie couldn't agree more. Though some warned treating workhouse residents at a premium would encourage them to remain rather than seek a better life, based on what little Lettie had learned, there was a slim risk of that occurring. The conditions inside were far from comfortable.

She believed if workhouse children received an education along with the basic necessities, they would be more likely to grow into productive members of society. It only made sense to lend a helping hand now with the hope of avoiding their return to the workhouse in later years.

Lettie was well aware she couldn't help everyone. But she could help one or two. While that might not make a big difference in the wide view of the problem, it would make a difference to that particular family. That was all she wanted.

After much deliberation, she'd decided to heed Mr. Hawke's warning and stay away from Blackfriars Bridge.

This area of the city seemed safer. At the very least, there were fewer people passing by. Tall buildings lined both sides of the street, perhaps they lent to the feeling of safety.

As she watched the entrance, a rather stout woman emerged and glanced up and down the street. Perhaps this was her contact, Mary Smith. At last the woman's gaze fell on Lettie, so she gave her a little wave and a smile.

The woman didn't return either gesture but crossed the street toward Lettie.

"Ye be the lady with the questions?" she asked in a gruff voice.

"Yes. And you are Mrs. Smith?"

The woman smirked. "Sure. That's me all right. Smith."

Lettie realized with dismay that wasn't her real name. How naïve of her to think the nurse would be honest. Yet Lettie didn't understand the need for secrecy. She wasn't doing anything wrong. At least Lettie didn't think so.

"What is it ye want to know?" The woman glanced around, pulling her shawl closer about her. "Let us walk down the street. I don't want to be seen lingerin' out here with the likes of ye."

Lettie frowned. What on earth did that mean? Not that it mattered. She needed to keep her goal in mind. "Have you noted any young girls in the workhouse who seem especially reluctant to stay there?"

The woman snorted. "No one wants to be there."

"I'm sure. But I'm looking for someone in particular who might be especially down on their luck."

Mrs. Smith stopped to stare at Lettie, frowning in disbelief. "Ye've no idea of what ye speak. They wouldn't be in the workhouse if they weren't havin' some bad luck. Except fer those in the imbecile ward. I assume ye aren't referrin' to them."

Lettie shook her head. "I don't believe I can help them." Many of those classified as such lived a terrible life. While they obviously needed assistance, that was more than she could manage.

"We ain't helpin' them much either." The woman gazed back at the building, making Lettie wonder of what she was thinking. "Some say they'll be building a new workhouse but that ain't fer a year or two."

"What I would truly like is the name of a young girl who might be in need of my assistance." Nerves tingled along Lettie's spine. She looked around, trying to determine what caused her unease.

"What sort of help are ye planning to give?" Mrs. Smith eyed her suspiciously.

Lettie hesitated. That was an excellent question. While she was prepared to give money, she worried as to whether it would find its way into the wrong hands. "I know of an apprenticeship that might be appropriate for the right girl. I suppose I would like to learn more about her situation before I determine how best I could aid her. I want to help in whatever way is best."

"Only a name? That's all ye need from me?"

"And an introduction?" A name would do little good without one.

"To the girl?" Mrs. Smith asked and frowned again, making Lettie realize how unusual her request must be.

Lettie suddenly felt a presence behind her. Her breath caught in her throat, and she spun to look, fearing the worst.

Mr. Hawke stood directly behind her, glaring at her in a most unwelcome way. "What do you think you're doing?"

Nathaniel could hardly believe it. Every place he went, there she was. Was Miss Fairchild following him?

Her eyes widened as she looked up at him.

He glanced at the woman with whom Miss Fairchild spoke. From the scowl on the woman's face, she didn't appreciate the interruption.

"Look here, mister. We're havin' a private conversation."

"Not any longer."

"What on earth are you doing here?" Miss Fairchild asked, her eyes still registering surprise.

"Escorting you home apparently."

"I haven't yet completed my discussion with Mrs. Smith."

"Yes, you have."

The stout woman looked back and forth between them before remaining on Miss Fairchild. "Ye promised me payment if I answered yer questions."

"Do you by chance know any young girls named Alice?" Miss Fairchild asked.

Nathaniel shook his head, unable to believe her tenacity. Why did she frequent the same places as he? She couldn't possibly be following him as had first crossed his mind. After all, she hadn't been here when he'd watched the place two days ago, and today she'd arrived before him.

"There are several girls named Alice. What does she look like?"

As the women discussed the mysterious Alice, Nathaniel glanced around to see if anyone watched. Miss Fairchild still didn't seem to understand the danger she was in. Several people walked down the opposite side of the street, but none seemed to take notice of them.

This workhouse was one of several Nathaniel had decided to watch. But there was only one of him. He was beginning to doubt whether he'd be able to make inroads into the problems he uncovered by himself. Yet what choice did he have?

Warenton had returned to Northumberland with his bride. Nathaniel could hardly involve Tristan. He couldn't see his perfect brother lingering outside workhouses in less than desirable neighborhoods. Nor did Nathaniel care to share with Tristan what he was doing or why.

Definitely not why.

Miss Fairchild might be willing, but that would be even less appropriate than having his brother aid him. But how could he make her understand that?

Deciding enough time had passed for the women to finish their discussion whether they agreed with him or not, Nathaniel took Miss Fairchild's elbow.

"I must insist we leave," he advised her.

"But I have more questions for Mrs. Smith," Miss Fairchild protested, digging in her heels.

"I'm certain you've taken enough of her time." He reached into his pocket to withdraw some coins to hand to the woman.

The glare Miss Fairchild sent him would've melted a less courageous man. Luckily, Nathaniel's years in the military had provided him with the ability to withstand such attacks.

Mrs. Smith took the coins and hurried away without a backward glance.

"Did you follow me here?" Miss Fairchild asked, her tone biting.

"No, I did not. I must say I'm surprised to find you here. I thought you agreed to take more care and stay away from places such as this."

"You advised me to stay away from Blackfriars Bridge, and I agreed. There was no mention of workhouses." She heaved a sigh at the departing back of the woman.

How could she not realize the danger? Nathaniel clenched his jaw, hoping to contain the anger swirling through him. The force of it surprised him. What was it about this woman that caused such a reaction?

"Have you nothing to say for yourself?" she prodded him.

He turned her, prompting her to walk the direction from which he'd come. "I hardly know where to start."

"I have a plan and you are interrupting it." She drew to a halt and shifted from his grip.

"I would say the same."

Her eyes narrowed as she stared up at him. "What was your plan?"

"It is of no consequence. What is important is your safety, which you so easily cast aside."

The frustration in her pursed lips might've amused him had the circumstances been different.

"Why is it that you are in constant need of rescue? Based on my brief acquaintance with you, I cannot understand how you've lived this long unscathed."

Those amazing eyes of hers lit with fire. Or was that ire? Difficult to tell, but the result was amazing. Suddenly he could imagine them lit with passion. Her face flushed with it as she—

"I would've gotten along just fine without you whisking me away." The fire dimmed a bit. "Although I do truly appreciate your rescue at the ball. But I have survived far worse encounters with Lady Samantha and her friends."

"That situation is not the one that concerns me. What truly bothers me is the way you continually put yourself in harm's way. What do you want with this Alice or any of the other young girls for that matter?"

She bit her lower lip for a moment then sighed. The look she gave him was guarded, as though she expected he wouldn't understand.

But he wanted to understand. He wanted to know what was going on in her mind. Why she'd take such risks to come to places like this and the bridge.

At last she said, "I would very much like to help someone in need. To make a difference, even in just one person's life." She again met his gaze. "That isn't so very much to ask."

"No, it isn't. But only if you ensure your own safety before you seek to aid others."

"I didn't think I was taking much risk coming here." She glanced around as though searching for a thief or vagrant who might be ready to accost them. "No one has bothered me. It is the middle of the day. At least I didn't come at night."

"I don't think you comprehend the desperation of people who come to the workhouse. They are willing to do nearly anything to put food in their bellies or that of their families. Just before the supper hour, a line will form, and the dailies will come. The street will fill with them."

"Who are they?"

"In exchange for some food and two nights shelter, these men will be given a job to do around the workhouse."

"Should I come back then?" she asked.

"Christ, no. Dailies are not simply down on their luck. For some, this is how they live, traveling from workhouse to workhouse unless a better opportunity comes upon them. An opportunity like you. They could easily steal from you—"

"I was very careful not to bring anything they might want to steal or that would even attract their notice."

He drew back to stare at her, incredulous. How could he get through to her? "One glance at you and they'd notice."

She scoffed. "I wear a plain, black cloak and simple shoes. I don't have fur trim or embellishments of any kind." She glanced down at her attire as though to check to make certain it was as she remembered.

"Miss Fairchild, have you looked in a mirror recently?"

She looked back up at him, clearly puzzled at his question. "Well, of course. Only this morning as I prepared for this outing."

He couldn't resist trailing a gloved finger along her cheek. "Your appearance in rags would draw attention."

Still she frowned up at him in confusion.

He paused, trying to decide how he could make her understand without saying things he shouldn't. Though he'd been away a long time, he remembered the conventions of society. They hadn't been formally introduced. Granted they'd kissed, so he'd already broken all the rules. How could he make her see what he saw so clearly? "You are an arresting woman."

He regretted the words as soon as he said them, for they didn't do her justice. She was uniquely beautiful. Why she hadn't already been snatched up by some lord was beyond him.

"Arresting?" She gave him a wry smile. "That's an interesting description."

Since words failed him, he longed to *show* her exactly how attractive he found her. But that would never do. Twice he'd kissed her, taking liberties he had no business taking. She wasn't for the likes of him. A second son who didn't matter, as his father had so often pointed out.

Miss Fairchild deserved a husband who would be her equal in all ways. Not one who was broken and filled with self-doubt. Who carried the marks of his father on the inside. No matter how hard he tried, how many risks he took, how many battles he'd fought, he'd never been able to remove his father's words or the feeling of inadequacy they gave him.

"Do you mean the style and fabric of my cloak? That is what makes me stand out?" she asked. When he didn't answer, she nodded. "I should've considered that. Perhaps next time I could borrow one of the maid's cloaks."

"No." Perhaps she'd understand the simple word since she hadn't caught on to the other things he'd said.

"No?"

He took her arm and turned her toward his carriage. If he stood here with her a minute longer, he'd find some deserted alleyway in which to drag her so that he might taste her once again.

Apparently he needed to find a way to end his celibacy since all he could think about when he was with Miss Fairchild was picking up where they'd left off—with another heated kiss.

"I don't want you to venture into any part of the East

End or any other street where anyone less fortunate than you lingers, lives, or passes through. Do I make myself perfectly clear?" Surely that covered the entire list of possibilities.

"While I appreciate you worrying over my safety, I am old enough to care for myself." She tugged at her elbow, but he refused to release her.

"No, you aren't. Not on these streets. The depravity of man knows no bounds. Believe me. I've seen it." That was one of the reasons he'd found himself wandering the streets at night, unable to sleep. Memories of what he'd witnessed, what he'd done, kept him awake at night.

"During your time in the military?" she asked.

He nearly took a misstep. "How do you know I was in the military?"

"It's obvious. The way you carry yourself, your posture, and especially your tendency to give orders. One has to assume you're used to being obeyed."

For some reason, those words from her aroused him to no end. He wanted her to obey him in ways he didn't dare say. He closed his eyes momentarily—anything to ease the sudden throbbing in his loins.

Why couldn't this woman be an experienced widow, a status that would allow them to explore their passion together rather than a miss who would be someone's wife one day?

He had to get away from her before he did something he'd regret.

"Where is your carriage?" he asked through clenched teeth.

"We're nearly there."

"Excellent." He kept walking, trying to focus on the ache in his leg instead of the ache elsewhere. How could he convince her to stay out of these areas?

"I don't see what's wrong with wanting to help," she muttered.

"It's not wrong. But you cannot come alone." He could

nearly hear the wheels his words had set in motion in her mind. His concern compelled him to clarify his order. "Nor can you bring a maid and hope to remain safe."

Her scowl confirmed he'd guessed correctly.

A carriage came into view. At the sight of them, a footman scrambled down from his post and held open the door. He eyed Nathaniel warily before turning to Miss Fairchild. "Is everything well, miss?"

"Yes, thank you, James." She paused before stepping inside. "Are you in need of a ride, Mr. Hawke?"

"No, thank you." He waited until she'd settled herself inside before waving away the footman and standing on the step to lean inside. "Heed my request, Miss Fairchild. Else you'll leave me no choice but to speak with your father about your recent expeditions."

Her mouth rounded open. "You wouldn't."

Pleased that he'd at last found a way to make her behave, he gave a nod. "Yes, I would. Your safety is that important."

"That is not fair."

"As you said, I'm a military man. Strategy is my specialty. Good day." He closed the carriage door and nodded at the footman to be on his way.

He watched the carriage pull away, part of him hoping that was the last time he'd see Letitia, part of him hoping she'd find a way around his blockade.

A few moments later, Lettie rapped her knuckles on the roof of the carriage. James complied, bringing the conveyance to a halt along the side of the street.

"Yes, miss?" he asked as he came to the window.

"Follow that man. Discretely, of course. I don't want him to know." It was time she did a little investigation on Mr. Hawke. He seemed to know far more about her than she knew about him.

Culbert Rutter remained in the shadows of an alleyway as he watched the man and woman leave separately, thoroughly unsettled to see Hawke again. His boss wasn't going to like this one bit.

"What is it?" Teddy asked from his side. The man was new to their business but had proven helpful thus far.

"I've seen that man afore. He was one of the blokes that caught us smuggling girls to Brussels. Him and that earl."

"I heard the story. It was what sent ye to prison last time, wasn't it?"

Culbert couldn't help but smile. Though he'd landed in jail two times of late, he'd been released when the police had 'misplaced' the evidence against him. But the ease of his release didn't mean he wanted to repeat the experience.

"Do ye want me to keep an eye on him?" Teddy asked.

"No." As clever as the bloke seemed to be, chances were he'd notice someone following him and Teddy was not yet experienced in such activities. Having someone watch him might make Hawke pay closer attention.

If Culbert had to guess, the man had been in the military. Something about the way he held himself, not to mention how he'd moved in the skirmish on the ship. That had not been his first fight, of that Culbert had no doubt. "But if ye happen to see him again, let me know, will ye?"

In the mean time, Culbert intended to do a little poking around and see if he could discover more about the mysterious man and what he might be doing near the workhouse.

CHAPTER FIVE

"I have seen one of these gaunt wolfish little children with his tattered cap full of plums of a sort one of which I would not have permitted a child of mine to eat for all the money in the Mint, and this at a season when the sanitary authorities in their desperate alarm at the spread of cholera..."

~ *The Seven Curses of London*

Lettie could see very little as they followed Nathaniel's carriage. Gradually, the dirty, crowded streets shifted to better groomed ones of the well-to-do neighborhoods. They passed a church on a street corner and still the carriage continued. She peeked out the window, wondering where the fascinating Mr. Hawke might live.

At last they pulled to a stop. From what little she could see, he had a modest townhome on the west side of Arlington Street. The three-story brick front revealed little of what might be inside. Then again, they couldn't draw too near without risking him seeing her. That would never do. She didn't want Mr. Hawke to know she was following him. Or curious about him. Or interested in him in any way. Not that she was. Nothing of the sort. She simply wanted additional details about him should they meet again.

With a shake of her head, she realized no purpose would be served in lying to herself. The man interested her on more levels than she cared to count. But she had to try harder to act as though he didn't, in order to protect herself.

Despite his kisses and comments, she would never dare to dream he might be attracted to her. After all, she was nearly on the shelf, past the point of drawing anyone's notice. Even *he* had called her "arresting". Which meant...

Well, she wasn't quite certain, but it was far from beautiful. She knew she wasn't the type to catch a man's eye. Besides, he'd been frustrated with her when he'd kissed her. That was a far cry from true desire.

The pang of disappointment had her closing her eyes briefly.

That was all the more reason to focus on her purpose. Gathering her resolve, she studied the front of the tidy home for a few minutes more, taking the time to note the neighborhood. The townhomes were nothing like those on Park Lane or the like, but still a very nice neighborhood with slightly smaller homes. Perfectly acceptable for an unmarried man.

Or did he have a family? Surely he hadn't taken such liberties with her if he had a wife and children at home. The thought made her ill.

She rapped her knuckles on the roof once more and the carriage eased forward. Her thoughts circled endlessly during the drive home to Grosvenor Square. In many ways, she wished she hadn't followed Mr. Hawke. Now she was even more curious about him.

The footman helped her down upon their arrival home. As she entered the foyer, she spotted Holly sitting on the steps.

"Whatever are you doing there?" Lettie asked as she removed her gloves.

"Waiting for you." Holly eyed her curiously. "No one

seems to know where you've been."

"Oh?" Lettie had been deliberately vague when she'd left, saying she had errands to run. How unfortunate Holly had noticed. The girl could be much like a dog with a bone. She'd taken to reading mysteries, which had fueled her imagination. Now she saw shadows and conspiracies where there were none. Just last week, she'd insisted one of the maids was spying on them. The week before, she'd suspected the cook of addicting them to sweets.

Lettie had no desire to find herself the focus of her sister's latest investigation.

"Were you meeting a man?"

Her sister's blunt question normally would've made Lettie laugh. Yet how could she when the image of Mr. Hawke appeared so vividly in her mind?

Well aware of her cheeks heating, Lettie feigned interest in her gloves. "I saw the dressmaker. Does that count?"

"*You* visited the dressmaker?"

At once Lettie realized her mistake. She would never venture there alone. In truth, she didn't like the woman her mother insisted they go to or the gowns she made. Lettie preferred Madame Daphne's, but the only thing her mother allowed them to purchase there were chemises and the like.

She frantically sought an excuse that made her lie plausible. "Rose needed an adjustment on one of her gowns, and I offered to deliver it."

Holly continued to stare suspiciously at her from her position on the stairs.

"Don't you have something more important to do with your time than watch the foyer?"

"Not really. I've finished my latest book."

"I'm certain if I mentioned that to Mother, she'd find something to fill the rest of your day."

Holly quickly stood. "No need. I've just remembered I left something in my room." She turned and ran up several steps before pausing. "Are you going to the ball this evening?" The wistful note in her tone made Lettie wish all the more that she was not.

"My presence has once again been requested."

"How much longer do you have to go to such events?" At Lettie's questioning frown, Holly explained, "Rose says you never dance, let alone speak with anyone. What purpose is there in you attending a ball?"

Lettie's heart squeezed. While Holly had said nothing that Lettie hadn't thought, it still hurt to hear that her family believed her marriage prospects were completely at end. She reminded herself this was what she wanted—to be a spinster in full. With that came freedom. She'd be that much closer to making her own decisions, perhaps even having a little cottage by the sea. And a pet. A dog. A large dog. She would love to have a great beast to keep her company.

Somehow, all that sounded less than appealing given the events of late.

Setting aside her feelings, she concentrated on answering Holly's question. "I believe I am there in case Rose or Violet or Dalia require my assistance."

"Or Mother," Holly pointed out.

"Yes, Mother sometimes has need of me as well."

"Lettie? Is that you?" her mother's voice called from the upper floor. "Please come here. I require your assistance."

"Ah. There she is now." Lettie forced a smile.

"Doesn't that grow old?" Holly whispered. "Someone always needs you for something."

"True, but it is also lovely to be needed." Lettie used to think that, but sometime in the past year or two, the feeling had faded.

"It just seems as if she could easily ask a maid to do some of the things she requests of you."

"That may be, but we like to pretend we aren't completely dependent on the servants."

"Why? We pay them to help us."

"Self-sufficiency is a trait to be admired." Lettie shook her head when Holly opened her mouth to argue. Holly's points were valid, but she was in no mood to discuss them further. "Why don't you bring up some of your questions with Mother?"

Holly scowled. "She'll only put me to work too."

Lettie hooked her arm through Holly's. "Let us see how we can help our sisters, shall we? If I have to suffer, it's only fair you join me."

When Holly groaned, Lettie had to chuckle.

Lettie gathered her resolve as the coach drew to a halt at the Smitherson's massive house that evening, hoping the ball would pass pleasantly. And swiftly. She had no desire to fence words with Lady Samantha again, or any of the other women who surrounded the unpleasant woman.

Rose was nervous once again. More talk of the duke's offer had taken up their preparations for the ball. In Lettie's opinion, their mother didn't help, telling Rose how she should and shouldn't behave. One glance at her sister as they entered the Smitherson's had Lettie pulling Rose aside, allowing their mother to proceed.

"Rose, you should relax," Lettie advised, offering a smile.

"It's impossible to. What if he doesn't ever offer? Then what shall I do? This is my third Season, you know. Soon I will be standing with the mothers and other chaperones with nothing to do but twiddle my thumbs." Rose looked distraught at the prospect.

"With me?" Lettie asked, brow raised as pain shot through her. She knew her sister had much on her mind, but that had been a hurtful thing to say.

Rose gasped in dismay and reached for Lettie's hand. "I never meant to offend you."

"Nor does anyone else in our family, but it still seems to happen on a regular basis," Lettie replied. She shook her head, annoyed she'd allowed the truth slip out. "Trust me, Rose. You will never become a spinster."

"I thought you looked forward to the time when you might live like Aunt Agatha."

I thought I did, too, but Lettie chose not to say the words aloud. Not when she had such mixed feelings on the matter.

"The reason you attracted the duke's attention to begin with was because you were being genuine. Your true self. You used to enjoy balls, remember?"

Rose nodded as she considered Lettie's comment. "I suppose you're right. I never thought of it like that."

"I wouldn't be surprised if it was your joy and happiness that attracted him to you. Don't become someone you think he would like. Just be you." Lettie squeezed her sister's hand.

Tears glistened in her sister's eyes as she held tight to Lettie. "What would I do without you, dear Lettie? You always know what to say to make me feel better. Thank you for that."

"My pleasure. Now let us take a breath and smile." Together, they drew as deep a breath as their corsets allowed then smiled at the same moment.

Rose immediately dissolved into laughter. She turned to enter the ballroom, Lettie's hand still in hers, only to see the duke standing there.

Lettie couldn't help but notice the light of interest that lit his eyes as he watched Rose. And she was especially proud of her sister when she greeted him with a curtsey and a genuine smile. Her sister had no need to play coy. It was not in her nature. Surely that set her apart from half the other ladies in the room.

The duke bowed in return and offered her his elbow, nodding briefly at Lettie who quickly curtsied.

Rose was out on the dance floor with him before their

mother realized what had occurred.

"They make a lovely couple," she whispered to her mother. "I think he truly cares for her."

"Well, of course, he does." Her mother said the words with a nod as though she had no doubt. "He'd be a fool not to. What were you and Rose speaking about in the foyer?"

"Nothing important. I just reminded her to be herself."

Her mother scoffed. "What sort of ridiculous advice is that, Lettie? For heaven's sake, she is trying to catch his eye."

"Being herself is what caught his attention at the start."

"Humph. Please be careful what you tell her. I will be most relieved when all this business is over and done."

Lettie could only shake her head. Once Rose was betrothed, her mother would shift her attention to Dalia, poor dear. She searched the ballroom for her, finding her across the room, visiting with friends. Dalia was enjoying her second Season immensely, from what Lettie could determine.

Violet, on the other hand, was still becoming accustomed to all the social activities as this was her first Season. Lettie hoped their mother wasn't applying too much pressure on her as to who she chose for friends. While appearances were important, it would be a shame if Violet didn't enjoy herself.

"Will you please fetch me a glass of lemonade? I find I am quite parched."

"Of course, Mother." Lettie perused the ballroom as she walked toward the top of it, realizing with a start for whom she looked—Mr. Hawke. With a reminder to herself that she needed to keep her distance or risk the wrath of her mother, she looked instead for Lady Samantha. If she could avoid her this evening, the night would truly be a success.

"Hello, Letitia," a friendly voice said.

Lettie turned to see Lady Julia approaching. "Lovely to

see you," Lettie greeted her with a smile.

Lady Julia was a bubbly, friendly woman who never seemed to stop moving. Her energy and happiness were catching. She brought smiles to the faces of anyone within arm's reach.

"How does this evening find you?" The unusual thing about Julia's question was that she expected an honest answer and waited patiently for it. At a time when many didn't bother to ask, let alone listen to the answer, Lettie found it charming.

"Quite well. And you?" Lettie asked.

She and Julia had become friends of a sort, but Lettie couldn't understand why Julia always made it a point to seek out Lettie when they attended the same events. She was a beautiful woman, popular among men and ladies alike, and an heiress. According to gossip, she'd had multiple offers, and this was her third Season.

"Very well," Julia replied as she scanned the crowd. "Is that Rose dancing with the Duke of Welbourne? How exciting."

She appeared truly delighted they were together, surprising Lettie, especially since the duke had shown interest in Julia during the last Season. Granted, she didn't come to many balls. Her elderly father was often bedridden, so she preferred to remain home with him.

"Rose seems to be quite fond of him," Lettie offered.

"He is very kind despite his quiet demeanor."

Lettie studied Julia once again, wondering if there was more to her comment than met the eye. But no, she smiled as she watched them twirl about the dance floor.

"Lettuce? Is that you?" The grating sound of Lady Samantha's voice had Lettie's smile fading.

"Good evening, Lady Samantha." Julia turned to greet her. "You already know my dear friend, Miss Letitia Fairchild?"

Samantha stared at Julia in astonishment. "Dear friend?"

Julia's smile brightened as she hooked her arm through Lettie's. "We've known each other for ages. We always seem to be together, watching the dancers, don't we, Letitia?"

Lettie couldn't help but smile. How kind of Julia to not only suggest she watched the dancing alongside Lettie, but to make light of it. Lettie could've hugged her. Julia had more dance partners in one evening than Lettie in her five Seasons combined. Her genuine kindness warmed Lettie's heart.

"How is your mother, Samantha? I understand she's been feeling poorly." Again, Julia kept her gaze on Samantha, showing interest in her answer.

The conversation continued until at last, Samantha stomped away to pick on someone else.

"Poor Samantha," Julia whispered to Lettie. "Her mother is putting so much pressure on her to make a good match. That must be very difficult for her." The genuine sympathy in her voice surprised Lettie.

"I wasn't aware," Lettie admitted.

"Between you and me, I think it is what puts her in such a foul mood. She seems to want to make everyone as miserable as she."

"She has never been nice to me. Perhaps I bring out the worst in her."

"I think she's rather jealous of you."

"Of me?" Lettie was astounded at the idea.

"You're intelligent, kind, and somehow you manage to make it clear you do not need a husband to make you whole. I believe many admire you for that."

Julia's insightful words made Lettie think. She wasn't quite sure why Julia had that impression. Perhaps they were better friends than Lettie realized. That was an unexpected gift.

"How fares your father?" she asked, more than ready to turn the conversation away from herself.

Julia's golden glow dimmed. "Feeling rather poorly, I'm

afraid. I didn't want to come tonight in case he needed me, but he insisted."

"I'm sorry to hear that."

"The doctor will be by on the morrow. Hopefully he'll have good news for us."

"I'll be thinking of you with the hope he does," Lettie offered. Her gaze followed Julia's to a man on the opposite side of the dance floor. "Who is that?"

"The Earl of Adair," Julia answered. "He rarely frequents balls. I understand he's looking for a wife this Season."

"He's quite handsome," Lettie observed. "If rather brooding."

"He could be a character in a Gothic novel, don't you think?"

A tall man with broad shoulders and dark hair, he ignored most of those around him. His demeanor alone would keep most people at a distance. He was attractive, but it was his obvious disregard for what anyone else seemed to think that drew her eye and others as well. Something about the shape of his brow seemed vaguely familiar, but she didn't think she'd seen him before.

"He apparently prefers gaming hells over ballrooms," Julia added.

"Who could blame him?"

Julia looked at her in surprise.

"Not that I've ever been to one, but it sounds much more exciting than a ball, don't you think?"

Julia chuckled and again, patted Lettie's hand. "You are a delight. I always enjoy speaking with you. Oh, here's an even rarer occurrence. His younger brother, recently retired captain from the Navy, a true hero by many accounts."

Lettie turned to look.

Mr. Hawke.

Or rather, Captain Hawke, if Julia was right. As she watched the two men together, she saw how the line of their brows matched. That was where the similarity ended. The earl had a solemn expression and appeared disinterested at the very least. Perhaps a cross between bored and irritated described him best.

His younger brother eyed the crowd as though evaluating each and every person.

"Do you know him?" Lettie asked.

"I've been introduced, but I wouldn't say I know either of them."

Lettie was amazed once again at how many people Julia was acquainted with as well as the interesting details she knew, especially since she attended fewer social events than Lettie. But when one was an heiress, one was introduced to many more people than someone like Lettie who had only a modest dowry.

"How long has the captain been back?" Lettie asked.

"Only a few months, I believe. From what his mother has said, she expects both men to marry this Season."

"I wonder if they know that," Lettie muttered.

Julia laughed. "Neither appear as though they want to be here, do they?" She sighed. "Here comes my next dance partner. Wish me luck, won't you?"

Though reluctance tinged her voice, her smile showed only delight to the man who approached.

Lettie watched the pair step onto the dance floor. Then she couldn't resist allowing her gaze to catch once more on Mr. Hawke. Or rather, Captain Hawke. She hardly knew what to call him now.

He frowned at his older brother, obviously less than pleased at something he'd said. The distance between the two suggested they weren't close. Had the captain's time away in the military contributed to that, or had it always been so? More questions came to mind that she wished she'd asked Julia.

Though she feared learning more about him would only increase her growing fascination with him.

With a start, she realized she still hadn't obtained a

glass of lemonade for her mother. Gawking at the brothers would only earn her a lecture about the rudeness of staring.

She wound her way through the growing crowd toward the refreshment table, already missing Julia's presence. As she picked up two glasses of lemonade, the hairs on the back of her neck tingled. She turned, not surprised to see the captain standing behind her.

"Good evening, Miss Fairchild." His blue eyes seeming to take her in with one, thorough glance.

What did he see? she wondered. Then she reminded herself she didn't want to know. Still holding two glasses of lemonade, she returned his greeting. "Captain Hawke."

Something shuttered across his eyes, giving her pause. When he didn't offer any apology for not giving her his true identity, she frowned. "It hardly seems fair that you've known my name this entire time but I only had part of yours. It makes me think you must be hiding something."

He reached out to take the glasses of lemonade from her hands then set them on the table from where she'd just retrieved them.

"One of those is for my mother," Lettie protested.

"She already has some," the captain advised.

Lettie studied the far end of the room until she found her mother, who did indeed have a glass in her hand.

The captain offered his elbow. "I'm pleased to see you are not in need of rescue for once."

She decided against responding as anything that came to mind would be considered rude. Funny how learning that he wasn't quite who she thought he was made her treat him differently. "Where are we going?"

"I thought we might have a word in private."

Lettie slowed her steps as regret filled her. Part of her longed to share another kiss with him. But the other part worried that he only intended to lecture her on staying safe.

"I cannot risk it," she said at last. "We have high hopes

my sister will receive an offer soon, and Mother was not pleased when I stepped out into the garden with you last time."

He scowled. "Then I suppose we must attempt another dance if we wish to converse."

Pleasure filled her. She so rarely got to dance that having a second one in the space of a few days was delightful. "I would like that very much."

He glanced at her, the uncertainty in his expression tugging at her. "Are you sure? My movements are clumsy at best."

" We managed to move quite well together last time, did we not?" She smiled up at him, hoping to ease his concern.

"Yes, I suppose we did." With a sigh, he moved toward the dance floor as though reluctant.

"Was there something in particular you wanted to discuss?"

"I have discovered the lodging house in which your Alice lives quite by accident."

"Oh?" Lettie asked with interest. "Where?"

Nathaniel smiled. "I'll merely tell you that she's safe, if in cramped quarters. If you feel the need to speak further with her, I'd be happy to deliver a message."

Lettie tried to scowl in displeasure, but how could she when the strains of a waltz filled the air as they reached the dance floor? She supposed she'd have to be satisfied with his offer.

When his hand came to rest on her waist with his other firmly grasping hers, her thoughts fell away. The intimacy of the dance engulfed her senses. Or was it Nathaniel who did so?

Waiting for his cue, she kept her steps small to match his, loving the sensation of gliding across the floor in his arms, even though their movements were restricted.

"So there is no need for you to put yourself at risk to locate her whereabouts," he continued as he became more comfortable with the steps.

Her gaze held his as she considered his words, trying to return her focus to the subject. "Are you simply making that up so I won't try to find her?"

He lifted a brow. "Are you accusing me of lying?"

The heat in his gaze should've warned her she was treading on thin ground. "No, of course not."

"Then what?"

"You seem quite determined to keep me away. Inventing an answer to one of my quests would be a simple method to do so."

"That would be lying."

"You never lie?"

"It would be an unusual occurrence. Something I avoid at all costs." A shadow cast down over his expression, making her wonder at the reason. "Do you lie often?"

She sighed. "It's nothing I'm proud of, but with four younger sisters, and overprotective parents, I fear I have told a falsehood once or twice."

"Such as your whereabouts of late?"

She reluctantly nodded, though it wasn't as if she were telling him something he didn't already know.

"If you'd stay away from the seedier parts of London, you wouldn't need to lie." His gaze dropped to her lips, and she found herself licking them. The heat returned to his gaze, but now it seemed to have an entirely different meaning.

She wished they were alone, dancing on a private terrace. Then she would know if he was thinking what she thought he was thinking—that he would like to kiss her. Because she would certainly like to kiss him.

The music swelled as though answering her desire. Nathaniel turned her, and her skirt swung out around his bad leg just as he stepped forward. He stumbled slightly, pulling her close as he caught himself. Their bodies touched from breast to knee for a long moment, the heat of him catching her by surprise.

The contact felt glorious. Her gaze lifted to his, and she wondered if he thought the same. But his expression was unreadable as he lowered his gaze, first to her lips, then to her modest neckline. Her gown was snug around her breasts, the pale fabric doing little to hide her generous curves.

His hand rose ever so slightly from her waist, up along her ribs, resting just at the swell of her breast as they faced each other.

She couldn't breathe, couldn't think. Nor did she know how to react. Her breast tingled, and she had the strangest urge to arch into his touch. But she was well aware of where they were—at the edge of the dance floor in plain sight of well over a hundred people, including her mother.

This man puzzled her to no end. She didn't understand what he wanted from her. And it seemed she no longer knew what she wanted for herself.

The music stopped yet he continued to hold her a moment more, his intense blue gaze remaining on hers.

"Thank you for the dance, Miss Fairchild. Be safe." He released her at last, bowed and turned away, disappearing into the crowd.

Her heart thundering in her chest, she returned to a position along the wall. A place eminently more suited to her as it was safe and familiar, a far cry from the danger her heart faced each moment she spent with Nathaniel.

CHAPTER SIX

"Nothing is more common than to discover a hideous stew of courts and alleys reeking in poverty and wretchedness almost in the shadow of the palatial abodes of the great and wealthy."
~ *The Seven Curses of London*

Nathaniel cursed as he lay in bed late that night, staring at the ceiling once again. Sleep was ever elusive. He sorely missed its company and the depths of escape it provided. Of late, nothing seemed to offer him reprieve from his thoughts or his memories or the damned ache in his leg.

Tonight, one more issue added to his sleeplessness—desire for Letitia pulsed through his body. That certainly didn't help him fall into slumber. Why couldn't he find a willing woman and be done with this lust? Yet the idea of anyone other than Letitia didn't sound the least bit appealing.

What was she doing at this moment? Was she still at the ball? He'd left soon after their dance.

With an oath, he shoved back the covers and swung his legs over the side of the bed. He wasn't certain why he bothered to attempt to sleep anymore. He rubbed his injured thigh and the jagged scar that marked it, wishing for a reprieve from the pain as well. The bone-deep ache never left, though at times it eased.

Like during his dance with Letitia.

He wouldn't question how the awkward dance with her reduced the pain. Perhaps it just helped him forget it for a short while because the rest of his body felt so alive while holding her in his arms.

He lit the lamp on his bedside table and rose. After pacing his bedroom, he decided his only hope for sleep was to tire himself further. Now was as good a time as any to take a closer look at the brothel he'd recently heard about.

He dressed in his street clothes, as he'd come to think of the worn tweed jacket and simple trousers. With his pistol in his coat pocket, one knife tucked in his belt and the other in the top of his boot, he retrieved his cane from the corner near the door and made his way down the hall to the stairs.

He let himself out the front door, locking it behind him. Dibbles would not be pleased when he discovered he'd taken yet another midnight stroll. But Nathaniel knew he could take care of himself. All his years in the military had proven that. Walking eased the stiffness in his leg, tired his body, and helped keep his memories at bay.

Though he'd expected a period of adjustment after leaving the Navy, he'd underestimated how difficult it would be. He relived certain events over and over, wondering what he should've done differently, how he could've saved more of his men. In many ways, he was grateful for the purpose that now filled his life. The numbness he'd experienced after leaving the service had eased, and his irrational anger was directed toward a specific target. But nothing seemed to halt his vivid dreams.

He shifted his attention to his surroundings, noting how the fog had settled in some areas. It swirled about his legs as he walked. The quiet streets of his neighborhood faded to a slightly more boisterous atmosphere despite the late hour as he limped toward one of the seedier neighborhoods of London. The damp air mingled with the smoke of coal fires and a myriad of other scents, most unpleasant, that filled the city.

With his destination in mind, he passed a tavern and a theater, both of which had closed for the night. That didn't keep people from roaming the streets in the area.

A woman who seemed a bit worse for drink approached him with a grin and only one or two teeth missing. "Aren't ye a totty? Do ye fancy a shag?"

"No, thank you," Nathaniel replied.

"A quick toss then? I know just how to please a fine man such as yerself." She gave him a wink and made a rude gesture with her hand that made her meaning clear.

"I'm certain you're quite skilled, but I must decline." Nathaniel kept walking, hoping she'd find another customer.

"Come on, now. I just need a little dust money." She drew her tattered shawl over her shoulders, covering her generous cleavage.

He resisted the urge to toss her a coin, knowing she'd only use it to buy more gin, based on her current level of inebriation. Giving a handout to some only encouraged them to pursue their vices. Luckily, she remained near the theater, no doubt hoping some randy toff would wander by in need of her services.

Soon he neared the brothel he'd heard referenced in a conversation on the street two days past. Apparently this one occasionally offered young girls touted to be virgins.

His friend, Marcus de Wolfe, the Earl of Warenton, had recently sent a letter, sharing additional information he'd uncovered from his encounter with those involved in using his ships to smuggle girls. Nathaniel knew Warenton hoped he'd continue his quest to stop the men entrapping young girls with false promises in order to sell them.

After learning the facts, how could he turn his back on

such an atrocity? Though he knew he might very well end up dead if he continued to pursue this problem, something had to be done to stop it.

Warenton had advised that he'd be here himself if it weren't for the fact that his new wife was expecting a babe. Traveling from Northumberland to London was made far more difficult with a pregnant wife. And after losing his first wife to an illness many years ago, Warenton wasn't taking any chances.

Still, the problem was too large for Nathaniel to solve alone. Warenton had written of Josephine Butler, an acquaintance of his who'd become an advocate for this issue. If she continued to bring it to the attention of others, using the media as well as helping to change legislation, progress could be made. So, in some respects, Nathaniel wasn't the only person fighting this battle.

That didn't mean he wouldn't appreciate having someone with whom to strategize. He feared involving Letitia would only give her a stronger desire to take action. That would never do. She'd already put herself at risk too many times.

The cool air soaked into his leg, tightening the muscles. His limp became more pronounced as he went, but still he continued to the brothel situated just off Vine Street. The location was ironic as a police station stood nearby. No doubt someone on the force had been paid well to look the other way.

Every window of the three-story house had a shade pulled low with a faint glow around the edges. After watching the front door briefly, he moved toward the rear entrance, accessible by an alleyway. He was more interested in the operation behind the brothel than its customers.

Nathaniel knew the madam who owned this brothel also owned others in the city. Rumor said she waited at train stations, watching for families with young girls and would offer to watch the children while the parents went to purchase tickets or collect their luggage. Once the parents stepped away, she took the girls, some as young as eight, and locked them in one of her brothels. The girls would be drugged and sold to the highest bidder.

The very idea turned Nathaniel's stomach. He shouldn't be shocked any longer at the atrocities people committed for greed. Not after all he'd seen. But somehow this, in his own country, blocks from where he lived, made him livid.

Though the urge was strong to break down the brothel's door, pistol in hand, and shoot those involved, he held back. Halting what happened this one night would not solve the bigger problem, and that was his true purpose.

So he watched, grateful for the gas lamp above the back door that would reveal the faces of those who aided in this terrible crime. Several men entered the walled garden with its wrought-iron gate then made their way up the path to the four steps at the rear entrance. Some he had a chance to study but not all.

A tall, stocky man with a round face and a bowler hat paused on the back step and glanced around before stepping inside. Nathaniel straightened. That was the same man he'd seen at Blackfriars Bridge when he'd come across Miss Fairchild. This was exactly what he needed. One person he could follow through the operation. Someone who had worked in this trade long enough to know the details of their activities, names of others involved, and those in charge.

Years of training had him drawing nearer as determination filled him to learn more. Yet he paused to weigh the risk as no good would come from gaining information if he was killed before he could make use of it. He was alone and couldn't forget that. Still, he couldn't allow this opportunity to pass by. He eased into the shadows, crossed the alley, and moved closer to the back door.

This certainly wouldn't be the first time the odds had been against him to complete a mission. He opened the garden gate, grateful it didn't squeak. Pausing to listen, he debated on the best method of entering. Had there been enough traffic in and out the back door that one more person coming in would draw little notice? While most people would be in the front where customers arrived, the men he'd noted would surely remain in the rear of the house.

He might've been better off posing as a customer interested in a maiden, but the idea of giving the madam money went against every bone in his body.

Slowly he passed through the small garden until he reached the back door. He considered extinguishing the light, but he might have need of it on his way out.

A test of the knob proved it to be unlocked, and he opened the door. Keeping his cane at the ready, he slipped inside. The hallway in which he found himself was dimly lit. Back stairs rose upward to his left, a closed door to his right. Laughter and music came from the front of the house. That was no doubt where customers were shown, where each man would select which woman he wanted for the night. Except for any maidens. They were kept locked away.

He listened at the closed door, barely able to make out the murmur of male voices. That would never do. He turned the knob slowly and cracked open the door. Much better. Now he could hear most of what the men said.

The room was a kitchen and the men were gathered around a table from what little he could see through the narrow crack.

"Are the two virgins locked in tight?" one of the men asked.

Nathaniel froze at the question. Had that man convinced some of the girls at Blackfriars Bridge to succumb to his ploy that day? *Damn.*

"I secured the doors to their rooms meself."

"Good that they're on the third floor. Less chance of us hearin' their screams."

"They'll make some lucky toffers happy tonight."

"And more the next night. How many times will the madam claim they're virgins?"

The laughter that followed made Nathaniel's stomach clench. An image of two terrified girls filled his mind, changing his plan completely. He reached out and quietly closed the kitchen door.

Tonight would no longer be spent merely gathering information.

The picture of those scared little girls locked away propelled him up the stairs. He couldn't live with himself if he didn't attempt to rescue them. Moving slowly, he kept his back to the wall, pausing on the second floor to listen.

Six closed doors greeted him. Light cast from beneath them, and muffled grunts and groans could be heard along with a few encouraging words that sounded false even from this distance.

He continued up the back stairs, moving as quickly as he dared. Another six doors marked this floor as well, but only two displayed light at the bottom. He listened at the first one, hearing nothing. He hoped she didn't yet have a customer. Or perhaps she'd been drugged to keep her quiet. With a shake of his head, he acknowledged it could be either or both.

The sound of footsteps on the front stairs had him searching for a place to hide, but he found none. He hurried back to the rear stairs and rushed down several steps, staying low, hoping whomever approached wouldn't come this way.

"She's a virgin, just as we promised," a woman said in the quiet hallway. "I know how much you like them." The jingle of keys could be heard. "I'll have you take a look at her and then we'll agree on the price."

"Excellent," a man said. Even from this distance, Nathaniel could hear the eagerness in his tone.

Did the man not realize the girl was here against her will? Or did he simply not care?

"If you don't like this one, I have one more you can peek at, though I can't promise anything as someone else requested her."

Nathaniel eased forward just as the two of them disappeared into the room.

"You there," a man's voice demanded from below Nathaniel on the stairs. "What do you think you're doing?"

Nathaniel rose but didn't answer nor did he turn to face the man. He lifted his cane, waiting for him to draw closer.

"I say, you there." The sounds of his steps on the stairs heralded his arrival.

When Nathaniel felt his presence directly behind him, he spun, raising one end of his cane to strike the man on the side of his head. The blow knocked him to the side, and he crumpled to the stairs, unmoving.

Well aware that the longer he was in this house, the greater the risk, Nathaniel hurried to the door the madam had gestured toward. A check on the knob confirmed it was locked. Still listening for the man and woman in the other room, he used his knife to unlock it, slipped inside, and closed the door behind him.

A young girl, perhaps ten or eleven years of age, lay on the bed in a white nightgown. Her eyes widened in fear at the sight of him but no sound escaped her lips nor did she move.

Nathaniel could only assume she'd been given something to calm her. An opiate of some sort, perhaps. He had to get her out of there. But the closer he came, the more frightened she appeared.

He held a finger to his lips, gesturing for her to remain quiet. "I'm taking you out of here."

The girl appeared even more alarmed at his words and shook her head frantically. He cursed under his breath, trying to think of a way to reassure her, but he had no experience in speaking with little girls. For the first time, he wished Letitia were here.

"You don't have to stay, no matter what they told you," he tried again. "I will help you return home."

"Truly?" she asked as tears filled her eyes.

"We'll leave immediately. But I need your help."

Still uncertain, she whispered, "With what?"

"Helping me free the other girl. Do you know her?"

She nodded.

The rattle of keys sounded at the door. Apparently the man had been less than pleased with the first girl and wanted to see his other option.

"Lay on the bed for a moment," Nathaniel ordered the girl.

She moved into the same pose as when Nathaniel had first entered, her face tightened in fear. Nathaniel stepped behind the door, cane in hand.

"What of this one?" the madam asked. "She joined us only yesterday. She's as fresh as the first snow."

"She's quite lovely." The portly, well-dressed man must've been in his early fifties. Certainly old enough to know better. "Yes, I'd prefer her."

"She's twice the price as the other girl."

"That's ridiculous. Why would one be worth more than the other?" the man sputtered as he stepped farther into the room.

"She's promised to another, and she's younger, fresher."

Nathaniel's stomach churned at her description.

"Very well. She'll do nicely." He rubbed his hands together eagerly.

"I'll leave you two to become acquainted then." She turned to the girl. "Anna, treat Mr. Jonesby real nice, just how we talked about it. He's one of our best customers."

The anger surging through Nathaniel was difficult to control. The man had eyes only for the girl as the madam closed the door. Nathaniel saw no point in questioning him. He didn't care to hear anything he had to say. As far as he was concerned, there was no excuse for his behavior.

Anna's gaze slid from the man to Nathaniel, and he turned to see what she looked at, catching sight of Nathaniel.

Nathaniel's anger erupted. Before Mr. Jonesby could utter a word, Nathaniel struck him over the head sharply with his cane. The man dropped to the floor like a sack of flour, landing with a loud thump.

The girl bolted upright, eyes wide. "Did ye kill him?"

"Unfortunately not, so we must hurry." Perhaps he'd think twice about returning.

She scrambled off the bed, obviously deciding that leaving with Nathaniel was a better option than anything that awaited her here. She stepped around the man on the floor, giving him as wide a berth as possible. Still staring down at him, she took Nathaniel's hand. "He's not nice."

"I would have to agree. Now let us get you out of here." He opened the door and peered into the hall, relieved to find it empty.

With his cane in one hand, and the girl's hand in the other, he crossed the hall and made quick work of the lock on the door.

A glance into the room revealed only a girl in it. Hoping to avoid alarming her, Nathaniel gestured for Anna to precede him. She hurried to where the girl lay on the bed. This one appeared to be asleep. When Anna shook her, she opened her eyes briefly only to close them again.

"Wake up," Anna demanded. "It's time to go. We've been rescued."

The other girl's eyes popped open. "Rescued?" The word was slightly slurred.

Nathaniel frowned. How was he to get both girls out without raising the alarm, especially when one was barely coherent?

Laughter and voices drifted up from the floor below.

There was no time to waste.

"Quickly now. We must be on our way," he bid the girls.

While Anna prodded the other girl to her feet, Nathaniel returned to the stairs, pleased to find the man he'd struck still unconscious. He lifted him under the arms and dragged him into the room as Anna and the other girl stepped into the hallway.

"We must hurry," Nathaniel told them both as he shut the door, leaving the unconscious man inside.

Too late, Nathaniel caught sight of the horror on the other girl's face. She burst into tears.

"Shh," Anna warned her sternly. "Come on with ye. Be brave like us." Anna gestured to herself and Nathaniel, almost making him smile. Then she took the girl's hand in her own. Nathaniel could've hugged her.

"Follow me," he directed as he hurried to the stairs, glancing over his shoulder to make certain no one followed. As they neared the landing of the first floor, he said, "Stay close."

He drew a breath of relief when he saw the hall was empty then continued down the stairs.

"What the—" A man stared in surprise at Nathaniel as he reached the main level, the girls directly behind him.

Nathaniel hesitated to strike him while the girls watched. They'd witnessed enough terrible things during their stay. "I'm taking them out for some fresh air," he told the man, doing his best to act casual as he gestured for the girls to keep moving to the back door and freedom.

"Says who?" he asked as he closed the door to the kitchen and approached Nathaniel.

"Me. They've been cooped inside far too long." Nathaniel shifted so he was between the man and the girls who had now reached the door.

"Ye need to approve that with Brigger before ye take 'em anywhere." The man started to turn away as though to find Brigger himself.

"I already did," Nathaniel said. He gestured for Anna to open the door.

"I don't think—"

Nathaniel didn't allow him to finish the thought but struck him with his cane alongside the head. The man howled in pain as he bent over. Wanting to shut him up, Nathaniel struck him again on the back of the head. The man slid bonelessly to the floor, quiet at last.

A quick glance down the hall showed no one else coming, but Nathaniel knew that would be short lived. The rush of footsteps sounded so he hurried out the door to find the girls waiting outside at the foot of the stairs. He held the door closed, listening. A muffled oath sounded when the unconscious man was discovered.

Nathaniel held the knob loosely, waiting for the feel of it turning. As the door began to open, he shoved hard with his shoulder. The door caught their pursuer unaware. Nathaniel repeated the gesture, pulling the door forward then shoving it back. By the solid thump, he guessed he'd hit something hard. Hopefully it had been the man's head. He risked a glance inside and confirmed his suspicion. A man lay sprawled on the floor near the door.

Where one pursuer was, another was certain to follow. Nathaniel closed the door and extinguished the gas light, leaving the entrance in darkness then turned toward the girls.

But they were gone.

Heart pounding, he hurried through the dark garden to the gate, searching as he went but still didn't find them.

"Anna?" he softly called out.

Only silence reached him. He passed through the gate and latched it, using his knife to twist the closure so it couldn't be easily opened. Anything to give them a few more minutes to make their escape. Assuming he could find the girls.

He looked up and down the alleyway but caught no sight of the small forms dressed all in white. His little ghosts were gone. He left the brothel behind, hoping he was taking the most logical path out of the area.

But he couldn't find the girls anywhere.

CHAPTER SEVEN

"It is in the infant labour market especially that this new and dashing spirit of commercial enterprise exercises itself chiefly. There are many kinds of labour that require no application of muscular strength; all that is requisite is dexterity and lightness of touch, and these with most children are natural gifts."

~ The Seven Curses of London

After Nathaniel left the ball, Lettie searched for Julia, hoping to speak with her again to find out more about the mysterious captain, but to no avail. The more Lettie learned of him, the more intrigued she was. Odd how thinking of him as a military hero was so intimidating. She had been prepared to argue with Mr. Hawke but was more compelled to heed the captain's requests.

Why hadn't he told her his true identity? She could understand why he hadn't at their first meeting, but why had he allowed the misconception to continue that evening at the ball? Did his military rank not matter to him? Or did he not care what she believed about him?

The latter thought was the more logical of the two but certainly didn't please her. Her focus needed to remain on his involvement with her goal rather than how many secrets his blue eyes held.

Why was he appearing in the same areas of the city as she? She should've pursued answers to that question during their dance. With a lift of her chin, she promised herself to ask him next time she saw him and not become distracted by the way he made her feel.

In truth, she wasn't used to speaking to a man such as he. It was no wonder that when he studied her so closely, she lost all her wits.

Did Rose have the same experience when her duke looked at her?

With a shake of her head, she reminded herself there was no comparison between the two. The duke was courting Rose, while the captain—

She stopped short. In truth, she had no idea what he was doing. Certainly not courting her. Perhaps warning her would be a better description. Or berating her. It was difficult to say.

At last she spotted Julia not far from the ballroom entrance. As she stepped forward, anxious to speak with her, Dalia placed a hand on her arm.

"I noted you shaking your head and frowning from across the room," she said. "People are going to start talking if you continue to act so oddly."

Lettie scowled at her sister both for her comment and for interrupting her hope to speak with Julia. "I suppose I forgot I wasn't invisible."

Dalia looped her arm through hers. "Never say such a thing. You are a wonder, and I refuse to allow you to forget it."

Lettie could only raise her brow. Dalia wasn't always kind. She spoke with blunt honesty that put off many people despite their mother's attempt to curb it. This sudden compliment made Lettie suspicious.

"What?" Dalia protested, eyes wide. "I truly adore you and I want you to know it."

"What is it you need?" Lettie asked cautiously, one eye

still on Julia, hoping she didn't leave before Lettie had a chance to question her.

Her sister scoffed in denial.

Lettie waited, certain there had to be more to her comment than a simple compliment. Not that Dalia didn't love her. But she knew her sister well.

"I merely wondered if you'd care to ride in Hyde Park early tomorrow morning with me," Dalia admitted.

"Who are you meeting?"

"Can't I want to spend time with you?"

"That is highly unlikely and we both know it. Explain yourself. Full details if you want me to consider agreeing."

Heaving a sigh, she admitted, "I intend to meet Mr. Brover there."

Lettie was even more suspicious. "Mother and Father wouldn't like you to do so because..."

"They haven't yet met him." The slight defensive edge to her sister's tone raised more suspicions.

Certain there was more to the story than Dalia was offering, Lettie tried to gather her patience. She wanted to speak with Julia, but once again, she had to put aside her personal wants and aid one of her sisters.

After several more questions, Lettie unearthed the fact that the man was a second son in a family with limited funds. Second sons of any sort were not to be considered as their mother would disapprove of such a relationship. Therefore, Lettie had to think long and hard about whether she should agree to accompany her. Encouraging rebellious behavior was not advisable.

But something in the depth of Dalia's dark eyes had her reconsidering. What if her sister was truly enamored with this young man? Shouldn't she have a chance at love, if that was what this was? Lettie felt obligated to help, or at least determine if the young man was sincere or more interested in the modest dowry marrying Dalia would provide.

"Very well. I will accompany you, but I want to meet

him. And the pair of you must remain in sight at all times."
Lettie thought she owed her sister at least that much. "But
if I don't care for him I will be forced to warn Mother."

Dalia's smile lit her face. "You'll like him, I promise."
She briefly squeezed Lettie's arm. "Thank you, dear Lettie.
I truly don't know what we'd do without you."

Convince a maid to serve as chaperone instead? The little voice
in her head was not always nice. But part of it was true. It
almost felt as if she were a maidenly aunt who served as
chaperone when no one else was available.

The idea hurt more than she cared to admit.

No wonder she enjoyed dancing with Nathaniel. He
didn't make her feel spinsterish at all. With him, she felt
vibrant and alive.

Fresh determination filled her to speak with Julia. She
had to learn more about him.

"If you'll excuse me, I need to speak with Julia," Lettie
said.

"Of course. Thank you, Lettie," Dalia responded with a
smile before stepping away.

But as Lettie moved toward Julia, her friend walked out
the ballroom door, leaving Lettie standing alone in
disappointment at the lost opportunity.

How often had she put her family before her own
wants? Too many times to count. This was simply one
more. She swallowed hard, uncertain why tonight felt so
painful.

The rest of the evening passed slowly. She caught a
glimpse of the man Dalia intended to meet when her sister
spoke briefly with him near the refreshment table. She was
certain it was him by the brightness of her sister's smile.
Lettie realized she wasn't the only one who needed to
work on better masking her emotions.

When her mother at last signaled it was time to leave,
she released a grateful sigh. She waited while her sisters
gathered in the foyer, and their coach was called to take
them home, surprised at the impatience filling her at the

whole process.

As always, her mother questioned each daughter for details on who they'd danced with or spoke to, either encouraging or discouraging as the case might be. Lettie listened long enough to note Dalia didn't mention the man in whom she was interested.

Her thoughts drifted as the conversation flowed around her. Perhaps it was best that Julia had left when she had. Lettie needed to put aside her curiosity about Nathaniel and focus on her original goal—to help someone. She had no choice but to take his threat seriously. If he mentioned to her father where she'd been, her mother was certain to hear about it as well. The two presented a united front to their daughters in all matters. Her father always sided with her mother even if he disagreed.

How else could she help if she couldn't venture to any of the areas where children in need lived? She had to determine a way to have them come to her. But how?

The book had mentioned ads that a family might place in a newspaper if they were willing to give up their child for adoption. That might be another way to find someone who could use her assistance. Obviously, Lettie couldn't adopt the child, but contacting such a family might provide a way for her to find a child to help. And she'd be keeping her word to Nathaniel.

A rather sharp elbow found its way into her ribs, causing her to yelp.

"Lettie, Mother has said your name three times now. What on earth is wrong with you?" Violet asked.

"I'm sorry." She offered a smile with her apology as she looked at her mother. "I'm tired, I suppose. What did you need?"

"I wanted to know of your conversation with Captain Hawke." The impatience in her mother's voice raised Lettie's guard.

She should've realized her mother would discover his

identity. After all these years of not having her mother's attention, it was a shock to feel her scrutiny now.

"Well," Lettie began, searching for a valid reply. She couldn't tell her they shared the same interest of helping those less fortunate. That would only bring about a lecture.

Before Lettie could come up with an answer, her mother continued, "Who introduced you?"

"Lady Julia. I happened to be speaking with her when he claimed his dance with her." Lettie held her breath while she waited to see if her mother believed her.

"Odd. I didn't see Lady Julia dancing with him. Only you."

Lettie glanced down at her lap, well aware that if she met her mother's gaze, she'd know Lettie wasn't telling the truth. Lettie was a poor liar in addition to not being good at hiding her emotions. One more fault on which she needed to work.

"Lady Julia's father is under the weather again. Poor dear," Lettie said, hoping to cast her mother's focus elsewhere.

"I'm surprised he's survived this long. He seems to have one illness after another. It's very kind of you to befriend her, Lettie.

Lettie wanted to laugh. If anyone was kind, it was Julia.

"She has excellent taste in fashion," her mother continued. "I wonder who her dressmaker is."

The conversation continued to other topics, allowing Lettie to breathe a sigh of relief. She didn't want to draw her mother's attention now. Not when she was on the verge of action. Granted, her mother wouldn't approve of those activities, but Lettie didn't care.

She wanted to make a difference, and for once, she was going to do what *she* wanted.

"Girls? Anna?" Nathaniel called out softly. He knew

the men from the brothel would burst out the rear entrance any moment and didn't want to draw their notice. But he also feared the girls had already been caught. Where could they be?

He strode past the rear entrance of two other houses before noting one had an unlatched gate. Easing it open, he called again, searching for their white gowns in the dim light.

"Here," a voice answered. The girls rose from their hiding place.

The relief he felt weakened his legs. He didn't care to question why it had become so important that this mission was successful, but it was.

"Allow us to hurry before they start searching," Nathaniel said, gesturing for them to come before realizing they probably couldn't see him in his dark clothing. "Come along."

The girls hurried forward, holding hands and shivering in the cool night air.

Anna placed her hand in his. "We're ready, sir."

The gravity of the situation struck him once more as he looked at the two expectant faces. He would do all in his power to save them. They could not be taken again. As he led them out of the gate, he made certain to leave it slightly ajar. Perhaps their pursuers would see it and stop to search the garden.

"I'm going to ask you to walk as quickly as you can for a time," he whispered.

Without waiting for their reply, he lengthened his stride, his injured thigh already protesting despite the assistance of his cane. He'd already walked too far and the altercation in the brothel had worsened it. He ignored the pain, casting his thoughts to where they could hide or if they should search for a cab. The best way to deal with the pain was to focus on something else as he'd learned on his many military missions.

Holding tight to Anna's hand, he glanced back as they

rushed out of the alley and onto the street to make certain the other girl was still with them. Well aware they were tiring, he offered as many encouraging words as he could but kept moving.

Their white gowns would make them an easy target even in the dark, so he took several turns down side streets and alleyways. No one shouted in protest as they hurried past.

By now, several men must be looking for them. They would most likely take a cab to search faster. The idea had Nathaniel moving faster.

"A little bit farther, and we'll rest," he promised the girls.

The smallest one was growing tired. She stumbled several times, crying out as her bare feet scraped the cobbles. They couldn't stop yet. Nathaniel lifted her into his arms. "I'll carry you for a bit, shall I? How nice will it be to see your mother and father again?"

When the girls starting sniffling, he realized he'd once again said the wrong thing. He offered what few words of comfort he could think of.

At last they came to a hansom cab stand, and to his relief, a cab and driver were there.

He assisted the girls into the cab as he called directions to the driver. "There's an extra shilling for you if you drive quickly."

The man flicked the reins and the horse started forward before Nathaniel had closed the door. The meager light inside the cab revealed the girls' frightened faces, their big eyes staring at him.

He offered a tentative smile. "Are you both well?"

Anna smiled back and ran a hand along the seat as she looked around the interior of the cab. "I've never ridden in a hansom afore."

That seemed to lighten the other girl's mood as they marveled at the experience.

"Ye're not just takin' us to some other place, are ye?"

the other girl asked.

"No. I am not. I promise on the Queen's honor." That didn't seem to impress her. "On my mother's honor."

She gave a nod. "That'll do," she said and leaned back against the seat.

"How did you come to be at the brothel?" he asked. If their parents had sold them, there was no point in returning them home. He'd have to find another place for them.

"We were promised jobs as maids," Anna said, sharing a look with the other girl. "But when we arrived at the house to work, a man was there waiting for us, and he took us to the brothel." She blinked back tears. "He said we'd never see our families again."

"You're safe now," he reassured them. "You'll be home soon."

Anna released the other girl's hand and shifted to sit beside him. She took his hand and held it tightly, smiling up at him. "We can't thank you enough, sir."

A tightness filled his chest, gathering in the back of his throat. He was a military man for Christ's sake. There was no place for such emotion in his life. But at this moment, something warm and sweet filled him all the same.

As Nathaniel looked at both of them, he realized this was a night he'd never forget. This mission had been far different than the ones he'd completed in the military. He was rather surprised to realize how satisfying it was to know he'd saved these girls from a terrible fate.

When the cab drew to a halt outside the lodging house in which both girls lived, he delivered them to the welcoming arms of their families. The joy on their faces was as all the thanks he needed. He gave each family several shillings, hoping it would help their situation.

A deep satisfaction filled him as he closed the door of the lodging house. The hansom cab awaited him, a good thing as his leg ached like the devil.

With a sigh, he leaned back against the seat, wishing he

had someone with whom to share the look of delight that had been on the girls' faces when they'd been reunited with their families.

He could only sigh again when Letitia came to mind.

CHAPTER EIGHT

"A human creature, and more than all, a helpless human creature, endowed with the noblest shape of God's creation, and with a soul to save or lose, is as much out of place grovelling in filth and contamination as would be a wild cat crouching on the hearth-rug of a nursery."

~ The Seven Curses of London

Lettie loved to ride. Everything about it appealed to her from her horse, to the scenery at Hyde Park, to the freedom. She rode her dappled grey mare as often as she could. The hill and dale and stately trees of the park made her feel as if she were in the country. She adored it all. All except the number of people on Rotten Row and how they looked each other over from head to toe. Lettie felt lacking as she always did in such situations.

Dalia had requested they go before breakfast, earlier than most would, making the ride more pleasurable as far as Lettie was concerned.

The park always smelled fresh—at least fresher than the rest of the city. But this morning's venture here wasn't simply for the joy of it. Lettie wanted to keep a very close eye on her sister and the man she was meeting. For the present moment, that was her responsibility and she intended do it well. Perhaps it was better that a maid hadn't accompanied her sister. Dalia might've managed to convince her to look the other way, but Lettie would not.

As they rode along the sandy tracks, she did her best to ignore her sister's obvious searching and focused on her enjoyment of the ride. Her mare tugged at the reins and seemed to be in high spirits as well. The morning was overcast but still quite pleasant.

"I can't imagine where he could be," Dalia said with a scowl upon her lips.

"Perhaps something came up and changed his plans," Lettie offered, trying to keep her tone neutral. But if he disappointed her sister, that made him a cad in her opinion. She was already prepared to dislike him for wanting to meet Dalia without her family's approval.

"There he is." The excitement in Dalia's face as she stared at someone in the distance made Lettie feel instantly guilty.

Attempting to reserve judgment, she followed her sister's gaze to see the same well-dressed young man she'd glimpsed the previous night riding toward them on a sleek black stallion.

Lettie watched the horse in admiration. It was a beauty. Full of energy, it jerked its head at the reins, but the man seemed to control it well. She reluctantly admired him for both his choice in horses and for handling it so well.

"Good morning," he said as he rode up beside Dalia. Mr. Brover was handsome with dark hair, brown eyes and even features. But there was a slyness to his smile that Lettie didn't care for. Or maybe it was in his eyes.

"Good morning to you as well," Dalia said with a bright smile.

His gaze shifted to Lettie, smiling as Dalia made the introductions.

"How kind of you to accompany your beautiful sister," Brover said to Lettie.

Dalia blushed at his words. Lettie thought them forward.

Brover guided his horse to ride alongside Dalia. "Do you have a preference as to where we ride?"

"Whatever you prefer."

Lettie frowned. Her sister always had an opinion. Always. Was she already trying to be someone she wasn't to gain his interest? That was just what she had warned Rose against. One of the many reasons she liked Nathaniel was because he didn't seem to expect her to be anyone but herself.

She wasn't certain why what Nathaniel thought of her mattered so much. But it did.

As the three of them rode, Dalia sent several glares at Lettie. Lettie looked at her wide-eyed as though she didn't understand what Dalia wanted, well aware her sister would prefer she drop back so the pair might have some privacy.

She had no intention of doing so. Dalia would no doubt be angry, but Lettie didn't care. Until she knew this man better, she wasn't allowing them out of her sight. The best she could do was feign interest in the scenery as though not listening to what they discussed.

Soon they chatted about an upcoming ball and who might be attending, none of which held Lettie's attention. With each Season that passed, she'd felt less and less like she fit in with other ladies. While they were concerned with who wore what and who was invited to which party, Lettie's focus had broadened to the world around her.

Her curiosity had started with her family's servants then grown to their families. She'd read many newspaper articles on the topic of London's poor. The more knowledge she gained, the less important the events of the Season seemed.

Whether she liked it or not, the world as she knew it was dominated by men. She often wondered how different life would be if she'd been born a male. The things she wanted to accomplish would've been far easier if she had.

And while she didn't feel completely fulfilled at the moment, she'd realized playing wife to a husband wouldn't necessarily make her complete either. It wasn't the act of marriage that brought happiness, but the man to whom one was married. None of the men she'd met had made her think twice.

Until now.

If only she could find a way to convince Nathaniel to help her. If she saw him again, she would implore him to do so. He was the only one in her acquaintance who possessed the ability and shared the same concern as she.

The whole process of attempting to find someone to aid had been frustrating thus far. She didn't know enough about the exact nature of the problem to offer real help. As Nathaniel had agreed, money didn't always solve the problem for such families.

Her search in the newspaper that morning had revealed two ads for children being offered for sale. She was tempted to contact both. After all, one might not be available anymore. And if neither had been sold, maybe she could assist both families. She'd saved her pin money for several months now and had enough to offer one-time modest financial assistance. Maybe she could help in some other way as well. Nathaniel would be the perfect person to aid her with this endeavor.

"Is that true, Miss Fairchild?"

Lettie turned to see Lord Brover had leaned forward in his saddle to look at her.

"I'm sorry?" she responded, ignoring Dalia's glare. Her sister should be pleased to know Lettie wasn't listening to their conversation.

"I asked if it was truly your fifth Season. You must have great experience with all these activities." The hard glint in his eye made her think he didn't mean the remark in a complimentary way.

"I'm sure you'll both be at ease with the pace of events soon." She refused to confirm his hurtful words. It was rude of both him and her sister to discuss the number of Seasons she'd had. She sent her sister a look of displeasure.

Dalia had the good sense to look sheepish.

Lettie did her best to pay more attention to their conversation. Did Mr. Brover not realize he would have a better chance of spending time with Dalia if he was kind? Based on their brief acquaintance, she didn't care for him.

After making plans to dance with Dalia at the ball that evening, he bid them goodbye.

"Why must you do that?" Dalia asked, her anger obvious.

"What?"

"Every time you meet someone, especially a man, it's as if you're keeping score."

Lettie considered the claim. To some extent, it was true. She did evaluate them. And thus far, she'd found most lacking.

"It would be refreshing to see you participate in a relationship rather than merely observe," Dalia continued.

"I hardly think—"

"I disagree. You think far too much. Sometimes you have to lead with your heart rather than your head."

Lettie sighed and didn't bother to raise her concerns about Mr. Brover. In Dalia's current mood, they would only fall on deaf ears.

They rode the rest of the way home in silence. She had to admit her social interactions weren't exactly interactive. It wasn't as if she wanted to watch life pass her by. She wanted to participate, but on her terms. Unfortunately, no one in her family understood that.

Only one person did, and that was Nathaniel. With his assistance, she could do far more than observe. Somehow, someway, she had to convince him to aid her.

Nathaniel didn't care to be incapacitated though he

supposed it was a small price to pay for what had been accomplished the previous evening. But lying in bed with a warmer along his leg for this long was frustrating.

He'd slept for a few hours after returning home, only to wake with his leg throbbing, warm to the touch, and swollen. Dibbles had tut-tutted in his usual way and sent for the doctor without Nathaniel's leave. As if Nathaniel didn't already know the doctor would suggest rest and heat. He'd lived with the damned leg for months after all.

It had been six months since he'd been discharged, and seven since he'd received the injury. The bullet he'd taken during a skirmish in India had shattered his thigh bone. He hadn't realized the severity of the wound until after the adrenalin rushing through him had eased. He'd hoped once the bullet was removed, he'd make a full recovery, but that wasn't to be.

The doctor had advised him that when a bone was shattered, the pieces shifted, preventing the bone from knitting properly. Apparently the pieces still moved after significant activity as his leg throbbed endlessly.

The laudanum his doctor had left on the bedside table remained untouched. He'd had enough of the nasty stuff after his first surgery on the leg. The side effects outweighed the benefits, in his opinion. He'd rather have a brandy and hope for the pain to pass.

Today it was taking a hell of a long time.

He read a few more pages of *The Seven Curses of London* in an attempt to take his mind off the pain. Reading that small amount was all he could stomach at a time. The atrocities the author noted made it difficult to simply lie there and read. He wanted to *do* something, to take action to prevent such things from happening within a few miles of his home.

But not this day. He was resigned to remaining in bed at least until the morrow. The doctor's threat of amputation if he didn't allow his leg to heal was enough to keep him in bed. He didn't want to lose his leg.

His bedroom door opened. Nathaniel didn't bother to look up as he expected it was Dibbles once again. The man had been hovering all day.

"What happened?" Tristan asked as he strode into the room. Both his presence and the concern on his face were surprising.

Nathaniel set aside the book, tucking it close to his body and out of his brother's sight. He didn't want to hear a lecture about how it was nonsense. That was certainly what his father would've said, and Tristan would most likely feel the same.

"Good afternoon." Nathaniel sat up as best he could. "I'm afraid I overdid things yesterday. My injury is acting up."

"Shouldn't it be healed by now? You've been back several months."

"I fear this is as good as it's going to get. I need to take better care, I suppose."

Tristan stepped forward and drew the covers back to look at his bare thigh.

"Jesus, man. Have you no manners?" Nathaniel was genuinely shocked that his conservative, stoic brother would do such a thing. Luckily, the loose undergarment he wore maintained his privacy.

"You're my brother. Surely manners are unnecessary."

"Please remember that next time I feel the need to take such liberties with you." Unable to bear his brother's scrutiny at what he knew to be a weakness, he jerked the covers back over his leg.

"As secretive as you are, you leave me no choice but to see the damage for myself. It looks terrible. What does the doctor have to say?"

"Rest, heat. Nothing I haven't heard many times over."

Tristan studied Nathaniel until at last Nathaniel raised a brow. "Have I grown horns?" He couldn't resist using Tristan's words back at him with the hope of shifting his brother's focus.

"I'm amazed my quiet younger brother can bear what must be causing him great pain. What did the military do to you?"

"I don't know that it was the military." He had his father to thank for it. After all, he'd borne emotional pain since he'd been old enough to remember.

From his youngest days, he had memories of his father dismissing him time and again, reminding him that he was the second son, the spare. That Tristan was the golden child and the only one worthy of his attention.

That Nathaniel didn't matter.

He'd heard that over and over until it was part of who he was. Until he'd nearly become numb from it.

Nearly.

But Nathaniel didn't care to discuss any of that with his brother. He waved a hand, wishing he could wipe away the words he'd uttered.

"What do you mean?" Tristan asked. He drew the chair from the desk closer to the bed and took a seat.

"Nothing."

"I wish you'd tell me."

Nathaniel didn't think he truly wanted to hear the answer. "Don't you have another ball to attend this evening?" he asked, more than ready to shift the focus from himself.

Tristan looked away, staring out the window. "I haven't decided if I'll be attending."

"Why not?" Nathaniel didn't understand why his brother wouldn't give into their mother's demands that he marry so she would cease her nagging. Marrying and providing an heir was part of the many duties he carried out so well in other aspects. "Marriage might suit you."

"I doubt that."

"Why?"

Tristan waved at the air, much like Nathaniel had only moments before, and smiled wryly. "Why don't we avoid the topics neither of us wish to discuss?"

"Very well." Though still curious, Nathaniel could hardly demand answers when he wasn't willing to give any of his own.

"What are you reading?"

"Nothing of import." Nathaniel nearly sighed, for he didn't care to discuss that topic either. This awkward conversation reminded him of how far apart he and Tristan were—had always been.

Tristan reached over the top of him and picked up the book. "*The Seven Curses of London.* Only seven? I would've thought our fair city would have a great many more."

"I'm sure none of them would interest you, regardless of the number."

Tristan looked at him blandly. "I believe you judge me and find me lacking, dear brother." He opened the book. "Chapter one. Neglected children." He read silently for a few moments before glancing at Nathaniel. "Do you believe this information to be true?"

"I know it is. I've seen it for myself."

His brother raised his brow, obviously taken aback. "Explain."

"Playing the lord today?" He'd said the one word with no doubt, as though he expected action with his order. It was a reminder how similar he was to their father. At Tristan's frown, Nathaniel offered, "I've spent a few sleepless nights walking. Sometimes those walks take me into areas I wouldn't have otherwise ventured."

"Such as?"

"Whitechapel, for one."

"What on earth would cause you to wander that way?" Tristan gave a mock shudder. "In the dead of night, no less."

"I don't know if I mentioned the scheme that one of Warenton's ships was being used for?"

"Marcus de Wolfe, the Earl of Warenton?"

Nathaniel nodded. "We've remained friends since our days at university together. He discovered cargo was being smuggled aboard his ship. Upon investigating, he realized his vessel was being used to haul young girls to Brussels for their brothels."

"You can't be serious." Tristan appeared incredulous.

"Surely you've read about the white slave trade in the papers."

"In truth, I don't normally pay attention to those sort of articles. It always seems as if they exaggerate the problem."

"In this case, they're not. I assisted him with part of the problem, but later we discovered a large group of men are involved." Nathaniel nodded to the book. "Warenton is the one who sent me that book."

"How interesting." Tristan turned a few more pages, glancing through it. "I might have to purchase a copy of this for myself."

Nathaniel couldn't have been more shocked.

Tristan looked up from the pages at Nathaniel's lack of response and noted his expression. "Why so surprised? Of course I care about what's happening in our city. Why wouldn't I?"

"I suppose I didn't think you would find it of interest."

Tristan scowled, his eyes going cold. "You mean because Father wouldn't have?"

Nathaniel decided it best not to respond.

"I am not his mirror image, you know." Tristan closed the book with a thump. "I should allow you to rest. Wouldn't want to tire my hero of a brother."

"I'm no hero," Nathaniel protested, uncomfortable at the term.

"It's an indisputable fact. There is written proof that you are. I believe Dibbles saved every newspaper article that lauded your efforts. I'm told you earned various medals as well."

Now it was Nathaniel's turn to scowl. He didn't care to be reminded of the honors he'd received. Those didn't change the belief he had of himself, the one tucked away in the depths of his soul.

"I will check on you again on the morrow, shall I? Perhaps we can continue this enlivening conversation." Tristan returned the book to the bed then gave a wave as he walked out the door and closed it behind him.

Still avoiding the laudanum, Nathaniel reached for the decanter of brandy and glass Dibbles had left for him, pouring himself a generous drink.

It wasn't only his leg that hurt.

He wished the brandy better helped either pain.

CHAPTER NINE

"It is only necessary to point to the large number of such children, for they are no better, who annually swell our criminal lists, to prove that somewhere a screw is sadly loose, and that the sooner it is set right the better it will be for the nation.

~ *The Seven Curses of London*

Culbert Rutter swallowed hard as he prepared to give the bad news to his boss, Jasper Smithby. He was almost grateful for the knot on his forehead. Surely it would show Smithby he'd done all he could to stop the bloke.

"What's eating you, Culbert?" Smithby asked as he shoved forkfuls of sausage into his large mouth. "Did someone die?" He paused with his meal to peer closer. "What happened to your head?"

"I fear I have bad news."

"Oh?" Smithby's tone held a warning note Culbert desperately wished he could heed, yet he had no choice but to continue, all too aware how angry his boss would be.

"We lost two of the girls last night."

"Which girls?"

Culbert braced himself. "The newest, young ones we took yesterday morn."

"*Lost them?* How?"

"Some bloke broke into the brothel, made his way to the upper level, and took them." Culbert looked down at the new hat he held to avoid seeing the rage in Smithby's cold blue eyes.

"Where were the guards?"

"He knocked several unconscious and injured others." He dearly wanted to point to his head to make it clear he was one of those.

"One man did all that?" Smithby appeared doubtful that he spoke the truth.

Culbert nodded, still having difficulty believing it himself.

"Who the hell is he?" Spittle and bits of sausage came out with his anger.

"I didn't get his name." Culbert frowned. He'd thought long and hard on the way here about whether to share the full truth. That Hawke was the same man who'd helped to bring their lucrative trips to Brussels to a halt. Based on Smithby's reaction thus far, he decided against it. Somehow, he was certain it would end up being his fault that this man was haunting them.

"I wasn't asking for an introduction." Smithby shoved his plate off the table, sending the utensils flying as well. The tin clattered on the floor, making Culbert jerk at the sound. "Who the hell is he?"

Culbert resisted the urge to press a hand to his stomach as it clenched something terrible. His last meal wasn't sitting well, and with the threat of Smithby's temper hanging over him, the cramps signaled he'd need to leave soon. "I seen him at Blackfriars Bridge a few days ago as well. He was speaking to some woman along with a few girls."

"And?" Smithby raised his brow. "How does that help identify him?"

"I don't know," Culbert admitted with a shrug. "He must've been sniffin' around is all I'm sayin'."

"Bloody hell." Smithby wiped his mouth with the back of his sleeve, much to Culbert's relief. The mix of sausage and spit around his lips was nauseating. "What did the madam have to say?"

Culbert rubbed his ear where she'd slapped him. "Nothin' good. She wants replacement girls by this evenin'. Says she has customers expectin' virgins and won't be disappointin' them, else they'll go elsewhere."

"Did someone leave the door unlocked? How did he get in?"

Culbert shook his head, mostly because he wasn't certain of the details. "He must've picked the lock on the back door as well as the bedroom doors as they were locked too. By the way he took out Johnny, I'd guess he's experienced at fighting." That part was true as he'd seen it for himself aboard the ship back in February.

"Why would someone take a sudden interest in the girls in a brothel?" Smithby rubbed a finger along his upper lip as he thought it over. He eyed Culbert closely, making him squirm.

"Don't make me take out the book, Culbert," he warned.

Culbert's stomach took a sharp turn for the worse. The damned book made all the men nervous, including Culbert. Ever since Smithby had acquired *The Book of Secrets*, he'd had some sort of dark magic that gave Culbert the creeps. It seemed to give him unnatural power to know all and see all.

"I'll find out eventually, so you might as well tell me now. Make it easier on yourself," Smithby warned, eyes narrowed.

"Maybe the fancy lord who owned the steamship has something to do with this." A partial confession was a risk, but it was as much as Culbert was willing to say despite the threat of the book.

"Why? That was months ago."

"I think the man who took the girls is the same one on

the bridge that day with the lord. He's a gentleman at the least, but one who knows what he's about."

Smithby nodded. "I see. We'll have to take extra care in case he shows up again. Double the guards. We must keep the madam happy, or she'll find someone else to supply her with girls."

"She's already threatenin' to find some herself."

"Christ. That's the last thing we need. If she goes to the train station and picks up one, she'll draw too much attention. It gives parents a chance to see her face."

"She insists she needs at least two for tonight."

"Then why are you standing here? Find some."

Culbert moved to turn away, only to stop when Smithby spoke again.

"Don't screw this up, Culbert, else I'll have your head."

"Yes, sir." He took his leave, realizing too late he'd nearly ruined the hat he'd purchased the previous day by gripping it too tightly. With one hand on his stomach, he hurried toward the nearest toilet before his bowels made a fool of him.

Lettie sighed as she glanced over the ballroom the next evening. The hostess for this one favored roses. Vases of the blooms dotted the large room, scenting the air. She was grateful the doors to the garden stood ajar as the combination of the crush of people and the smell of the flowers would've been overwhelming otherwise.

Still no sign of Nathaniel. He hadn't been at the previous evening's event either. Not that it was the only party being held. But if this continued, she'd have no choice but to seek him out at his residence. That was a bold step for a woman, even if she was almost a spinster.

No. She couldn't risk it, she realized. Not with Rose and her duke still undecided.

Perhaps she could send him a message and request his

presence at the ball she'd be attending tomorrow night. While still a forward move, it wasn't nearly as risky.

She had to find a way to speak with him.

After much thought, she'd decided against contacting the people noted in the ads. Each time she read them, a feeling of unease came over her. She could hardly lecture Dalia about propriety if she didn't act above reproach as well. While she knew she was a bit naïve, she was well aware the ads could be some sort of scheme.

That was one more reason she needed Nathaniel to aid her.

As though her thoughts had conjured him, he walked through the entrance to the ballroom. His limp was more noticeable than normal, and his lips had a pinched appearance.

What had happened? She curbed the urge to go to him to discover the cause. Instead, she waited, not far from where many of the chaperones chatted. Though quite certain no one watched her, she tore her gaze away from Nathaniel to glance about the room before looking his way once again.

When his blue eyes locked on hers, she wasn't surprised. He had the uncanny ability to find her, even in a crowd. Her pulse quickened and her mouth went dry as he started toward her. What was it about him that caused her reaction? True, it wasn't as if she met the gaze of very many men. Their glances usually swept right past her, as though she were merely part of the décor.

Was that the cause then? Just having a man's undivided attention, however briefly, made her heart pound like mad? Unable to resist experimenting, she looked about, at last catching a man's gaze nearby. He looked at her briefly then returned to the conversation he was having.

Nothing. No change in her physical being in any way. A glance toward Nathaniel had the whole process starting again. Heat in her cheeks, dryness in her mouth, and a pounding heart.

Before she could reflect on the question any further, he had arrived at her side.

"Good evening, Miss Fairchild." That incredible blue gaze of his swept over her face, as though by simply studying her, he could determine everything he wanted to know.

"Captain." She curtsied. "Has something occurred?"

He frowned. "What do you mean?"

"I couldn't help but notice your limp has considerably worsened."

"It's nothing." He glanced away, but the muscle in his jaw tensed.

"Obviously it's something."

When his eyes met hers once again, she saw the lines around his eyes. She could only assume he was still in pain.

"I overused it."

Somehow she was certain there was more to the story. But she could hardly force it out of him.

The corner of his mouth quirked with the hint of a smile. "Actually, I believe you are the one person among my acquaintances who would truly appreciate the reason."

She gave a little gasp, catching the attention of two elderly women who chatted nearby. Trying to be more circumspect, she demanded, "Now you must tell me. Was it on Blackfriars Bridge? Or at the workhouse? What happened?"

He chuckled softly as he glanced about the room. "Another time perhaps, when we won't be overheard."

"That is exactly why I hoped you would be here this evening."

"Oh?" Funny how the raise of his brow like that made her stomach dance.

She drew a step closer, well aware of the stares from some of the chaperones. Was it because she was speaking with a man or because they found Nathaniel as handsome as she did? "I am in need of your assistance in my quest."

Immediately he frowned. "Based upon my limited

knowledge of your last two quests, I am paralyzed by fear as to what the next one might be."

She tried not to take affront at his comment. "I am still determined to find someone to help." She raised a finger to halt his response. "This option does not take me to any dangerous neighborhoods."

His bland stare caused her to scowl but she forged ahead.

"I have found two advertisements in somewhat respectable newspapers that offer children for sale."

"You jest."

"I don't mean to buy them. I merely want to reach out to the families and see if I can help. If they're interested in selling their young ones, they must be in desperate need."

The muscle in his jaw tensed once again.

Lettie felt the need to further explain herself. "I intend to offer to meet them in a place that would prove safe to all involved."

"Where might that be?" At her lack of an answer, he asked, "And offer to do what?" His eyes dared her to continue.

"I will inquire as to how I might be of assistance."

"What form of 'assistance' do you think might be requested?"

Her confidence wavered. "That is the point about which I am still unclear. What would you suggest?"

"I would suggest you do nothing. Those ads might be a scheme of some sort."

"I thought as much, which is why I have not yet taken action." She looked up at him from beneath her lashes. "Would you consider aiding me?"

He glanced away, watching the dancing couples twirling about the floor.

Hope rose inside Lettie. At least he hadn't immediately said no.

"I will think upon it." He looked quite displeased. "That is all I can offer."

"Is there anything I could do to sway you?"

He closed his eyes briefly before his gaze tangled with hers. She was unprepared for the heat in them. "Do not offer what you cannot give."

For a brief moment, she had the craziest notion—

That he might be suggesting—

But no. How silly. Though they'd shared two kisses, that didn't mean he desired her. Both times, he'd been frustrated with her. Somehow his frustration had twisted into a kiss. She didn't care to analyze the reason he'd done it. After all these years as a wallflower, she knew her limitations. She wasn't the type of person to catch a man's interest in that way.

"I don't know what you mean."

"I suppose you don't."

The sick feeling of embarrassment coursing through her was all too familiar. This was the part of social functions she detested, when it seemed as if everyone was speaking in a foreign language she didn't understand. She felt even more isolated than normal.

With a sigh, she pushed all the uncomfortable emotions aside to focus on her goal. "I would very much like your assistance to find some way to aid a neglected child."

Nathaniel turned to study her more closely. "Where did you hear that exact term?"

Though reluctant to reveal how much she depended on books for her knowledge, no other ideas came to mind. "I happened upon a book called, *The Seven*—"

"*Curses of London*," Nathaniel finished for her.

Lettie stared at him in surprise, unable to hide her smile. "You know of the book?"

"A friend sent it to me."

"Isn't it fascinating? I mean, the information shared is terrible if even half of it is true. But I confess to being riveted by it."

"Why do you find it so interesting?" He seemed truly curious as to her answer. "I can't believe other ladies your age would agree."

"No, I don't suppose they would. My sisters certainly don't." She wondered for a moment if Julia would, not that she had any intention of asking. She'd learned long ago not to bring up books she'd read with friends. No one seemed to share the same interests as she. "I find it interesting to learn how others live when it's so different than my life, I suppose. But even more, it makes me want to help."

"On that we agree, but do not underestimate the danger involved."

"All the more reason for us to work together, don't you think?" She couldn't resist attempting once more to convince him.

"I will consider it. That is the most I can promise at the moment. Isn't that your mother staring at us?"

Lettie glanced at where Nathaniel was looking and sighed at her mother's frown. She'd thought their position hidden from her view. "I suppose I've been speaking with you overlong."

"Is that what her look means?"

"My mother's look matches your brother's."

Nathaniel turned to follow her gaze and scowled at his brother's approach.

Lettie decided it was time to take her leave. His brother did not look pleased. "I look forward to hearing from you as to your answer. The sooner the better I might add." She curtsied and walked toward her mother, hoping he'd agree.

"Who was that?" Tristan asked.

"Letitia Fairchild." Nathaniel didn't offer anything further.

"Isn't she the same one you've been dancing with of late?"

"Yes."

"Twice?"

"Yes." Nathaniel refused to be baited into sharing more information. His brother was the one who was supposed to be dancing.

"Do you expect this relationship to progress?"

"No."

Tristan frowned. "Why not?"

Because I don't intend to marry. The words almost spilled out of Nathaniel before he stopped himself. If he admitted that, his brother would want to know why. Nathaniel didn't care to discuss the reason behind it. Instead, he changed the subject. "Have you fulfilled Mother's requirement to dance with three ladies?"

"No."

"Why not?" Two could play at this game.

"Touché." Tristan smiled. "How is your leg doing?"

"Improving. I don't intend to stay long."

"You've spoken with Miss Fairchild so your mission has been accomplished? Attending a ball for the purpose of speaking briefly with one lady, eh? Despite your denial, I can only assume she is special to you."

"We share some common interests."

"Truly?" Tristan gazed at him as though genuinely curious.

His question made Nathaniel realize how unusual it was to find anyone who shared his interests, let alone a woman. He also realized Tristan never seemed to speak with anyone, male or female. Nathaniel thought back over his brother's time at university. As Tristan was several years older than he, he hadn't paid much attention.

They'd rarely brought friends home. Their father's reaction to others was never certain. Best to avoid having to explain his deplorable behavior and verbal tirades. He and Tristan had never discussed it—it was an unspoken rule.

"What sort of interests?"

"For one, *The Seven Curses of London.*" Nathaniel could

119

only shake his head at the coincidence, still amazed by it.

"That book you're reading?" Tristan's gaze sought Lettie once again. "A bookish sort, is she? I'm surprised such a thing appeals to you."

Nathaniel thought that an odd thing to say. "What sort of lady do you prefer?"

"One I don't have to speak to." Tristan's expression chilled. He gave Nathaniel a nod. "I see someone I know." Without any further comment, he walked away.

His brother seemed to have more secrets than Nathaniel had realized, and Tristan didn't seem the least inclined to share any of them. In the past, that would've been fine with Nathaniel, but of late, he found himself wanting to know what his brother was thinking.

That was odd indeed.

CHAPTER TEN

"Although it is not possible, in a book of moderate dimensions, such as this, to treat the question of neglected children with that extended care and completeness it undoubtedly deserves, any attempt at its consideration would be glaringly deficient did it not include some reference to the modern and murderous institution known as "baby farming.""

~ The Seven Curses of London

Lettie and her maid, Cora, entered Madam Daphne's seamstress shop the next morning. She'd told her mother she was in need of new undergarments, but in truth, she wanted to see if the shop still needed apprentices.

If Nathaniel refused to help her, she was considering another visit to Blackfriars Bridge to find girls who might welcome a seamstress apprenticeship. While not easy work, it had to be better than a job in a factory.

"Good morning to you, Miss Fairchild," Molly, the new proprietress, greeted her. She and her mother had taken over the shop from Miss Maycroft and her aunt earlier this year.

Lettie hadn't known the former owners well, but she knew Tessa Maycroft had married an earl and moved to

Northumberland along with her aunt, who had been her partner in the shop. Molly continued the longstanding tradition of offering apprenticeships to girls eager to learn a trade and unique seamstress skills that might provide a better living.

"Good morning, Molly. I wanted to see if you had any openings." Lettie glanced toward the back of the shop where several girls sat around a long wooden table lit with lamps. Each girl worked on a garment.

One of the girls glanced up, caught sight of Lettie, and rose with a smile on her face.

Lettie recognized her instantly from a few days ago on Blackfriars Bridge. "Alice? You came." Happiness flooded her.

"Hello, miss." With a hesitant glance at Molly who nodded permission, she came forward. "Miss Molly has been ever so kind as to give me a job."

"I'm so pleased. How do you like it thus far?"

"Very well. There's much to learn, but Miss Molly is an excellent teacher and patient with me clumsy fingers."

"Alice is being modest," Molly offered. "She's a quick learner and has done well on her mending projects. Soon she'll be learning the more intricate embroidery stitches."

"Well done," Lettie exclaimed.

"Thank ye again for risking so much to speak with me that day," Alice continued. Again she looked at Molly as though for permission.

"I think you should tell her," Molly encouraged.

"What is it?" Lettie asked.

"That man you were speaking with at Blackfriars? The one who interrupted us?" At Lettie's nod, she continued, "He rescued two girls from a brothel two days past."

"He did?" Lettie knew her mouth was agape, but she could hardly believe Alice's words.

"The girls live in the same lodging house as me. Anna said they took positions as maids, but it was all a terrible trick. A man took them to a brothel instead and locked them in rooms at the top of this big, fancy house. She was scared out of her wits as they told her she'd never see her family again. Yer Mr. Hawke showed up, and Anna feared he was some man come to take her virginity as that's what the brothel madam told her was going to happen. But instead, he says how he's taking her home."

"Oh, my goodness," Lettie exclaimed, goose flesh spreading up her arms as she shared an incredulous look with Molly.

"Anna said how it got worse when some of the guards tried to stop them. Yer man fought them off single-handed."

Your man. The words echoed in Lettie's head even though she knew they weren't true. "They escaped?"

"Yes. True to his word, he took them both home and gave them some money to help their families."

A warm glow filled Lettie. Nathaniel was a hero. To take such a terrible risk by himself, find the girls and free them... She could hardly take it in. "Those girls were brave to have the courage to follow him."

"Anna said she could tell just by lookin' at him that he was no ordinary toff."

"I know just what she means," Lettie agreed, well aware of the curious look on Molly's face.

"Anna and Tillie are so grateful. They said if I was to see you, I was to ask if ye would tell him again how thankful they are. They'd be trapped in that brothel for the rest of their lives if it weren't for him."

"I'll be sure to tell him next time I see him."

"Is he your man then?" Alice asked with a shy smile.

"No. Nothing of the sort. We are merely..." She wasn't quite certain how to define their relationship. "Friends, I suppose you could say."

A glance at the rest of the girls in the shop showed them all avidly listening.

"I'll be certain to pass the girls' message to him."

Alice went back to work while Molly showed her some

of the chemise choices. As Lettie selected one, Molly said, "Forgive me for saying so, miss, but have you ever thought about wearing brighter colors?" She tilted her head as she looked over Lettie's pastel gown. "I think something like this would be more becoming on you." Molly reached for a vibrant silk scarf in royal blue and held it up to Lettie's face then nodded for her to take a look in the mirror.

The image reflecting back at her startled Lettie. In truth, it made her uncomfortable. "Oh, well, bright colors are reserved for married ladies and widows, aren't they?"

"Not always," Molly countered. "Some of the ladies have realized pastels don't suit their coloring. Just something for you to consider. After all, it isn't your first Season."

Heat stole through Lettie's cheeks.

"Oh, miss, I meant no harm. I'm only saying that if you were presenting at court, you would need to wear pastels but as that's behind you, you have more choices."

Lettie smiled. "Of course." It was only her own insecurity that made her uncomfortable at the reminder. "I will keep it in mind."

Lettie was lost in thought as they returned home, imagining the events Alice had described. Nathaniel was an amazing man. All the same, Lettie was concerned. He'd risked his life to save the girls. No wonder his leg hurt so badly. Why hadn't he taken someone with him for added protection? His brother surely would've aided him. Then again, rescuing young girls from brothels was not proper behavior for an earl.

If only Nathaniel would confide in her so she knew what he was doing. That would allow her to aid him when needed. Perhaps she could force him to allow her to help. She might have to attempt that next since he was being so stubborn.

"Set out my other suit as well, Dibbles," Nathaniel ordered as he dressed for the day.

"Why?"

Nathaniel could only shake his head at his butler's impertinence. "Because I intend to venture out this evening."

"To where?"

Nathaniel leveled a gaze at the older man.

"I'm merely asking to confirm to which suit you're referring."

Well aware the old man was lying, Nathaniel tried to hold onto his patience. "You know which suit."

"I must protest. You should not be venturing to places like you did the other night. Not by yourself. 'Tis not safe, not to mention the additional harm it might cause your leg."

"It will be fine. It's not as if it truly matters." The words were out before Nathaniel realized he'd uttered them. And Dibbles was all too aware of the significance of those exact words. "Not compared to the lives of others," he continued, hoping he hadn't caught Dibbles' interest.

When Dibbles cleared his throat, Nathaniel turned to face him. The older man had witnessed many of his father's tirades. He knew what Nathaniel had been taught since he was old enough to walk. "I beg to differ, Captain."

Nathaniel shook his head. "Those young girls I saved matter a great deal more than I do."

"Forgive me for saying so, but your father was not sane. He couldn't have been more wrong."

"I've tried to tell myself that, and while I know it to be true here," he touched his temple, "I don't believe it here." He placed a hand over his heart. "As crazed as he may have been, he was in part right."

"Captain—"

"I only feel worthy when I help others. I feared that would be over once I left the Navy. After all, how often does the average man have the opportunity to make a difference? But I have found it."

"I applaud your efforts, but I disagree."

Nathaniel nodded. "Thank you for that. I appreciate it. But it is far more important to me to somehow show the neglected children that they matter."

"You are right in that they, too, matter. But with each risk you take, it lessens the likelihood of you helping others. Please remember that for them and me, you do indeed matter."

"I'll keep that in mind." That was the best Nathaniel could offer.

"Very well. I'll ready your suit."

As Nathaniel finished preparing for the day, he ran the conversation through his mind again.

Dibbles had a valid point. It had been a near miss the other night. Then again, he hadn't intended to perform a rescue. But tonight he wanted to see if he might find one of the men who'd guarded the brothel. Either to follow him or bribe him or whatever it would take to gain more information.

Each step he took dragged him deeper into the scheme, but as Warenton had discovered a few months ago, there was far more to the white slave trade operation than they'd realized.

Did he dare involve Lettie in one of his investigations?

He immediately dismissed the idea. The risk was too great. He had no choice but to refuse her request.

But he wasn't certain if she'd take no for an answer.

Lettie tucked the advertisements for children for sale in her purse as she prepared to leave the house to meet Nathaniel. Her heart had pounded in anticipation since she'd received his message earlier, suggesting they meet at a bookstore that afternoon.

She could only hope he intended to tell her he'd assist her with her goal. Surely that was the reason for the meeting. While she didn't know why they didn't simply speak at the ball tonight. Perhaps he thought their conversations were drawing too much attention.

She wondered if his leg was better. The way he'd clenched his jaw and the tightness around his eyes had told of his pain. At least now she knew why. What Alice had told her shocked her. The first thing she intended to do was ask him to be more careful. How could he insist she wasn't taking proper precautions when he took such risks?

"Where are you going?" Holly asked from the doorway of her bedroom.

"To the bookstore."

"Again?" Her little sister eyed her suspiciously.

"I like books, therefore I spend quite a bit of time at bookstores." All of that was true, Lettie reminded herself. She did her best to meet Holly's gaze. The girl remained suspicious. Unfortunately, she was right, but Lettie didn't dare admit it.

Holly turned to stare at the books Lettie had purchased a few days ago, which sat on her desk untouched since she'd brought them home.

Lettie smiled brightly. She only hoped it wasn't too bright. "I do enjoy books."

"You've been gone so much the past week. You're hardly ever home anymore."

"It's June, my dear. That's when the social Season is in full swing. In a few more years, you'll be joining the madness."

"But by then, you won't be. Either you'll no longer attend or you'll live with Aunt Agatha."

Lettie paused in her movements. Where would she be in a few years? The answer wasn't as clear as it had been even a week ago. But now was not the time to dwell on that.

"I won't be gone long," Lettie promised. At least she

didn't think she would be. "What are your plans for the day?"

"Nothing exciting, although Mother says I can accompany the family to the Robinson's gathering on the morrow."

Lettie had nearly forgotten about it. "What are you going to wear?"

Holly's eyes narrowed as she considered her options. "I'm not certain."

"Why don't you pick three gowns, and I'll help you decide upon my return?" Lettie patted her little sister's cheek as she passed, noting how tall she was growing. "I'm wondering if you have any gowns that are long enough."

Holly smiled proudly. She had high hopes to be the tallest of her sisters. "I suppose I'd better make certain."

"I'll see you shortly."

"What is this?" Holly asked as she moved toward a piece of paper on the corner of Lettie's bed.

Lettie grimaced. It was Nathaniel's message, asking to meet at the bookstore.

"Who is N?" Holly asked, a scowl upon her lips.

"A friend. You don't know her." Lettie walked over and plucked the message from her sister's fingers. "I must be going. I'll see you soon."

She breathed a sigh of relief as she walked down the stairs, hoping Holly would focus on which gown to wear on the morrow and not on Lettie's whereabouts. Even if Nathaniel did agree to aid her, Lettie would need to be careful about what excuses she used to leave the house with Holly interested in her every move.

"Lettie?" Her father's voice called from the library doorway as Lettie stepped into the foyer.

Lettie nearly groaned. If these interruptions continued, she was going to be late.

"Yes, Father?"

"Are you going out?" he asked as he looked at her purse in her hand.

"I'm meeting a friend at the bookstore. Did you need something?" She crossed her fingers that he didn't.

"I was looking for the book you gave me, but I can't find it. I finally have time to review it more closely."

Lettie hesitated. In all honesty, she doubted he'd follow through. How many times had they already had a conversation with no results? On the other hand, if he was bringing it up, then maybe he would truly take an interest.

But she wanted to work with Nathaniel.

No offense to her father, but between the two men, she'd prefer Nathaniel for this particular task. He was the one who truly understood and had already taken action.

With a sigh, she relented. She didn't know for certain if Nathaniel would agree to help her. If he declined, that left only her father. "I'll bring it down for you. Thank you for taking the time to have a look."

He stepped closer to reach out and squeeze her hand. "Anything for my eldest daughter."

Once again, she was reminded that he truly did love her even if it often felt as though she took second place to the rest of her sisters.

She could only hope Nathaniel would wait for her.

CHAPTER ELEVEN

"This is the unhappy fate that attends nearly all our great social grievances. They are overlooked or shyly glanced at and kicked aside for years and years, when suddenly a stray spark ignites their smouldering heaps, and the eager town cooks a splendid supper of horrors at the gaudy conflagration; but having supped full, there ensues a speedy distaste for flame and smoke, and in his heart every one is chiefly anxious that the fire may burn itself out, or that some kind hand will smother it."

~ The Seven Curses of London

Nathaniel perused the shelves at the bookstore while keeping an eye on the door for Letitia. Where could she be? He checked his pocket watch. It was nearly ten minutes past the time he'd suggested they meet.

Granted, ten minutes was nothing for most members of the *ton*. That wasn't even considered fashionably late. But his years in the military had made punctuality a habit.

The bell above the door tinkled, and he glanced up to see her enter the shop. Her maid waited by the door while Letitia searched the store for him. Her bonnet today was once again fawn colored. He scowled at the annoying shade.

Her hazel gaze landed upon him, and her face lit as she hurried forward, causing a similar reaction in him. "My apologies for my delay."

"It's of no consequence."

"My family picks the worst times to need me."

Nathaniel couldn't imagine what it must be like to live with four other females plus her parents and a houseful of servants. Though he'd lived side-by-side with his men in the Navy, that had been different. The idea of having them all invade his house made Nathaniel shudder. In the few months he'd been out of the military, he'd come to enjoy spending time alone.

"I was pleased to receive your message," she said, her expression hopeful.

That made him feel all the worse for what he was about to tell her. He reminded himself it was far too dangerous. This was no game he was playing. He'd had several close encounters with armed men, and he refused to allow that sort of danger close to her. Or any sort of danger for that matter.

"Can I assist you in locating something?" the shop owner asked as he appeared at Nathaniel's elbow.

"We're going to browse for a time," he answered, hoping the man would leave them in peace.

"Of course. Let me know if I can be of help." He moved to the counter to speak with another customer.

Nathaniel led the way to the rear of the store, away from the other customers so they might have some privacy. The shelves reached the ceiling along the wall. The aisles of books narrowed at the back as though the shopkeeper had run out of room. The tall rows suited Nathaniel's purpose quite well. The only danger was in being overheard by other customers.

He turned toward Lettie in the shadowed area. "I appreciate you meeting me here." The enclosed, dusty space made Letitia's orchid scent smell all the better. Unable to help himself, he breathed it in.

"I was pleased to hear from you. Might I hope you've decided to assist me with my...endeavor?" She glanced around at the last word as though she was well aware of the risk of being overheard.

Her caution pleased him as it showed that she realized how careful she needed to be. But it didn't change his answer. "I have given the matter considerable thought. While I appreciate your wish to help others, your best option would be to choose a charity that aligns closely with your ideas and donate funds."

The disappointment in those amazing eyes nearly had him changing his mind. What was it about her that made him want to please her?

"I see." Her gaze lowered, stealing his pleasure at looking into them.

"Do you? The streets are far too dangerous for a lady such as yourself. The things that happen..." He decided against completing the statement. During his years of service, he'd never failed to be surprised at what acts men committed in the name of greed or a shared cause. He thought he'd put those encounters behind him when he returned home to London, but that didn't seem to be the case.

"I have come to realize the situation on the streets is more dire than I'd imagined even after reading the book," Lettie said. "But that is the very reason I feel compelled to help." At last she looked back up at him, her gaze meeting his. "I ask again if you would please consider assisting me. I wouldn't do anything to put you or myself in harm's way. I only request an escort for a limited time so that I might find a way to help."

Damn. She made her request sound almost reasonable, as though it would only take an hour or two of his time. In all honesty, he was sorely tempted. For reasons he didn't care to examine, he liked Letitia. He enjoyed her company on every level—from her intelligence to her humor to her kindness. And if the opportunity arose, he would certainly enjoy kissing her again. But that path held a danger of its own. She was a young lady of the *ton*, therefore searching for a husband.

He didn't want to give her any ideas by spending time with her. He was not husband material. Leading her to think he might have that sort of interest in her would be unfair. Not when he had no intention of marrying any woman.

No. This was for the best all around. No matter that it didn't feel like a good decision.

"I fear I must decline."

Her full lips twisted, tugging at something deep inside him. Surely it was only desire.

"I see. Then I suppose I have no choice."

The look in her eyes gave him a moment's warning, but he wasn't certain what it warned him of.

"I wonder what your brother, the earl, might think of your recent activities." She raised a brow as though expecting a reaction.

"Ah. You think to force me into aiding you?" He nearly smiled. Such a clever woman. He admired her strategy.

"I wouldn't dream I could force you to do anything." She grinned, and desire coiled deep inside him.

Did she realize the double meaning of her words?

He cleared his throat in an attempt to regain control of his body. "Good. Because that would be impossible."

She nodded as though she'd expected as much. "I'm certain the earl already knows of your efforts to save our city though you don't appear to be close from the little I've observed."

If he didn't know better, he'd guess her trap was closing, but she'd said nothing he couldn't easily avoid thus far. Fascinating.

"You and he probably had a lengthy conversation about how you entered a brothel and saved two young girls from a life of prostitution."

Nerves tingled along his spine. How had she found out

that? And hell no. He had no intention of sharing those sorts of details with Tristan.

She tapped a finger on those luscious lips as she studied the books on the shelves before them. "Perhaps a word to a reporter about how one of England's finest military heroes is now performing those same heroics at home in London. Wouldn't that be an intriguing story?"

He frowned, no longer troubled by desire. He couldn't imagine a worse fate. "You wouldn't."

She looked up at him and blinked oh so innocently. "Which one wouldn't I do?"

"Either. Neither."

With a gloved hand, she retrieved a book from the shelf and opened it, paging through it. "Wouldn't I?"

He hadn't given her nearly enough credit. He'd always considered himself a good strategist but she was amazing. Who knew?

"Letitia."

She glanced up in surprise at his use of her given name.

"Surely I have permission to call you by your first name if you intend to blackmail me."

"I am not blackmailing you." She replaced the book with a thump. "I am only asking for a few hours of your time," she added with a disgruntled expression.

"Or else you'll reveal my recent activities to my brother and perhaps even an interested reporter. How did you find out about the girls?"

She smiled, clearly pleased with herself. "I had the pure luck of running into Alice, the girl on Blackfriars Bridge that I spoke with the day we met."

"Where did you come across her?" He immediately pictured Letitia loitering about in the very places he'd asked her to avoid.

"At Madame Daphne's, the seamstress shop. You may remember I gave Alice her card. She took an apprenticeship there. And one of the girls you rescued lives in her lodging house. She guessed it was you from her friend's description of her rescuer."

Nathaniel could only shake his head. "What are the odds?"

Letitia's eyes gleamed. "I couldn't agree more. Needless to say, when this information was shared with me, two things came to mind."

"Oh?" Nathaniel wasn't certain he wanted to know what they were.

She stepped a little closer, within inches of him, her gaze holding his. "You are a hero."

He frowned, disliking the label. "I did what anyone would've—"

"Don't discount your efforts. You were truly amazing from what little Alice told me."

He shook his head. He was never amazing. Never.

"But the story also tells me you take far too many risks." Her expression grew serious. "You could've been killed."

He didn't consider what he did risky. He'd only wanted to save those girls from the terrible fate awaiting them. They mattered just as much as he. More even. Why should he take care when those girls couldn't?

But he didn't tell her any of that.

Instead, he offered, "We managed to make it out of there together. That's what is important."

"I disagree." Her somber expression surprised him. Normally people brushed aside his comments without further analysis. But she continued to study him as though trying to absorb what he was truly saying.

"Nathaniel." Shivers coursed down his back at her use of his first name. No one called him that. "I am asking you to please be careful. The more I learn of the problems noted in that book, the more I believe a significant number of people must be involved to run these schemes. That also means there is money involved."

Nathaniel was nonplussed at her words. How had she come to those conclusions based on the little she knew and even less that she'd experienced?

She reached up to run her fingers under his lapel, such a sweet, feminine gesture unfamiliar to him. "I don't want anything to happen to you." Her lashes lifted to reveal those beautiful eyes, and he was mesmerized.

He drew closer until their breath mingled, until her heady fragrance filled his senses and desire pulsed through his body.

Her gaze dropped to his lips and all thoughts fled. He couldn't remember ever wanting someone so desperately as he wanted her. She appealed to him on every level—physically, emotionally, and intellectually—a heady combination.

"That is why I must insist on us finding a way to work together." Her gaze captured his again. "I want to help keep you safe."

He tried to clear his head, to make sense of the words she'd uttered. But he could only think of the taste of her lips. How she'd feel in his arms. Slowly, tentatively, he pressed his mouth to hers as though kissing her for the first time.

Her lips were soft and warm beneath his. She made a tiny sound in the back of her throat. He captured it with his mouth, turning his head slightly to better fit with her.

She drew back with a gasp, eyes wide then glancing about as though suddenly remembering where they were.

"Letitia, you are sweet." He couldn't resist touching her cheek with his bare finger. Her skin was warm and soft. "No."

"No, what?" She blinked in confusion.

"No, we cannot work together."

The determined glint in her eye gave him pause. "I beg to differ."

"No."

"Yes."

"Letitia."

"Nathaniel."

He released an exasperated breath, unable to remember when he'd had a more frustrating conversation.

"I'm pleased that is settled," she announced. "What is your next step?"

"I don't have a set agenda."

"I see." She frowned. "I am more of a planner, but I will try to adjust to your schedule, or lack thereof, as best I can."

He placed both hands alongside her face, holding her still. "I appreciate your wish to help. But it is too dangerous. I don't want you anywhere near these men. They are capable of unmentionable deeds."

"I know." She patted one of his hands. "It seems as though you should have one more day of rest before any action is taken to make certain your leg is better. How does your schedule look for the morrow?"

At his look of disbelief, she smiled. "I'll allow you to think upon it. Will you be attending the Ainley's ball this evening? We could discuss it further there."

When he merely stared at her in baffled silence, Letitia continued, "I'm certain it will take time to grow used to the idea of having a partner." She retrieved a piece of paper from her purse. "What do you think of this? Is it safe to contact them?"

After a glance at the ad offering an infant for sale, Nathaniel's stomach churned. The idea of Letitia speaking to whoever placed the ad made him ill. "No." At her crestfallen expression, he relented. "Perhaps it would be best if we did work together on an occasion or two." He didn't add that the reason behind his change of heart was his desire to keep her safe.

"Excellent. I look forward to it."

The shopkeeper entered the row in which they stood, eyes narrowed with suspicion as he peered at them. "Did you find something of interest?"

"Yes," Letitia answered as she glanced at the shelves. "We're narrowing down the options at the moment."

"Very well," he said as though doubtful it was true.

After he stepped away, Letitia leaned forward. "Perhaps we'll need to find another place to meet. The shopkeeper is far too suspicious."

One of the many challenges he faced in working with her would be to find ways to speak with her that wouldn't draw attention. His mission of helping the children was growing more complicated each day. Military operations had been conducted with more ease than this was proving.

But as he watched Letitia glance at the books on the shelves, her head tilted to the side as she read the titles, a tiny corner of his soul was pleased at the twist his life had taken.

He merely had to make certain to keep her at arm's distance from the dangerous situations as well as from himself. He didn't care for the doubt that filled him as to whether that was possible.

Lettie returned to the carriage with a smile upon her face. She gave a little cheer as she took her seat, pleased at her progress with Nathaniel.

"Did you find the book you were looking for, miss?" Cora asked as she settled onto the opposite bench.

Realizing she'd forgotten to purchase a book, she shook her head. "I'm afraid I'll need to try another bookstore some other day." Perhaps that would provide an excuse to meet him again.

There was more to subterfuge than she'd realized. She blamed the tingle of excitement she felt on that rather than the sweet kiss they'd shared.

Could he truly not see how amazing he was? No other man she knew, not that she knew many, would've bothered to investigate the brothel let alone rescue those poor girls. While she didn't know anything about houses of ill repute, she knew men paid for certain services there.

That meant money was being exchanged, and that meant guards. Armed guards.

She couldn't help the shudder that passed through her at the thought of Nathaniel in that house alone. They could have easily shot him and dumped his body in the Thames with no one the wiser.

Yet he appeared to sincerely believe the risks he took were nothing. She didn't understand that. While she knew he had most likely faced dangerous missions during his time in the Navy, this was different. He was working alone.

She was no closer to understanding his dismissive attitude by the time she arrived home. The footman advised her that her mother and Rose were entertaining guests in the drawing room. That rarely required her presence, so she went upstairs to her room.

Holly sat at the chair in front of her desk when Lettie entered.

"What are you looking at?" Lettie asked as she removed her gloves and set her purse on the bed.

"I believe it's something you left behind." Holly held up a newspaper clipping.

Lettie's heart pounded. How had she managed to leave behind one of the ads for a child for sale? "What is it?" she asked, hoping to fool her youngest sister.

"You know very well what it is." Holly's eyes narrowed with suspicion.

Funny how often that was happening of late.

Lettie continued playing innocent, though she held doubt Holly would let it go. "Why don't you tell me?"

"It's an advertisement for a child for sale." The outrage in her sister's tone nearly made Lettie smile. "Why do you want a baby? Shouldn't you find a husband first and then have a baby the normal way? Why would you pay for one?"

"I am only keeping my options open." Lettie turned away to hide her expression. "You know how unlikely it is that I will marry. I'm nearly on the shelf already. Five Seasons and no offer."

Holly mistook the amusement in her voice for emotion. She rushed over to wrap her arms around Lettie. "Do not give up hope. There are many things to love about you, and someone will see them like I do. Perhaps if we make a few changes, those silly men at those silly balls will see the true you."

Lettie gave her sister a squeeze, touched by her words. "What changes would those be?"

"When you brought home that blue scarf from the dressmaker's, I realized how pretty it looked on you." She drew back to look at Lettie's gown. "Brighter colors would be much more becoming. I'll speak with Mother. Maybe I can make her see that her choices in dresses do not suit you."

Lettie could only stare at her sister in disbelief. "That's the second time someone has told me that."

"What?"

"That I should wear brighter colors."

"Well, it's true." Holly folded her arms across her chest. "You are pretty in your own way."

That comment made Lettie sigh. "That really means I'm not pretty at all."

"Yes, you are."

At least this argument was making her sister forget about the advertisement. "Thank you, Holly. I appreciate your attempts to make me feel better." But she well knew a different dress wouldn't change her label as a wallflower.

Holly hugged her tight again. "Promise me you won't buy a baby. I'll come live with you if you become a spinster, living by yourself in a little cottage."

Lettie returned her hug. "You are far too pretty to grow old with me. Men will be vying for your attention, and soon you'll have your own family to worry about."

"Not if you're still alone. I promise not to like any of them and I'll stay with you instead."

Lettie drew back and met her sister's gaze. "Very well. We shall make a pact. If you are not married by the time you're five and twenty, you shall come and live with me."

"What if *you* are married by then?"

The question brought a lump to Lettie's throat, but she did her best to hide it. She'd long ago given up hope of such occurrence. "Then you shall still come and live with me."

"It's agreed." Holly picked up the newspaper clipping and tore it in half and then half again. "We have no need for this."

"No. We do not." Lettie hoped Nathaniel would keep his word and aid her as well as allow her to help him. If they could save a few of those neglected children, Lettie would be happy. That would be enough to fulfill her.

And she could think of no better way to take on such a noble task than with Nathaniel. For a brief moment, she thought of their kisses, wishing he truly cared for her. Perhaps he was attracted to her on some level.

No. She was a wallflower and he was a hero. No matter how much she stretched her imagination, she couldn't see any world where they were more than passing acquaintances.

She blinked at the tears that filled her eyes at the thought. She'd known all along he was not for her. He was only in her life for a short time. The knowledge made her even more determined to hold on to the special moments she shared with him. Surely they would give her pleasure in the years to come. She would think of the days ahead as a grand adventure.

She forced a smile, but it didn't reach her heart.

Chapter Twelve

"Instructive and interesting though it may be to inquire into the haunts and habits of these wretched waifs and "rank outsiders" of humanity, of how much importance and of useful purpose is it to dig yet a little deeper and discover who are the parents—the mothers especially—of these babes of the gutter."
~ The Seven Curses of London

Nathaniel read the report from the man he'd hired to assist him. Robert Langston was a former detective who continued to make his living chasing down unscrupulous characters who escaped the law. But now he did so outside the boundaries of the police department.

No longer believing in the justice system, he'd decided to bend the rules he'd previously lived by. From what little he'd told Nathaniel, it seemed he'd had one too many criminals go free despite evidence pointing to their guilt.

One of those criminals was Culbert Rutter. Enough evidence had existed to arrest him. It had only been later—too late—that Langston had been advised his sentence was overturned due a sudden lack of evidence. Someone higher up in the justice system had chosen to release Rutter.

Nathaniel had been given Langston's name by the man he'd befriended on the Metropolitan Police Department and had liked him immediately. In his mid-forties with a receding hairline and impressive sideburns, Langston was a no-nonsense individual. Nathaniel had no problem with the man's bent rules. He'd had to do the same a few times during his time in the service. As long as Langston's unconventional actions didn't attract interest from the police, all was well.

Though he preferred to work alone, doing so in this case wouldn't suffice. There were too many schemes and too little he could do alone to stop them.

Since the former detective had begun working for him two days ago, Nathaniel had been pleased with Langston's work. He was thorough, patient, and stubborn. All of which were excellent traits for the job before them. With so many brothels to watch, not to mention checking ships crossing the Channel, advertisements in papers...truly the list was endless. Having assistance in determining where action should be taken was helpful.

They'd discovered more details on the new brothel said to specialize in virgins to which Culbert and his cohorts supplied girls.

Now Nathaniel needed to decide what to do about it.

After much thought, he'd avoided attending any social engagements since his last meeting with Letitia. She'd invaded his dreams at night, pulling him along on erotic adventures she would've been appalled to know about in reality.

The less time he spent with her, the better.

Yet he couldn't allow too much time to pass. Else, once again, she'd be taking matters into her own hands. That would have terrible ramifications. Though tempted to have Langston keep an eye out for her, he'd decided against informing the man of Letitia. Surely she wouldn't do anything rash now that she believed she'd forced him into aiding her.

If only he could convince himself of that with greater certainty. The woman was unpredictable to say the least.

He needed to attend whatever event she was this evening. Putting in a brief appearance would surely bring a halt to any wild schemes she'd concocted.

A knock sounded on the front door, startling him out of his reflections. Who could that be? He rarely had unexpected visitors. He listened from his desk in the library as voices filled the foyer.

With a groan, he realized who it was.

As she entered the room unannounced, he rose to his feet. "Good day, Mother." He didn't bother to come around his desk for any sort of greeting. She didn't care for displays of affections.

"Nathaniel, I am most displeased."

"Of course you are," he muttered, bracing himself for her latest complaint, which was surely about Tristan not making progress in gaining a wife.

She'd aged relatively well for a woman of her advanced years. Her dark hair held touches of grey at the temples and lines bracketed her mouth. A few wrinkles marked her blue eyes but, as she rarely smiled, they were minimal.

"What did you say?" she asked, the violet feather on her bonnet bobbing alarmingly.

"I asked what has you so upset?" He already knew it had nothing to do with him and everything to do with his brother. If only Tristan would do her bidding as he'd so willingly done their father's, Nathaniel's life would be much easier.

"Your brother—"

Voices echoed in the foyer once again. Nathaniel had a good guess as to who his second guest was.

Tristan strode into the room, only to stop short with a scowl at the sight of their mother. It seemed his brother had come to complain about her as well.

"Good day, Tristan. It seems Mother has something to say to you." He raised a brow toward her, hoping she'd address her concerns directly rather than insisting he be the messenger.

"I have already heard what she has to say," his brother said tightly. The disdainful look he sent their mother was surprising. "I've come to speak with you," he told Nathaniel.

He'd always thought the two were on the same side. The side without him. He didn't belong with any of his family.

Tristan and his mother both glared at him. With a sigh, he took a seat, hoping they'd do the same so they could resolve whatever dispute they had like reasonable adults.

"Mother, why don't you share your concerns with both of us?"

"Humph." She took a seat in one of the chairs before his desk, completely ignoring Tristan. "Your brother doesn't seem to understand how important it is for a woman of a certain age to see her sons settled."

Nathaniel chose to ignore the fact that she'd never suggested he settle down. He already knew she believed exactly what his father had—that he didn't matter. He expected nothing less and told himself the tightness in his chest was from their unwelcome presence in his home. Surely he'd long ago put aside the hurt these sort of discussions caused. The sooner he settled this, the sooner they'd take their leave.

"Tristan, surely you understand why seeing you married is important to Mother."

"No, I don't." He sat in the other chair and looked at his mother. "What difference does it make to you?"

She opened and closed her mouth like a fish. "I shouldn't have to explain. It is your duty as heir—"

Tristan leaned forward, the anger on his face surprising. "I have always done my duty. But I am weary of it. No more."

Their mother jerked back as though he'd slapped her. "How can you say such a thing? Your father—"

"Damn my father." The cold voice Tristan used shocked Nathaniel.

Never in all their years had Tristan ever spoken a word against their sire. What on earth had gotten into him?

As though he'd only just realized what he'd said, Tristan sat back in the chair, his jaw clenching.

His mother's knuckles turned white as she gripped the chair arms, her lips forming a tight line.

Nathaniel felt the sick and all too familiar sensation he'd grown up with filling his belly. He swallowed hard. How many times had such tension filled the room in his youth? Except it used to involve their father belittling him for one reason or another. Or for no reason at all.

He did his best to keep his mask in place, to not allow either of them to know how much this conversation upset him.

"Your father only wanted what was best for—"

"For him, Mother. Only for him. You know what a selfish bastard he was. Why are you suggesting otherwise?"

Nathaniel waited, wondering if she would actually answer.

"There may have been a few times when he was unduly harsh, but I hardly think that is cause to speak ill of him."

Tristan stared hard at Nathaniel, but Nathaniel had no idea what he wanted him to say or do. Nor did he understand the purpose of this conversation. As far as he was concerned, their mother could believe whatever she wanted. He knew the truth. What Tristan believed was still a mystery, but it didn't matter to Nathaniel nor did he care to discuss it. His father had taken up far too much of his thoughts for years. Nathaniel was doing his best to put that part of his life behind him.

If only he truly could.

Nathaniel waited, his gaze meeting Tristan's.

With an oath, Tristan rose and stormed out, leaving silence in his wake.

"I have no idea what's gotten into your brother of

late," his mother said, her eyes watering suspiciously.

"Nor do I." He looked away from the tears. They did no good now. She should've used them while his father was alive to see if they would've worked on him.

She sat forward in her chair and looked at Nathaniel beseechingly. "All I ask is for you to encourage him to find the appropriate lady and offer for her. The line must continue."

"Why don't you allow Tristan to do so in his own time, Mother?"

"It's not as if it has to be a love match," she continued as though he hadn't spoken. "He can do what he wishes after he begets an heir."

Nathaniel closed his eyes for a moment. How many times did they have to discuss this? She said the same thing time and again. It only seemed to anger his brother. Why, he didn't know.

"It was your father's dying wish that Tristan marry before he turns five and thirty. I don't ask much of you, Nathaniel. Can't you assist with this one request?"

"I'll speak with him again," Nathaniel lied. He would indeed speak to him, but not of this. He didn't care what their father wanted. Tristan could make his own decisions. No doubt he had little interest in Nathaniel's opinion anyway.

"Thank you." She blinked rapidly, causing Nathaniel to rise with the hope that she'd leave now that she'd accomplished her mission. "I'm sure you're busy."

"I am." He didn't feel the least bit of remorse for his lack of civility toward her. Not after all the times she'd stepped aside so his father could berate him. Especially since she'd paid no attention to him his entire life.

She rose. "Very well then. I hope to see you this evening at the musical."

"Certainly. Good day." He'd promise nearly anything to get her to leave.

After glancing at him uncertainly, she departed. The

tension in the room fell away as he heard the front door close behind her.

He had no idea what had made Tristan so angry, but he had enough problems of his own with which to concern himself. If Tristan wanted to talk about something, he knew where to find him.

With a deep breath, he sat in his chair and picked up Langston's report again, wondering what would be the wisest path to put an end to this group that involved Culbert Rutter, a welcome task after the unsettling business with his family.

When Nathaniel arrived at the musical that evening, he didn't see either of his family members, much to his relief. Perhaps they were avoiding each other and had decided not to attend.

In truth, Nathaniel wouldn't have attended if not for needing to see Letitia. Social events felt frivolous when he knew his time was better spent elsewhere. But Letitia was no doubt creating a scheme to act on her own. He'd decided to pretend as though he intended to help her but would draw it out as long as possible with the hope that she'd lose interest in the project. Based on what little he knew of other ladies in the *ton*, that shouldn't take long.

He ignored the fact that Letitia was unlike any woman he'd ever met with her unselfish nature, relentless bravery, and, most of all, how she made him feel.

The musical was a large affair with well over fifty people in attendance. Chairs were set in rows for the guests but few had taken a seat. Instead they gathered along the edges of the room to visit until the performance began. He spotted Letitia immediately as he so often did. Somehow his senses were set for her like a compass was set to north. The idea made him smile.

"Captain Hawke, how nice to see you this evening."

He turned at the unfamiliar voice to find a lady who appeared vaguely familiar addressing him.

At his blank look, she smiled. The underlying meanness to that smile stirred his memory, the lady who'd called Letitia Lettuce. He did not return her smile only gave her the barest nod and continued walking. Why would she attempt to speak with him?

When he reached Letitia, he chose to exaggerate his greeting, well aware the other woman watched.

"You look lovely this evening," he said with a smile.

She blinked up at him as though confused. Had he never told her that? He realized he hadn't the last few times he'd seen her. How remiss of him.

"Thank you." Her smile was sincere. Despite her lack of dance partners, she remained a genuinely kind person, not bitter like some who were overlooked in life, and he respected her for that. "I'm glad you're here."

The warm feeling that spread through his chest at her words alarmed him.

"Do you have news?" she asked then glanced toward the area where the musicians were warming up.

Her tone belied the casualness of her behavior. It would take some time before she forgot her quest. Far longer than he'd originally expected. Doubt filled him at the wisdom of his plan. Perhaps he needed to offer some small task so her need to help would be fulfilled.

"I don't," he answered at last.

She turned quickly to search his face as though wondering if he told the truth. Her expression dimmed as though disappointed at his reply.

"Actually, I do have one piece of news."

"Oh?" Immediately her eyes lit again.

He chose not to question why he preferred that expression so much more. "I've found another man whose interests are aligned with mine. He is a former police detective pursuing the same group of men I am." He didn't mention he'd hired him.

"That is wonderful. The more you have to aid you, the better. Hopefully that means you'll be safer as well."

That was nothing Nathaniel cared about. He only wanted to find Rutter's boss and put an end to his efforts. That was proving more difficult than he'd expected, but having another set of eyes on the street who had an even better feel for the people involved would help considerably.

"Won't it?" she asked, eyes narrowed as she watched him.

"Certainly." He chose not to meet her gaze as he told the lie.

"I feel compelled to advise you it doesn't change our arrangement."

"Of course not." He knew sarcasm laced his tone but he couldn't help it.

"Shall we meet near Blackfriars Bridge on the morrow? Perhaps we can find another girl to whom I could offer help?"

He nearly groaned. What simple task could he find for her that would both keep her safe and fulfill her desire?

"Excuse me." A footman stood at Nathaniel's elbow. "A message was delivered for you, Captain Hawke."

Grateful for the interruption, he turned to see the man held a silver tray with a sealed message on it. An uneasy feeling crept over him as he retrieved it. There was little chance the note held good news.

He nodded his thanks to the footman and opened the missive.

"I hope all is well," Letitia offered, her tone laced with concern.

After reading one of Langston's reports, Nathaniel immediately recognized the handwriting. If the man had made the effort to send a message here, something was amiss.

CHAPTER THIRTEEN

"Work hard and win a fortune," has become a dry and mouldy maxim, distasteful to modern traders, and has yielded to one that is much smarter, viz., "There is more got by scheming than by hard work."

~ *The Seven Curses of London*

Lettie watched Nathaniel's face as he read the missive, but his expression revealed little. Receiving a message at a social event rarely resulted in good news.

"I must leave." Nathaniel stuffed the paper into his jacket pocket.

"Is all well?"

His gaze held hers.

She drew a quick breath at the concern in his eyes. "What's happened?"

"Mr. Langston needs assistance. Someone's been injured."

"I'm coming with you. If someone is hurt, I might be of help. As the eldest of four sisters, I've tended many injuries." She was exaggerating, but she wanted a chance to help.

"No need." Nathaniel stepped toward the door, but

Lettie moved to remain at his side.

"I'll tell my mother I'm not feeling well and a friend is giving me a ride home." Lettie kept her voice low, not wanting to draw attention.

Nathaniel stopped. "Letitia, this is far too dangerous. I don't know what the situation is. Langston didn't provide details. I don't know what trouble awaits us."

"All the more reason I should come. You can deal with the trouble while I help whoever is hurt."

As his mouth opened to protest further, she shook her head. "You're wasting time. I'll meet you outside."

She quickly found her mother who was visiting with friends and made her excuses. Luckily, her mother hadn't seen her speaking with Nathaniel so didn't question her wish to go home early.

After retrieving her cloak from a footman, Lettie stepped outside, half expecting to find that Nathaniel had left without her. She knew he wasn't pleased she insisted on accompanying him, but the man took far too many risks. She was determined to make him take more care.

To her relief, his black carriage awaited her. With a glance around to make certain no one she knew watched, she approached it. The footman hopped down from his perch and held open the door, assisting her into the dim interior.

The soft glow of the carriage light revealed Nathaniel in the far corner, his expression once again unreadable. She took a seat beside him and the carriage immediately departed.

"What do you know thus far?" Lettie asked.

"Langston has been following Culbert Rutter, a man we know to be associated with the taking of young girls. Rutter was waiting outside a shop this evening and followed a young girl into Whitechapel. He beat her."

"What? Why?" Lettie could not contain her shock. A grown man beat a young girl?

"I don't know. Langston is with the girl now, waiting

for me."

Lettie could feel the weight of Nathaniel's stare. She needed to gather herself. If she truly wanted to help in difficult situations, she had to remain calm and use her intellect and logic to be of assistance.

With a lift of her chin, she said, "Then it's a good thing I came along. I'll comfort the girl. She might appreciate another female being there."

Nathaniel pulled aside the curtain to check their progress. "I don't think you understand the type of situation we might be walking into."

Lettie refused to be intimidated. "I will soon enough. What do you intend to do?"

"Find Rutter."

The certainty in his tone concerned her. "Nathaniel?" She said his name softly, almost as a whisper.

He glanced at her, his gaze holding hers.

She reached out and touched his hand with her gloved one. "Please take care. You are important to me."

With a brief nod of his head, he glanced back out the window. Disappointment washed through her at his lack of response. That was why she needed to guard her heart from this man. He wasn't interested in her in that way.

The ride seemed endless as the carriage paused in several places due to traffic. But as they drew nearer to Whitechapel, the streets were quieter. Lettie realized most of these people would rise early for work and so had sought their beds.

Soon the carriage slowed, the clopping of the horses' hooves echoing on the cobbles between brick buildings. The evening air felt cooler here, or perhaps it was just Lettie's nerves getting the better of her.

Nathaniel didn't wait for the footman when the carriage finally drew to a halt. He eased past Lettie and stepped down. "Wait here."

She remained there a moment. Barely. Then followed.

She'd never been to this area before and couldn't help

but glance about as she stepped into the foreign landscape. The tall buildings seemed to absorb the light cast by the gas street lights. A few windows glowed, revealing tattered curtains. The stench was...indescribable. Soot and waste coated with a foul odor. In truth, she didn't want to know what caused the terrible smell.

With a glance over his shoulder at Lettie, Nathaniel muttered an oath then waited for her to catch up to him, taking her hand in his.

Somehow, she felt the darkness of this place in her very bones and was grateful to have Nathaniel at her side. How could this dreary, depressing neighborhood be part of the same city where she'd spent her entire life? She couldn't imagine living here, never escaping the bleakness.

"I believe I warned you," Nathaniel said even as he held her hand tighter.

"Over here," a voice called out.

Nathaniel hurried toward the mouth of an alley from where the voice had come, Lettie at his side.

"What happened?" he asked as he released Lettie to kneel beside a man who held a young girl in his arms.

It took a moment for Lettie's eyes to adjust to the dim light.

The man glanced at Lettie then back at Nathaniel. At Nathaniel's nod, he said, "I was following Culbert Rutter as discussed. He spent a long while outside some shops just off Bond Street. Then when this young woman came out of Madame Daphne's..."

Lettie stilled at the familiar name. Her gaze sought the girl, trying to see her face. "Alice?"

The girl looked up, and Lettie swallowed a gasp, stunned at the sight of Alice's battered face. Her cheek and eye were swollen twice the size of normal, making her barely recognizable. Tears streaked down her reddened face.

"Oh, miss," the girl whispered between sniffles as she caught sight of Lettie. "I'm ever so...sorry."

"You've nothing to be sorry for," Lettie reassured her, reaching out to take her hand. "What happened?"

"Culbert—" she hiccupped a sob, her words difficult to understand because of the swelling. "He said as how I talk too much, that I was interferin' with his business."

"What?"

"And how I was...actin' better than I should. That I needed to learn to keep my mouth shut as I was spreadin' rumors the jobs he's offerin' girls weren't real." She sniffed, still trying to control her tears. "But they aren't, miss. They aren't real. He's takin' girls to—to brothels. He's not really givin' them jobs."

"I know, Alice. You are right." Lettie shared a glance with Nathaniel before looking back at Alice. "I'm so sorry this happened."

"I must warn...my family," she said, her voice hitching. "He threatened to hurt them. He said my little sister will be the next one he takes."

"We'll make certain your family is safe," Nathaniel reassured her. "Mr. Langston will see to that."

Lettie couldn't stop staring at Alice's swollen face. She'd never seen such a thing. Dalia had fallen from a chair when she was only four or five and struck her face, causing it to swell terribly. But to know a man had deliberately hit little Alice, and not just once, appalled her.

Nathaniel touched Lettie's arm, one brow raised as though asking if she was all right. She nodded, swallowing the lump in her throat. "Can you stay with her while I speak with Langston?" he asked.

She nodded and eased into Mr. Langston's place as he stood, Nathaniel joining him. Wrapping an arm around the girl's shoulder, she asked, "Can you tell me where you're hurt?"

"My stomach hurts something awful. He punched me twice there." The girl gave a shiver and Lettie shifted to put her cloak around Alice with the hope her own body would warm the girl.

"Can you move?"

"Mr. Langston tried to help me earlier, but I must've twisted my ankle. It's throbbin' terrible." The girl coughed several times.

"We'll have a doctor check to make certain nothing serious is wrong," Lettie said, her stomach clenching when she saw the blood around Alice's mouth from her coughing.

"No, no doctor. We don't have the money."

"We'll pay for it, Alice. You need only try to rest. Soon we'll have you somewhere safe and warm."

"But my sister—"

"Mr. Hawke and Mr. Langston will see to your family. Do not worry." Lettie had no doubt Nathaniel would make it right.

Tears continued to track down Alice's face, squeezing Lettie's heart. Her throat tightened. What had she done? She couldn't help but feel she was partly to blame for Alice's injuries. Her ignorance had caused this. If she hadn't spoke to Alice, she'd be unharmed. Culbert wouldn't have been able to find her so easily if she wasn't working at Madame Daphne's.

Nathaniel was right—she hadn't understood what she was doing. The idea of her attempting to help someone, only to indirectly hurt them, was intolerable.

She glanced up to see Nathaniel conferring with Mr. Langston a short distance away. She couldn't hear what they said from her position, but merely having Nathaniel in sight reassured her. A more competent man she'd never met. If anyone could help right this situation, it was Nathaniel.

Nathaniel was enraged to think Culbert Rutter had gone to the extent of beating a young girl to make his point. But now was not the time for that. Nathaniel needed to see Alice and Letitia to safety, determine how severely the girl was injured, and then turn his anger on Rutter.

He made arrangements with Langston for him to explain to Alice's family what had happened, reassure them she would be well taken care of, and relocate the family to a better neighborhood. Perhaps he could obtain a job for Alice's father on his brother's estate. That would take the whole family out of town, which was the only way he was certain he could protect them until he dealt with Rutter.

Langston left to speak with Alice's family, enough money in hand to rent a room for several nights until other arrangements could be made.

Nathaniel returned to Letitia and Alice. "Does she need a doctor?"

Letitia nodded even as Alice protested.

"He hit her in the stomach," Letitia advised.

"We'd best make certain you aren't seriously injured," Nathaniel said, doing his best to keep his tone even. "Let us see you to the carriage, Alice."

"Her ankle is injured," Letitia advised.

Nathaniel lifted her and carried her to the carriage, his leg protesting from the extra weight. The footman hurried to open the door at their approach.

Nathaniel set Alice down on the seat then offered a hand to Letitia to assist her. "Take us home," he advised the footman. "Then you'll need to fetch the doctor."

After taking a seat inside, he leaned forward. "Mr. Langston will speak with your family and tell them what's happened. We're going to find another place for them to stay for a time so they'll be safe."

Alice nodded. Letitia had already placed her arm around the girl and shared her cloak with her but still Alice shivered. Within a few minutes, the carriage pulled to a halt outside his modest townhome.

Before Nathaniel could object, the footman opened the door and lifted Alice out of the conveyance.

Nathaniel couldn't help but glare at the man.

"My apologies, Captain, but Dibbles will have my head if you're sore on the morrow," the footman offered then walked toward the front steps.

"Who is Dibbles?" Letitia asked as Nathaniel handed her out of the carriage.

"Butler, valet, surrogate mother," Nathaniel muttered. "Depends on where he sees fit to stick his nose."

Letitia smiled. "I believe I will like Dibbles. I'm most anxious to meet him."

"Perhaps you should return home now. I wouldn't want to risk your reputation with all this." The idea of her and Dibbles comparing notes made him uneasy.

"Nonsense." She drew up the hood of her cloak. "Alice will no doubt feel better if I'm here. I would like to hear what the doctor has to say. Besides, no one seems to be about."

Nathaniel followed her gaze along the quiet street. "Very well." He escorted her up the walk to the steps where Dibbles held the door. The footman had already entered with Alice.

"Good evening. I didn't realize you were bringing home company." Nathaniel could only shake his head at the man's reprimand.

"Nor I," he offered. Once Dibbles had closed the door behind him, he said, "Miss Letitia Fairchild, this is my..." He debated which title would least offend Dibbles. "This is Dibbles."

"I'm pleased to meet you," Letitia said with a smile as she lowered her hood. "I'm relieved to hear someone is watching out for the Captain's welfare as he seems to have little regard for it."

Dibbles' stiff expression shifted into one far warmer. "I'm honored to think you might understand my burden."

Letitia grinned as she slanted a glance at Nathaniel. "I can only imagine the challenges you face."

Dibbles took her cloak only to study it with a critical

eye. "We'll have this cleaned while you're seeing to the girl's welfare." He turned to Nathaniel. "I had the footman take her to the yellow room on the third floor."

"When he comes down, he's to fetch the doctor."

Letitia caught his arm. "I fear she's coughing up blood from the blows she took to her stomach."

Nathaniel shook his head then turned to Dibbles. "Make certain he returns from the doctor as quickly as possible."

"May I sit with her now?" Letitia asked.

"Of course. I'll show you where she is." Nathaniel gestured toward the stairs. He nearly groaned at the thought of climbing to the third floor with Letitia at his side. His injured thigh did not care for the motion required to ascend stairs.

"It is very kind of you to send for the doctor," Letitia said as they walked. "I doubt we could've convince one to see her at her lodgings."

Letitia continued her casual comments as they made their way to the third floor, never once asking if he was all right, much to his relief. He appreciated her not fussing over him, but rather allowing him to progress at his own pace.

The small bedroom at the top of the stairs was modestly furnished and rarely used. It wasn't as if he ever had guests. One of his maids was seeing to Alice. Already the girl was sitting on the bed with her shoes off. Her eyes were big—or rather, the eye that wasn't swollen was. She stared about the room as though she'd never seen one before. He well knew how different his home was from hers.

"Thank you for seeing her settled," Letitia said with a smile to the maid as she took a seat beside Alice on the bed. "Why don't you rest, Alice?"

The girl eased back against the pillow, looking very uncomfortable.

"Are you in pain?" Letitia asked as she took the girl's

hand.

"I shouldn't be here," the girl whispered. "I don't belong in such a place."

"You are welcome to stay, Alice," Nathaniel reassured her. "I want you well before you return home."

"Yes," Letitia agreed. "The doctor will be here soon to see to your injuries."

The girl held a hand to her stomach. Perhaps the pain was forcing her to realize it would be wise for her to stay for a time.

Letitia glanced at the maid. "Would you please bring some warm towels so we can clean off the worst of the mud?"

"Of course, miss," the maid said and departed.

By the time the doctor arrived, Letitia had wiped the girl's face and hands and helped her don one of the maid's nightgowns. She was resting, but still held her hand on her stomach and frequently coughed.

Nathaniel stepped out of the room to speak with the doctor privately to explain the situation. Then he waited outside the bedroom until the man finished examining her.

"How does she fare?" Nathaniel asked as the doctor closed the door behind him.

"It doesn't seem as though she's broken anything, but with her coughing up blood, her internal organs may have been bruised. Her ankle is sprained, and overall, the less she moves for the next few days, the quicker she'll heal. By tomorrow, the coughing should ease. If not, you'd best send for me again."

"Thank you for coming so quickly."

The doctor looked him up and down. "How is your leg? I hope you're taking care of it."

"It is better than it was."

"And the swelling?"

"Mostly gone."

The doctor shook his head. "I hope for your own good, that's true. Keep the girl in bed with her ankle elevated. I left her something for her pain."

Nathaniel walked him to the top of the stairs then returned to the bedroom, only to find Letitia standing outside of it with the door closed behind her.

"Swelling?" she asked with a glance at his leg.

Obviously she'd overheard what the doctor had said. "Nothing with which to be concerned."

"Rest?"

"I did and now my leg is much improved." By the look on her face, he hadn't reassured her. "Truly, I'm fine."

She studied him for a long moment until he wanted to squirm. "Perhaps I should speak with Dibbles about this."

Slight panic filled him at the thought. "He will tell you exactly what I told you."

"Hmm..."

"How is she?" Of course, he wanted to know the answer, but even more, he wanted to shift her attention to something else.

"She's resting now. The maid said she'll stay with her since the poor girl is so nervous. She feels a little out of her element. What did the doctor say?"

"Let us discuss this in the drawing room so we don't disturb Alice." He didn't want the girl to overhear what he said.

They made their way down to the drawing room, and he closed the door behind them.

"The doctor doesn't want her moving for the next few days." He told her the doctor's concerns.

"Poor dear. I can't imagine what she went through. That terrible man." Lettie's outrage was evident in the fierce look in her eyes and clenched fists. "Who does he think he is?"

Nathaniel appreciated her anger as he felt the same way. "He will receive his due. Have no doubt." Rutter and whoever he worked for had to be stopped.

Tears filled Lettie's eyes.

"What is it?" he asked as he drew closer to take her

hands in his.

She blinked, shaking her head.

"Tell me," he urged, trying to resist the desire to take her into his arms.

"What happened to Alice is my fault." The emotion in her voice caught him off guard, as did her words.

"Why would you think that?" He couldn't help but pull her into his arms. Her upset caused the same within him.

"If I hadn't drawn attention to her on Blackfriars Bridge or given her the information on the seamstress apprenticeship, none of this would've happened."

"Or it might be that instead of some bruises, Alice would find herself stuffed in a ship's cargo hold and on her way to Brussels."

"What?" Letitia drew back to look at him.

"Rutter was involved in a scheme several months ago to lure young girls into accepting high paying jobs as maids in Belgium. But they were actually being taken to Brussels to be used in the brothels. We thought Rutter was in prison, but twice now, he's managed to be released."

"That's terrible. I can't imagine the horrors those poor girls go through, especially when they're so far from home." Letitia laid her head on his shoulder. "I never dreamed my actions could cause harm to someone."

"They didn't. What happened to Alice was a terrible coincidence. And it certainly doesn't mean you shouldn't help." He nearly bit his tongue as he realized what he was saying. But if she decided not to become involved any further, he understood. "I'll find a safer way for you to make a difference."

She bit her lip, obviously tempted by his suggestion. Then she shook her head. "That feels like allowing Rutter and his cohorts to win. The man is obviously a brute and must be stopped."

Nathaniel lifted her chin with his finger so she would meet his gaze. "He truly is a brute, and you must treat him with the utmost caution. He has no qualms about striking young girls, nor would he think twice about hurting you."

"You must take care as well."

"Of course. With Mr. Langston's help, we should be able to discover the ring leader of this scheme and bring down the entire operation."

But with the passing of each moment, he became more aware of Letitia in his arms, and the fact that they were alone. His gaze dropped to her lips. The lure of them proved far too strong for him to resist.

He drew her closer, ever so slowly. It didn't seem to matter how often he told himself to keep his distance from this woman—he couldn't. Their lips met, and it was no surprise when desire shot through him. As his tongue sought hers, he stopped thinking. She was warm and willing but the passion pulsing through him wasn't due to only that. Letitia was special in so many ways. How could he possibly resist her?

With no answer, he deepened the kiss, his tongue seeking hers. The sweet taste of her was something of which he'd never grow weary.

She placed her hand on his cheek, the heat of her palm seeping into his bones. He hadn't realized how cold he was deep inside until he'd met her. Her unique fragrance teased his senses until his head spun.

"You are so lovely," he whispered before kissing the sweet dent in her chin then along her jaw and down her neck. "So brave. So determined."

She stiffened as though to deny his words, but he didn't allow that. He moved his hands to her waist, bringing her against the length of him before grasping her hips. He held her tightly until her body relaxed once again. Still she wasn't close enough. He ran his hands along her bottom beneath the bustle there, annoyed by the extra fabric and padding in his way. Her breasts pressed against him until his chest ached with the need to feel her soft skin against his.

She wrapped her arms about his shoulders, and her

fingers tangled in the hair at the nape of his neck. When her lips sought his, he couldn't deny her. He ran his hands along the length of her, loving how well she fit in his arms, as though she belonged there.

He drew her toward the settee near the fire and continued to kiss her as they sank onto the cushions.

When she pulled back from their kiss, he groaned in protest. She pressed kisses along his jaw and down his neck as he had done to her. Nothing had felt so good in a very long time. Or perhaps ever. Letitia did things to him, made him feel noble and heroic. Made him believe in things he had no business believing in. Made him long for them with his whole being.

"I want you," he murmured, wishing desperately there was a way he could have her. At the moment, he needed her as much as he needed air.

"Oh, Nathaniel. I want you as well. I—" She stopped abruptly as though unable to put words to what she felt.

He understood completely. He took her lips with his again and gave in to the temptation of her curves. Giving her a moment to grow used to his touch, he held his hand just beneath her breast then captured the soft mound.

Her gasp was just what he wanted to hear. The idea of giving her pleasure only increased his own. He cupped her breast, squeezing gently. The way she arched into his embrace had him aching with need. With a gentle hand, he lifted her breast from her bodice to run a finger back and forth across the tip. Then he leaned down to kiss the swell of it, drawing another gasp from her.

"Letitia, I must touch you. I fear I'll go mad if I don't."

She opened those amazing eyes now glazed with passion. The desire in their depths was all the answer he needed to proceed. He kissed her again and shifted a hand to the hem of her skirt, easing up the fabric as anticipation throbbed through him.

When his fingers grazed her bare leg, she gave a tiny gasp but he continued upward until he reached the thin fabric of her knickers. With determination, he found the opening and eased past it to her bare skin. The feel of her soft, warm thigh made him grow heavy with need.

"Nathaniel," she said with a moan as he caressed her.

He kissed her deeper, that moan making him want her even more, to possess her in every possible way. But he'd settle for touching her for now.

He let his fingers dance along her soft skin, back and forth, teasing, growing ever nearer to the apex of her thighs. When he finally touched the curls at the top of her thighs, her body jerked in reaction. Yet he continued to caress her, seeking her very center, the dampness there sending a surge of desire through him that had him drawing back to watch her.

"Nathaniel?" she whispered as her head tipped back.

"Yes, my sweet?" He'd known she'd be responsive, passionate, but this was more than he could've hoped for.

"That—that is magic."

"Yes." He couldn't agree more. It was magic. She was magic. More than anything, he wanted her to understand how special she was and how much she pleased him. He nibbled along her neck as his fingers continued to move along her body.

"I didn't know..." Her voice was full of wonder.

To know that she trusted him, allowing him to touch her where no one else had, showing her the pleasure possible between a man and a woman, was a gift beyond price.

"There's more," he promised then pressed his fingers against her more firmly, slipping one finger inside. "You are so hot."

"Oh my." Her lips parted in response as her breath came faster. Her hand tightened on the back of his neck. Suddenly her eyes widened even as he felt her body arch.

He kissed her, taking her soft cries into his mouth. As her body softened against him, he held her tight, wishing he could carry her upstairs and make her his own. He wanted the chance to take his time and show her how happy he could make her.

His body ached with desire, and his chest had an odd echoing pang. He didn't care for the feeling at all. What was he going to do with her? This couldn't happen again. He couldn't allow desire to steal his common sense and so should keep his distance. Yet he needed to keep an eye on her and make certain she stayed safe.

"Nathaniel?"

Reluctantly he eased back to look at her, wondering what he'd find there. Her expression glowed with happiness. That pang in his chest shifted, spreading.

He could only close his eyes in response, for he knew the truth. She deserved someone far better than he. Someone who could give her a family. Someone who wasn't damaged both physically and emotionally, and who could give her the life she deserved.

But was he truly strong enough to release her and walk away?

CHAPTER FOURTEEN

"There are many kinds of labour that require no application of muscular strength; all that is requisite is dexterity and lightness of touch, and these with most children are natural gifts. They are better fitted for the work they are set to than adults would be, while the latter would require as wages shillings where the little ones are content with pence."

~ The Seven Curses of London

Lettie paced her bedroom the next morning, restless after the events of the previous evening. She'd barely slept a wink, for each time she'd closed her eyes, she relived being in Nathaniel's arms. What she'd experienced made her even more curious as to what it might be like to make love with Nathaniel, to become his in full.

Though she tried to downplay what had occurred, her heart raced with the possibilities. Yet part of her was scared to death. He hadn't suggested a deeper relationship last night, so what hope was there that he ever would?

How did she proceed from this point forward? Act as though nothing untoward had occurred? Or—

No. She paused mid-stride as a terrible thought occurred. Something about the way he'd said goodbye the previous evening had felt very final. Her heart squeezed at the thought. She shook her head. Surely it hadn't meant anything. She refused to accept such a quick end to their relationship.

At the very least, she needed to visit with Nathaniel so she could learn how Alice fared. If necessary, she'd visit his house of her own accord if he didn't contact her soon. She could always wear some sort of disguise. Perhaps a—

"What on earth are you thinking?" Holly asked from the doorway.

Lettie startled in surprise, so deep in her thoughts, she hadn't heard her sister open the door. "Why didn't you knock?"

"I did."

"I'm certain I didn't tell you to come in."

Holly gave a delicate shrug. "You weren't in the drawing room, and the rest of our sisters are. What else was I to do when you didn't answer?"

Lettie could only shake her head. "Return to the drawing room?"

Holly scowled her displeasure. "You didn't answer my question."

In all honesty, Lettie hoped she'd forgotten. "What was it?"

"What are you thinking?"

"What sort of question is that?"

Holly came in and sat on the bed. "I can see you're plotting something. It's obvious from your expression."

Lettie turned away before she revealed anything else.

"Aha. I knew it." Holly jumped up to face Lettie and study her more closely. "You're avoiding answering. That means I'm right."

"It merely means you're being a nuisance. Aren't you going to the Taylor's party this afternoon?"

"Yes."

"Don't you need to prepare for it?"

"No."

Lettie scowled at her sister. "Why don't we join the others in the drawing room?"

"You'll only make some excuse to leave once we're there." Holly stuck out her lower lip. "You have been very distracted of late. Everyone has. Rose with her duke and Dalia with whoever it is that has her attention."

Lettie reined in her impatience. "A bit lonely now that the Season is underway?"

"Maybe." Holly trailed her finger along Lettie's desk, a wistful look upon her face.

A sudden realization struck Lettie. Alice and Holly were nearly the same age. How different their lives were in every possible way, from the food they ate to the how they spent their day to the clothes they wore.

Lettie couldn't help but give Holly a hug.

"What's this for?" Holly asked as she returned the embrace.

"For being a great little sister."

Holly leaned back and smiled up at Lettie. "Thank you."

"You are welcome. Now, let us find the others and see what trouble we can cause, shall we?"

The poignant moment convinced Lettie even more that all the girls threatened by Rutter and whoever else was working with him needed to be saved. Those girls were someone's daughters, sisters, or nieces. They mattered, despite what some members of society might believe.

She had to find a way to become more involved in helping to save them.

Nathaniel watched the street carefully, waiting for Rutter's cohort to make an appearance. He didn't want to miss him. Langston had followed the man to this lodging house, and his observations suggested he lived there.

After much consideration, Nathaniel had decided

eliminating Rutter wasn't enough. He needed to discover who gave the orders and destroy that man. Even after all this time, he had yet to discover who the man was.

Rutter certainly wouldn't be willing to give him a name. The man appeared to be deeply embroiled with the whole scheme. He'd managed to escape prison twice and admitted to having contacts who'd gained his freedom. To Nathaniel, that meant his loyalty was firmly on the side of those running the scheme.

Therefore, Nathaniel had decided his best chance of gaining information was to question one of the men he'd seen accompany Rutter.

But Nathaniel still intended to make Rutter pay for what he'd done to Alice.

The injured girl seemed to be resting comfortably. The maid reported that though she'd coughed on and off throughout the night, it had subsided this morning. Nathaniel hoped that meant her internal injuries were minimal and would soon heal.

Langston had helped settle her family into a new lodging house and paid the rent for the next month until Alice was well enough to rejoin them and the family could decide where they wanted to go.

Unfortunately, it appeared Alice would have to give up her apprenticeship at the seamstress shop. Rutter might leave her alone at this point, or he might seek her out again to make certain he'd made his point. The risk was too great for the young girl.

But those decisions could wait for when she was feeling better. Today, his focus was on learning more about the operation in which Rutter was involved.

Once again, Nathaniel had dressed down for the occasion. His tattered bowler hat was pulled low over his brow as he leaned against the building across the street from the lodging house.

Nathaniel was grateful for this morning's task as it helped keep his thoughts from Letitia. It had been incredibly difficult to see her home the previous evening when everything in him wanted her to stay. And not just for one night. The way she'd responded to him made him long to further explore their passion. No matter how many times he told himself she wasn't for him, he hadn't yet convinced himself of it.

For now, the only thing he could do was to shift his attention to his anger at Rutter and the others involved.

From what Langston had learned over the past few days, the man left the lodging house relatively early and ventured toward Blackfriars Bridge most mornings.

After nearly an hour, Nathaniel's patience paid off. The tall, stocky man ambled out of the lodging house, hands in his pockets, and made his way down the street, crossing to Nathaniel's side.

Nathaniel followed at a discreet distance, cursing his thigh once again as it had tightened up while he'd stood waiting. Glad he'd brought his cane with him, he leaned on it rather heavily. It eased the pain, plus it made him appear less of an adversary if the man looked back.

The streets were busy this time of the morning. Everyone seemed to be in a rush. Nathaniel had no desire to draw attention to his conversation with the man so bided his time, hoping the man would venture into a more deserted area. In this particular neighborhood, Nathaniel would bet the man had more friends than Nathaniel.

At last the man turned down a crooked side street with few passersby. Nathaniel hurried his pace and caught up with him.

"Excuse me," Nathaniel said, trying for the friendly approach first.

The man frowned at him. "What is it?"

"I'm looking for some information."

"Leave off." He turned and started to walk away.

"I'm prepared to pay well for it." Nathaniel hoped that would be enough to catch the man's interest. It was easier when an informant was willing rather than reluctant.

The man glanced about and looked at Nathaniel again. "What sort of information?"

Nathaniel guessed the man's nose had been broken at one time or another. His features were dark from time spent outdoors. Long, rather unruly sideburns marked his jaw line. He was slightly taller than Nathaniel and certainly stockier. The man's clothes had seen better days, showing signs of wear. Hopefully money would appeal to him.

"You know a man named Culbert Rutter?"

The man frowned. "What about him?"

"I want to know what he's up to and with whom."

"Oh?" The wheels were turning behind the man's narrowed eyes.

"Can I buy you a meal so we can visit for a time?"

The man warily glanced about again as though expecting Rutter to jump out from a doorway. Yet temptation sparked in his eyes. "I'm not interested." He started to turn away.

"I'd pay well." Nathaniel kept his voice casual, as though it didn't matter if he said yes or no.

"How well?"

When Nathaniel named a price, surprise registered on the man's face. "I only need a few minutes of your time."

After several moments of consideration, the man asked, "How do I know you're good for the money?"

"I'll pay half now and the rest at the end of our conversation." Nathaniel held out his hand. "My name's Hawke. What's yours?"

"Teddy," the main offered reluctantly.

"Do we have a deal, Teddy?"

"All right. I have a bit of time before I'm expected at my job. No need to buy me a meal. I'd rather just have the money."

Nathaniel withdrew the coins from his pocket, counted them out, and handed them to Teddy. By the look on his face, it had been some time since he'd held that much. Did that mean he wasn't paid well? That would work to

Nathaniel's advantage.

"What is it you want to know?" Teddy asked, pocketing the shillings.

"Who does Rutter work for?"

With a scowl on his face, Teddy shook his head. "That would cost you extra. There's too much risk speaking his name. He has eyes and ears everywhere."

Despite his refusal, Nathaniel was pleased. At least Teddy knew who it was. Perhaps he needed to gain the man's trust before he asked for the name again.

"What role do you play?" At Teddy's frown, Nathaniel rephrased his question. "What do you do for Rutter?"

"I offer jobs to girls at Blackfriars or wherever else I find them."

"What sort of jobs?"

Teddy smiled, but it wasn't pleasant. "What do you think?"

"Brothels?"

"Well, we never tell the girls that, but yes, that's where they'd be taken."

"Just one brothel?"

"No. There are three or four, plus he has an operation that hauls them across the Channel, to Brussels. The men there pay high prices for English girls."

Nathaniel's stomach clenched as anger filled him. Obviously the operation he and Warenton had stopped was only a small part of the whole endeavor. "Why?"

"The money. Why else would we do so?"

"How many are involved in the operation?"

Teddy chuckled. "More than I can count."

The man seemed to be relaxing. Hopefully that meant he'd share more easily.

Yet his answer disturbed Nathaniel more than he cared to admit. He was only one man. He had Langston to aid him, but the odds were not in their favor. This operation was even larger than he'd anticipated. How could he possibly make a difference in this fight? Warenton remained in Northumberland and as his wife was expecting their babe, Nathaniel didn't anticipate him venturing to London any time soon.

Who was he to think he could make a difference, that who he was or what he did mattered? He shoved back the voice in his head. It always sounded in his father's voice, telling him that he didn't matter, that he was of no use. He'd spent his military career proving otherwise to no avail. None of that silenced the voice.

He took a deep breath, well aware of Teddy's stare. He needed to gather himself and focus on the moment.

"Anything you can tell me will be helpful. The more the better," Nathaniel said, still trying to keep his voice light.

Teddy shared far more than Nathaniel hoped, giving Nathaniel a good idea of how the network operated. Rutter played a central role as Nathaniel had expected. But Nathaniel needed to know to whom he reported. Rutter had escaped their clutches far too many times.

As the conversation drew to a close, Nathaniel retrieved more shillings from his pocket and paid Teddy the agreed upon price. Then he held out another ten schillings. "These are yours if you tell me to whom Rutter reports."

The man stared at the money for a long moment, obviously weighing his options. Whoever the leader was, he obviously instilled fear in his men.

Teddy glanced around once more, searching the area carefully. "Jasper Smithby." He grabbed the schillings from Nathaniel and stuffed them in his pocket. "But you didn't hear it from me. The man's a nasty character."

"How do I find him?" Nathaniel asked.

"There's no amount of money that will have me telling you that."

"No one will hear it from me," Nathaniel reassured him.

Teddy shook his head adamantly. "The man uses

special...powers. He knows all."

"What do you mean by special powers?"

"Unspeakable, dark powers. He has a book. *The Book of Secrets*. It tells him everything and gives him the power to do terrible things."

"Such as what?" Teddy was clearly frightened of Smithby and his ridiculous book. Nathaniel couldn't imagine how Smithby had convinced the men who worked for him that he had some sort of dark magic.

Teddy visibly paled. "I'm not saying anything more." He backed up a step. "If you know what's good for you, you'll keep your distance. Stay away from Smithby."

Nathaniel watched him hurry away then turned in the opposite direction and walked, his mind churning. The next steps in this fight would need to be planned carefully. First he needed to make certain Alice and her family were safe, preferably far away from here until this was all resolved. He also needed to make certain Langston understood the risks they faced.

In truth, they needed more men for this fight to improve the odds. But who? He considered many of the men with whom he'd served, weighing their availability, willingness, and trustworthiness. One man came to mind, but he'd left the Navy nearly two years before Nathaniel had. They hadn't stayed in touch.

A particular nasty operation he and Oliver Bartley, Viscount Frost, had been in together had seemed to change his friend's attitude. At the time, Nathaniel thought he'd work through it, but Frost had left the service soon afterward. Perhaps it was time to see if he still lived in London. And more importantly, if he was willing to help.

The true question was how could he make certain Letitia remained safe, that she kept her distance from the situation. Somehow he didn't think explaining the danger they faced when they stopped this operation would do any good. Then an idea came to mind that would keep her safe but allow her to aid him. Could he convince her to agree to it?

He certainly hoped so because the idea of Rutter ever getting his hands on Letitia was unthinkable.

Lettie's mother hovered at her side as the Grant's party dragged on that evening. The Grant's gathering was one of the highlights of the Season. A smaller party of just under one hundred people, it involved supper, music, and conversation on a more intimate level than a ball.

Lettie found her mother's presence quite annoying and couldn't understand what she was thinking. After all, Rose, Violet, and Dalia were there. They normally took her full attention.

"Is all well, Mother?" Lettie asked at last.

"I want you to introduce me to Captain Hawke when he arrives," her mother replied as she glanced about the room.

Lettie felt her cheeks heat. "I don't know if he's coming this evening."

"His brother is here, so I thought he'd come as well."

"May I ask why you want to meet him?"

Her mother gave her a bland look. "Surely that is obvious, Lettie. If he has some sort of interest in you, I intend to meet him."

Lettie couldn't help her surprise. "He isn't interested in me as anything more than a friend." Too late, she heard the bleakness in her own tone.

"Why do you say that?" Her mother raised a brow.

Unable to explain why they had developed their unique relationship without revealing how she'd met him, she shook her head. She had no idea how to explain their friendship—if that was what it could be called.

"We have some mutual interests." Lettie kept her voice casual, hoping her mother wasn't truly listening. "Who is speaking with Rose?"

In truth, no one unusual was, but a man stood near her sister, and Lettie hoped that was enough to distract her mother.

With an almost comical movement, her mother quickly turned her focus on Rose. Unfortunately, Lettie's relief was short-lived.

"I don't believe he's speaking with her." After a long moment, she turned back to Lettie. "Now then, what were you saying about the captain?"

Lettie decided there was nothing to be done but share as much of the truth as she could. "It's the strangest coincidence, but Captain Hawke is reading the book I gave Father last week."

Her mother looked incredulous. "That terrible curses book?"

"Yes." Lettie nodded enthusiastically, well aware how much this information would annoy her mother. She disliked Lettie speaking about books. "He is quite concerned with the problems in London."

Her mother sighed. "I believe we've spoken about this many times over the years, dear. One simply does not discuss books with men. They do not find it attractive in the least."

"I'm not trying to attract him." She'd given up on such attempts shortly into her first Season.

"Why else would he be speaking with you if he isn't interested?"

Lettie sighed. "Because we're friends of a sort." She refused to consider the passion she'd found in his arms as she had no idea what to make of that. After all, it wasn't as if he'd declared his affections for her despite the intimacy they'd shared.

Yet she couldn't set aside the hope that it *had* meant more.

What if—no.

She couldn't possibly allow herself to hope.

But what if—

She swallowed hard, trying to set aside the idea that he was the first man who'd looked past her appearance and truly seen her for who she was. Hope was dangerous. She'd learned that all too well during her first Season.

In truth, she very much enjoyed their time together. Conversing with him was infuriating at times, but it also made her think. He seemed to appreciate her opinions, even if he didn't always agree with her. He treated her as a person with a right to an opinion.

Certainly her heartbeat sped when he was near, but that was only because...

Her shoulders sagged in defeat.

Because she was growing to care for him.

Her mother at last gave up and moved away to speak with Rose. Lettie was quite relieved. The evening was proving to be endless.

A tingle of awareness teased the nape of her neck. Before she could turn to confirm the cause, she felt his presence at her side.

"Good evening, Miss Fairchild."

She glanced toward him, all too aware of the heat in her cheeks as her pulse sped. "Good evening." She dipped into a curtsey as he bowed.

"I trust the evening finds you well?" His observant gaze swept over her face, making her feel like she couldn't hide anything, including her growing feelings for him.

"Quite. And you?" The pain that sometimes lined his eyes had eased, much to her relief.

"Well." His gaze shifted to take in the other guests.

"How does the patient fare?" she asked after making certain no one was listening.

"Alice is recovering. Her family has settled into their new lodging house, at least temporarily."

"When will she be able to join them?"

"The doctor wants her to remain in bed for at least two more days. If her symptoms have eased, she should be well on the mend."

"That is excellent news." Relief filled Lettie. The poor girl had been through far too much. A movement out of the corner of her eye revealed her mother making her way toward them. "I have a small problem I feel I should warn you about."

"Oh?" The concern lacing his tone warmed her.

"My mother is approaching."

He stilled for a moment, making her wonder if he'd heard her.

There was no time to repeat the warning as her mother halted at her side.

"Captain Hawke, my I present my mother, Mrs. Thomas Fairchild."

After the pleasantries were exchanged, Lettie hoped her mother would be satisfied, but her mother remained firmly at her side.

Lettie sent a look of apology to Nathaniel.

He appeared rather disconcerted and remained silent for a long moment. Lettie could only guess he wasn't used to conversing with mothers, though she knew he had one.

"Your brother is the Earl of Adair?" Lettie's mother asked. "I believe I saw him earlier this evening."

A small muscle in Nathaniel's jaw pulsed. Lettie had to wonder why the question upset him.

"Yes." The terse answer had her mother glancing at him inquiringly. The smile he gave her looked forced. "He is several years older than me."

"Perhaps you might introduce Lettie and her sisters to him," she suggested. Lettie was appalled at the idea, especially since she knew the reason behind it.

"I'd be pleased to do so." He glanced at her, and she shook her head ever so slightly, trying to signal that she had no interest in meeting his brother.

"I understand you were in the Navy. How exciting." Her doubtful expression suggested it had been anything but.

Lettie wanted to put her hand over her mother's

mouth. Anything to stop her from sounding so insulting.

"Options for second sons are limited." The tightness in his voice caused Lettie to watch him closely. "The Navy was the best choice for me."

Though she knew her mother's words might be appropriate on the surface, she also knew her meaning was disrespectful at the least. But Nathaniel's reaction held some underlying pain she couldn't identify.

She didn't care to see him unhappy, especially if her mother was the cause of it. If only they could have a moment alone so she might explain that he should ignore her mother. Maybe then she could discover why her mother's words bothered him so much.

CHAPTER FIFTEEN

"This, perhaps, would be tolerable if their earnings increased with their years; but such an arrangement does not come within the scheme of the sweaters and slop-factors, Jew and Christian, who grind the bones of little children to make them not only bread, but luxurious living and country houses, and carriages to ride in."

~ The Seven Curses of London

Nathaniel reined in the helpless anger and feelings of inadequacy that always poured through him when his position as second son was mentioned. It wasn't as if Mrs. Fairchild had directly referred to it. But there was no denying she thought less of him as he was the spare heir. It only made sense as most of society did the same.

But the emotions remained.

He could feel Letitia's questioning gaze. She had never made him feel less than worthy. His status didn't seem to matter to her. For all of those reasons, he appreciated her all the more.

"Will you be attending the Maverson's ball tomorrow night?" Letitia asked.

"I am not yet certain." He appreciated her attempt to change the subject. "I have one other engagement that may take my time."

A subtle look of disappointment crossed Letitia's face. The idea of her missing him helped to calm his roiling emotions.

"Fine weather we've been having," he said. The weather was the only subject he could think of that might interest Mrs. Fairchild.

"Yes, today was especially pleasant for June," she agreed.

After several more moments of awkward silence, and a few pointed looks between mother and daughter, Mrs. Fairchild finally departed to speak with a friend. He breathed a sigh of relief.

"I'm terribly sorry about that," Letitia offered with a look of apology. "I don't know why she's suddenly taken an interest in you. I suppose it's because I don't normally speak with..."

"With men?"

"With anyone, really." The note in her voice did not beg sympathy. She was merely stating a fact.

"Why?" Nathaniel truly didn't understand it. She was an attractive, intelligent woman. How had the men at these events passed her by?

The look on her face was one of confusion. "For any number of reasons. I don't care to name them." A rosy hue filled her cheeks, and he realized with remorse he'd embarrassed her.

"I truly don't understand." He turned to face her, wanting to erase any possible insult. "You're attractive. You've an excellent mind. You're interesting and have a sense of humor."

Her eyes went wide. "Thank you. Those are very kind words."

But a shuttered look came over her expression, and he knew without a doubt she didn't believe him.

He glanced about, wishing they had some privacy so he could make it clear how he felt about her. He stopped short. If he had time alone with her, he knew exactly how he'd spend it. Her passion hadn't surprised him in the least. It was exactly what he'd expected from his interactions with her—that she'd be responsive.

But he couldn't dwell on how she'd felt in his arms. He had no intention of marrying. His father had made it clear that would be a waste. And in truth, society reinforced that opinion. He knew he'd do more good spending his days helping others than married and trying to please a wife.

"I discovered some new information today," he said, needing to change the subject. "I wondered if you might assist me with it."

Her face brightened at his request. "I'd be delighted to help in any way. What is it?"

"Apparently one of the leaders in this group uses the supposed powers he receives from a book to frighten his men into complying."

Lettie looked as confused as he was on the topic. "That is unusual for a book. What is it called?"

"*The Book of Secrets*. Have you ever heard of it?"

"I can't say that I have."

"I thought that perhaps as much reading as you've done—"

She closed her eyes for a moment, making him realize that his comment was not a compliment to her.

"I find your intelligence and knowledge to be a good thing, despite what your mother might think," he added, hoping to clarify his words.

She met his gaze. "Thank you."

"At any rate, I thought perhaps one of the bookstores you frequent might have information on such a book. I'm assuming it's older, so maybe one of the shops that specialize in rare books?"

"I will make some inquiries." She looked quite pleased to have a task.

"Do be careful." He hoped to emphasize his point. "Caution is needed in this endeavor. We cannot underestimate the people involved or the lengths they're willing to go to keep their operation thriving."

"I understand completely. I shall begin tomorrow."

"Excellent. I look forward to hearing what you find. If possible, I'll attend the ball tomorrow evening so we can discuss it."

The pleasure on her face was his reward. Though he did his best to tamp down his reaction, he couldn't stop it. Nor did he know what to do about it.

The next morning, Nathaniel sat at his desk in the library, reading the newspaper, hoping new information might come to light.

"The Earl of Adair to see you, Captain," a footman said at the door.

Nathaniel didn't have a chance to rise before his brother entered the room, a book in his hand.

"Tristan," Nathaniel greeted him, unable to hide his surprise. "What brings you here so early this morning?"

"I have several questions I feel compelled to ask."

Nathaniel could only assume it had something to do with their mother. He hadn't spoken with her since their last uncomfortable family meeting, but he couldn't think of any other subject Tristan might want to discuss.

Tristan turned to make certain the footman had left before he approached the desk and took a seat. He studied Nathaniel closely.

"Do I have crumbs on my face?" Nathaniel asked, a brow arched at the seriousness of Tristan's expression.

"Have you officially retired from the Navy?"

Nathaniel frowned, uncertain what was on his brother's mind. "Yes. My injury prevented me from remaining in the service."

"But you're still involved."

"Involved in what?"

"In the government."

He could only stare at Tristan, confused by his comments. They couldn't be called questions as he wasn't wording them as such. When Tristan didn't continue, Nathaniel said, "No, I am not involved in the government."

Tristan scowled, looking doubtful at his response. "A secret government agency perhaps?"

"Tristan, what on earth are you about?"

"I know you're involved in something." He set the book he'd been holding on the desk.

A glance at it had Nathaniel staring at the familiar cover in surprise. *The Seven Curses of London.* "Doing some light reading, are you?"

"Tell me the truth."

"I don't know what you mean." He'd already told his brother much of what he was doing. What more did he want?

"I think you do." Tristan leaned forward. "You've gained a purposeful attitude that has only grown in the past few months."

"And?" Even if he had, what difference did it make to Tristan?

"I want to know what you're involved in."

"Why?"

"I'm certain you're putting your life in danger."

Nathaniel scoffed. Though that was true, he wasn't prepared to discuss it. He well knew he wasn't only putting his own life in danger, but others as well. Yet he could think of no other way to stop these men than by taking the steps he had thus far. He feared it would grow worse before it became better.

"Who are you working for?" Before Nathaniel could respond, he continued, "You're secretive. You're taking late night walks in Whitechapel. What are you and Warenton up to?"

"Warenton is in Northumberland as his wife is

expecting a child. I am not working for anyone." He didn't bother to respond to the other statements.

"Are you trying to tell me that you're attempting to investigate the issues noted in this book out of the goodness of your heart?"

"It's more about righting wrongs."

"Damn, you really are a hero," Tristan said as he sat back with a look of annoyed disbelief. While the words were nothing his father would've offered, the look reminded Nathaniel so much of him that he had to look away.

"What is it?"

Nathaniel hesitated before answering, "You remind me of Father at times."

Now it was his brother's turn to look away, which surprised Nathaniel. Had his words displeased Tristan? Nathaniel had always believed his brother took great pride in how much he looked and acted like their father.

Tristan turned back, holding Nathaniel's gaze. "You truly are doing this on your own?"

"I'm not involved in the government in any way. There is no secret agency or such thing."

"Based on what I read thus far in that book, there should be some formal organization combating all these problems."

"You'd have my agreement on that. I'm merely doing what I can to improve the lives of some." Nathaniel leaned back in his chair. "You know the conditions of the slums in this city are appalling."

"I suppose that must be true." The grudging tone in his voice grated on Nathaniel.

"But it doesn't concern you." Nathaniel knew that as a fact and stated it as such.

"I send money to several charitable organizations."

Nathaniel wanted to shake his head in disappointment, but he resisted. That would've been too much like their father's reaction. "Do you know where your donations are spent? Or how?"

"What difference does that make? Others oversee such details."

Once again, Tristan's attitude reminded him of their father, which he didn't appreciate. Yet it didn't seem worth arguing about. Tristan had been molded by their father to continue on as he had done.

Unwilling to waste time arguing, Nathaniel held his silence, waiting to see if Tristan had anything more to say. By the determined glint in his eye, Nathaniel assumed something else bothered him.

"Are you planning on proposing to Miss Fairchild?"

"Heavens, no." The very idea made Nathaniel shift uncomfortably in his seat. "You're the one who is supposed to marry. Not me."

"Your behavior suggests otherwise." At Nathaniel's puzzled look, Tristan continued. "You've danced with her on at least two occasions, and to my knowledge, not with anyone else. At every event where both of you are in attendance, you speak with her. Someone even told me you spoke with her mother last night."

Nathaniel nearly groaned. He should've realized what his actions might be suggesting. In all honesty, it hadn't crossed his mind after being absent from society for some time. His attention had been on stopping the brothel operation, not on what the *ton* might be thinking.

"Her mother would be more pleased if I introduced her to you," Nathaniel said. "As would our own mother."

Tristan only shook his head. "I am in no hurry to marry, despite what Mother says. I have done my best to avoid women who might expect more than a dance from me."

"I don't believe Miss Fairchild expects anything out of me." Nathaniel was quite certain of it.

"That no longer matters. Tongues are wagging over your conversations with her."

"We're merely acquaintances who share a mutual

interest."

"That's more than most marriages are based on," Tristan said with a smile. "Sounds like you're well on your way to walking down the aisle."

"Marriage is not in my future."

"You should've thought of that before you began this association with Miss Fairchild. It may no longer be your choice."

Nathaniel sat back in surprise. He had never intended to harm Letitia's reputation. She was a lovely woman, inside and out and deserved to be happy. Yet imagining her with another man who might make her so made him scowl with displeasure.

Before they could discuss the matter further, Dibbles appeared in the doorway.

"My apologies, but the captain's presence is required in the kitchen."

Nathaniel stared at the odd expression on Dibbles' face. He knew the man well enough to tell something was terribly wrong. As casually as possible, he stood, hoping his brother would take his leave. "I suppose I must see what's wrong. If you'll excuse me?"

His brother nodded and rose. "I must be going anyway. I do hope you'll consider what I said."

"Of course." Nathaniel breathed a sigh of relief as he followed his brother out the library door. He bid Tristan goodbye and followed Dibbles down to the kitchen. He couldn't imagine what had the man so upset. Nothing ruffled him.

When Nathaniel entered the kitchen, two maids and a footman stood near the back door. At the look of shock on the footman's face and the tears on the maids', Nathaniel slowed his steps. The cook stood at the work table in the center of the kitchen, her hands idle, a rare occurrence.

"This way," Dibbles directed him as he gestured toward the kitchen's rear entrance.

All the servants drew back as Dibbles opened the door.

A man lay sprawled on the ground, his face pale, his eyes staring unseeingly at the sky.

Teddy. The man he'd spoken with the previous day who'd given him Smithby's name as well as the title of the book. Remorse filled him. Obviously whoever had killed the poor man had discovered he'd spoken to Nathaniel. Teddy had been right to be afraid.

As many dead men as he'd seen over the years during his military career, he wasn't completely shocked at the sight before him. But finding a body on his doorstep was a different matter entirely.

He drew nearer, noting the man's jacket and shirt were covered in blood. The metallic scent of it hung in the air. He squatted down beside the body, noting a piece of paper sticking out of the man's jacket pocket. With careful fingers, he withdrew the paper.

"What the hell?"

Nathaniel turned to see his brother standing behind him. "I thought you left."

"I nearly did. But curiosity got the better of me."

"I believe someone is sending me a message." Nathaniel said the words more to himself than to Tristan.

"You know this man?" The incredulous note in Tristan's voice did not go unnoticed.

"I met him yesterday."

"Are you certain he's dead?"

Nathaniel stared incredulously at his brother, only to realize he probably hadn't seen a murdered man before. "Yes. He's dead."

"Should we send for the police?"

Nathaniel sighed and ran a hand through his hair. "In time, but first I want to see what this message says." He needed a moment to think, to decide who he was going to tell at the police department as he was convinced not all of them could be trusted.

With slow movements, he unfolded the paper, reluctant

to read it. The handwriting was rough, the words written in pen.

Mind your own business.
Asking questions gets people killed.

No signature. No hint as to an identity.

Only a warning. But Nathaniel had to guess this was Jasper Smithby's doing. By itself, the note would've meant little, but delivered with the body...

"What does that mean?" Tristan asked as he looked at the message over Nathaniel's shoulder. He placed a hand to his nose as though the odor was getting the better of him.

"It means I'm moving in the right direction."

"With what?"

His heart heavy, Nathaniel leaned over and closed the dead man's eyes. Someone must've seen them speaking and reported it to Smithby. Or Rutter. Either man was no doubt capable of this. He refused to believe it had anything to do with the power Smithby supposedly had from *The Book of Secrets* as Teddy had seemed to believe.

Lettie entered one of the bookstores that she knew specialized in ancient texts. With luck, the proprietor could tell her about *The Book of Secrets* or, even better, find a secondary copy of it. There was a chance it was a single edition or only one copy remained as happened with some old books. She hoped that was not the case.

She didn't care for this particular store—the place smelled dank and musty, no doubt a result of the ancient tomes that lined the shelves. While she had a deep affection for books, this shop was a challenge in which to browse.

Mr. Stapleton, the proprietor, wasn't the friendliest

person. He had narrow, thick spectacles that sat on the end of his hooked nose and peered down at her through them. His nasally voice was difficult to understand at times as he tended to draw out his ss's.

"May I asssist you?" he asked as she and Cora entered.

She never understood how he knew customers had arrived without a bell to signal him, but without fail, he came from the back of the store when a customer arrived.

"I am in search of a book titled *The Book of Secrets*."

"Who isss the author?"

"I don't know."

"To what isss the book pertaining?"

"I'm afraid I don't know that either." She was tempted to tell him it pertained to secrets, but she didn't think he'd appreciate her attempt at humor.

"I don't know that I can aid you. I'm not familiar with sssuch a text."

In some ways she was relieved. The less she had to deal with Mr. Stapleton, the better. Still, she hesitated. What if the book was tucked on the back of one of those shelves, and he'd simply forgotten about it? "Would you mind if I looked around?"

He paused as though he'd prefer she didn't.

That was another reason the man annoyed her. At times, he seemed to forget he was in the business of selling books. She smiled politely, waiting. She hoped she was making it clear that she wasn't leaving until he agreed.

"Certainly." The word was friendly enough, but the tone was not.

"Why thank you," she said and moved away before he changed his mind. She waved at Cora to remain near the door as she knew the maid didn't care for books and would much rather watch the people passing by outside than peruse the shelves.

It would be impossible for Lettie to search the entire store. The only hope was if she came upon it by accident, but as she was already here, having a look was worth a try.

She started at a nearby shelf and worked her way toward the rear of the store. Many of the books didn't have a title on their spine, making her search all the more difficult. She couldn't possibly look through each of them. Plus Mr. Stapleton would not appreciate her touching his precious books. Already he watched her closely from the front counter.

With a sigh, she perused the next row, refraining from touching the books and instead, studied them, hoping inspiration would strike and she might be able to select one that would provide a clue.

She heard Mr. Stapleton greet another customer and realized the woman's voice was quite familiar. With a smile, she returned to the front of the shop.

"Greetings, Julia," she said as Mr. Stapleton withdrew to the back room to collect whatever Julia had requested.

"Lettie, how lovely to see you." Julia reached out a gloved hand to grasp Lettie's arm, her smile a bright light. "What brings you to Mr. Stapleton's shop?"

"I was hoping to discover some information on a book, but it doesn't seem as though he can assist me. What of you?"

"My father is a collector of old books. Mr. Stapleton was able to locate a rather rare one for him, so I've come to retrieve it."

"I didn't realize your father was interested in such things. Would it be possible for you to ask him a question for me?"

"Why certainly. He'd be delighted to help if he could. He doesn't venture out often anymore, so it's lovely if he can still feel needed."

Lettie hesitated, glancing toward the rear of the store. She didn't want to share this information with the proprietor. "Perhaps we can discuss it outside when your business here is finished."

After Julia agreed, Lettie returned to her browsing but to no avail. When Julia had completed her business, Lettie left as well with Cora trailing behind.

As Lettie gave Julia the information she was seeking, an odd feeling of being watched came over her. She turned to glance around but couldn't see any cause for the uncomfortable feeling.

"What is it?" Julia asked.

Lettie shook her head. "It feels as though someone is watching us, though I can't imagine why." Yet as she continued to converse with Julia, the feeling persisted.

"I will ask Father upon my return home and notify you if he has anything helpful to share."

They chatted a few more minutes before saying goodbye.

Lettie visited two more bookstores without any success. Disappointment filled her as obtaining news would've given her a reason to seek out Nathaniel. She knew she was becoming far too dependent on him. When all of this came to an end, and he was no longer in her life, it was going to hurt dreadfully.

And she knew it would end.

If only she could find a balance between enjoying each moment with Nathaniel to the fullest and keeping her defenses in place so that she didn't completely lose her heart to him when it was over.

But that was beginning to feel impossible.

CHAPTER SIXTEEN

"When their "hands" cease to be children, these enterprising tradesmen no longer require their services, and they are discharged to make room for a new batch of small toilers, eager to engage themselves on terms that the others have learned to despise, while those last-mentioned unfortunates are cast adrift to win their bread— somehow."

~ The Seven Curses of London

Lettie arrived at Nathaniel's home that afternoon, torn between being pleased and worried that he'd sent a message asking her to come to him. Pleased he might need her in even the smallest way, and worried Alice had taken a turn for the worse.

She'd sworn Cora to secrecy, hoping the maid was loyal enough to keep quiet about Lettie's whereabouts. She hadn't told her the full truth—that she was visiting Nathaniel's home—only that she was visiting a friend. A twinge of guilt nudged at her for the small lie. But Nathaniel was a friend of sorts, at least she liked to think so.

"Good afternoon, miss." Dibbles greeted her at the door with a smile—something she thought might be rare for him based on its tightness.

"And to you, Dibbles. The captain requested I visit."

"Of course." He showed her into the library. "Captain Hawke will be with you shortly."

"How is Alice faring?" she asked, worried the girl had worsened.

"Continuing to improve. I believe she's resting at the moment."

"I will visit with her after I speak with the captain." Lettie breathed a sigh of relief at the news, but couldn't stop wondering why Nathaniel wanted to see her. Expecting him to walk in at any moment, she sat in one of the tufted chairs before the desk, waiting patiently. But as the minutes ticked by, curiosity got the best of her, and she rose to wander about the room.

Few personal effects were displayed. A brass statue of a ship rising high on the crest of a ferocious wave. A china figurine of a dog that looked eagerly at something in the distance. The books on the shelves were much like the ones in her father's library, covering a wide variety of topics. The most prevalent were those on the sea. She wondered if he missed being on board a ship or if he was pleased to be home on solid ground. She made a mental note to ask when she had a chance.

A small sitting area graced the space near the fireplace, the wine-colored fabric covering the chairs and matching settee appropriate for a man's study. A desk and chairs took up the other end of the room near the window.

Listening for any sounds coming from the hall, she moved closer to study his desk. The black walnut had simple yet elegant lines. Not so massive that it took up the entire room, but large enough to provide sufficient space to work.

She glanced out the window and saw her own carriage waiting a short distance away. She'd requested the footman to avoid waiting directly in front of Nathaniel's home, not wanting to take any chances.

Sheets of correspondence of some sort lay on the desk. The bold, strong strokes of the letters made her certain it was Nathaniel's writing. A drawer was several inches ajar. Gold glinted off the objects inside, catching her eye. A closer look revealed ribbons as well, and she realized they were military medals.

She stared at the contents, wanting to examine them. Yet it seemed like a terrible intrusion to do so. Nathaniel was a private person. She had no right to look closer but couldn't help herself. Why would he tuck away the medals?

With another wary glance at the door, she eased open the drawer another inch to study them. There were easily a dozen medals inside. She couldn't tell what they were for, nor did she know much about the military, but she knew they didn't give everyone medals simply for participating. What had he done to earn so many, and why didn't he display them in a case as most men would?

The quantity of awards suggested he'd taken the same ridiculous risks in the Navy as he did on the streets of London. The very idea gave her the shivers.

"I'm sorry to have kept you waiting." He strode into the room, only to stop short when he saw her near the open drawer.

"What are these?" No longer concerned with getting caught snooping, she lifted one out, holding up the medal. Guilt shot through her at his tight expression, but she pushed it back, wanting to understand why these were hidden away.

"Searching through the drawers of my desk?" Nathaniel shook his head as embarrassment flooded him. "I must say I'm surprised."

"The drawer was ajar," she quickly responded.

"I suppose I have Dibbles to thank for that." It would be just like the man to leave Letitia alone in the library long enough for her to have discovered the open drawer.

He forced himself to step forward despite the discomfiture sweeping through him. The medals were kept in the drawer for a reason. He didn't want anyone to see them. They were reminders of his many attempts to make a difference, to somehow prove to himself and his father that he mattered.

Unfortunately, none of his efforts had proven successful. He still hadn't been able to convince himself that he mattered. His achievements in the Navy had certainly never impressed his father. Even Letitia's mother had made it clear that second sons didn't count.

"Do these mean what I think they mean?" she asked.

"They mean nothing." He walked closer to take the one she held, return it to the drawer, and firmly shut it.

"I disagree." She lifted her chin as though daring him to argue.

That gesture stole his breath. Or perhaps it was the way the light in her eyes shone into his soul, casting away the darkness, the doubt. Making him feel as if he truly did matter. She believed in him, worried over him. The knowledge had him swallowing hard.

"You were awarded those for bravery. For taking risks. For saving lives. How can you say they don't matter?" She opened the drawer again to stare at them, touching several.

He couldn't take his eyes off her fingers as they ran along the medals, wishing her hands were on him instead.

"Nathaniel, you are a hero." She whispered the words reverently as she looked up at him.

"No. I merely did what the task required." He couldn't meet her eyes, not wanting to see the disappointment in them when she realized the truth. The commendations meant nothing.

She turned to him, lifting her arms around his shoulders. "They mean something. If not to you, then to the others you aided. Why do you deny it?"

He shook his head, unable to explain.

"You're doing the same thing now that you've returned home. You should be relaxing and enjoying yourself after all you sacrificed during your time in the service. Instead, you're once again risking your life to save others."

"Hardly. Those girls are the ones whose lives are at risk. They matter."

"So do you." She took his face in her hands, forcing him to look into her eyes. "Nathaniel, you matter."

He closed his eyes, hardly able to bear to hear those words. Yet slowly, despite his denial, they sunk deep inside him. To think he mattered, at least to her, was a tremendous gift. One he didn't quite know how to manage.

"You matter to me." She lifted up on her toes and kissed him.

This he could manage. He drew her into his arms and returned the kiss, well aware of the passion that simmered within him whenever she was near, and even when she wasn't. He lingered long over the sweet taste of her, drawing comfort from the feel of her in his arms. She felt so good there, heating him from the inside out.

Her tongue met his as he deepened the kiss. The problems ahead of them fell away as he indulged his desire. Somehow when Letitia was with him, he felt whole. And when she kissed him, he felt far more. She drew back and held his gaze once more, the emotion shining in her eyes causing him to catch his breath. What was that in the depths? Faith? In him?

He released her, uncomfortable at the thought. Once again, he'd become distracted in her presence. He needed to focus on the reason he'd asked her to come. It certainly hadn't been to show her the medals. Dibbles had to stop interfering.

"I wanted to speak with you," he began, still uncertain how best to raise the subject without giving her the wrong idea. In truth, he wasn't certain what her reaction would be. Yet they couldn't continue on as they had been.

"Is it Alice? Dibbles said she was doing well."

"She continues to improve." He took her hand, closing the drawer before leading her to the settee before the fireplace. "I hope she'll be able to join her family within the next two days."

"That is excellent news. Unfortunately, I was less than successful on my quest for information on the book."

He nodded. "These things take time. I didn't expect immediate results."

Her head tilted to the side as she studied him. "What is it?"

The clever words he needed to convince her to see his side of the situation had not yet come to him. He could only hope they would trip off his tongue as he spoke. "It has come to my attention that we can't continue seeing each other the way we have without it harming your reputation."

A blush stained her cheeks. "I don't understand."

"It seems our conversations are starting to draw attention. Even my brother has noted that you're one of the few people I speak with at social events." He shook his head. "If my brother noticed, you can be assured others have as well."

She frowned. "I can hardly believe that. It's not as if this is my first Season. I'm practically on the shelf. Those rules don't really apply to me."

"Of course they do. You're an attractive woman of marriageable age."

She stared at him as though he'd lost his mind.

He closed his eyes for a moment to keep his patience. "Despite your view, you must rely on my experience in this matter."

"Is this a way for you to force me to stop my attempts to help others?" She folded her arms across her chest. "I'm warning you now not to bother. I am determined to continue to help with or without you."

"Yes, I'm well aware of that," he answered dryly. The

woman was a force of nature when she set her mind to a course. He drew a breath to gather his thoughts. "I have a suggestion for your consideration. It will allow us to continue working together, perhaps even more closely, without drawing unwanted attention. And it will protect your reputation."

Her eyes narrowed. "It sounds too good to be true. What is it?"

"I suggest that we become engaged..." He did his best to set aside his personal feelings for her to focus on the practical aspects of his proposal. This was a business arrangement after all. "On a temporary basis."

She stilled at his words. "Engaged?" The word was but a whisper. The way she said the term made it sound as though she was pronouncing it for the first time.

"An engagement would allow us to proceed with our investigation without drawing unwanted attention. Your mother's worries would be calmed, for the most part, though I fear my status as a second son is undesirable compared to what she'd hoped for her eldest daughter."

"What?" She appeared confused at his explanation. Or was it his proposal that puzzled her?

"I'm merely suggesting that while I'm not the ideal candidate for your hand, perhaps she would find it acceptable."

Letitia continued to stare at him as though he'd grown two heads.

"Once we've accomplished our mission, you would end the engagement, claiming whatever reason you wish, and we would proceed with our lives."

"A temporary engagement." She said the words carefully, as though still absorbing the concept.

He watched her closely, trying to determine her reaction, nerves chasing down his spine at the thought of her refusing him. "This arrangement would be the best way to stop others from concerning themselves with the amount of time we spend together."

"Forgive me. I've never been proposed to before. It's a bit much to take in." She rose and walked toward the desk, her back to him.

Remorse filled him. He hadn't given any thought to that possibility. After all, he wasn't experienced in proposing. "Surely you've received other offers."

"Actually, I haven't." She turned to face him again, but her pale face didn't ease his concern. "I must say, I didn't think it would be quite like this."

"Consider it more as a business arrangement." Why did the description sound less than satisfactory to him when he'd convinced himself earlier it was the best option?

Her mouth tightened, causing something to shift in his chest. "A temporary one," she repeated in a breathy voice.

"Yes." Odd, but his confirmation didn't seem to reassure her either. What was going on in that mind of hers?

"Yet we would have to act as though it were real," she continued, her hand trembling as she raised it to touch her chest. Surely her heart wasn't pounding as hard as his.

"Yes, I suppose we would. Perhaps we could tell your family we have not yet set a date. That way, they wouldn't begin to plan the event."

"I'm afraid you'll have to give me some time to consider all the ramifications of this." Her cheeks were flushed as she held his gaze for the briefest moment. If he didn't know better, he'd think her eyes held a stricken look, but that made no sense.

"Certainly. I wouldn't want to pressure you into any sudden decision that you would come to regret." In all honesty, he was puzzled by her reaction. He'd explained it was a business arrangement. Didn't she understand he was a mere second son and not a worthy husband for many reasons?

Or perhaps that was the problem.

The hollow feeling engulfing him as she quickly said goodbye and walked out the door was a sharp contrast to what he'd felt earlier. The emptiness left in her wake was something with which he should be familiar, as was the disappointment. But this felt different—far worse.

She took the light with her when she left, leaving him alone in shadows once more.

Lettie moved through the rest of the day as though in a trance. She felt numb, unable to process even the simplest information.

Part of her wanted to shut herself in her room and cry. How could the moment she'd dreamed of, that she'd nearly given up on ever happening, have gone so wrong?

A temporary business arrangement?

No, she wanted to scream.

She saw Nathaniel's logic. Even her mother had noted Nathaniel's attentions, and that was saying much. Rarely did her mother's focus shine its beacon on her. If his brother, whom she had yet to meet, had also noted it, then they did indeed have a problem.

She wasn't willing to stop her quest. Nor did she care to do it alone. Her attempts to do so had proven futile and dangerous. She supposed she could try once again to involve her father.

But she wanted Nathaniel.

In more than one way.

And that was truly the heart of the problem, she realized with a shaky breath. Her feelings for Nathaniel deepened each day. The way he touched her, the way he made her feel when she was in her arms, had given her hope their relationship was growing into something more, something deeper.

He'd dashed all that with his proposal. No, she refused to call it that. It was a business arrangement. Nothing more. Her hurt at the truth was difficult to conceal.

As the remainder of the day proceeded with her

helping her sisters with this and that, Lettie tried to determine her answer. With each hour that passed, she attempted to narrow her options.

She could refuse, but she was convinced that response would remove Nathaniel from her life. He would walk away without looking back, of that she had no doubt.

She could accept his proposal and the risks that went along with it. Those risks were so high. Could she keep her heart whole if she agreed? Or would she be left in pieces when the engagement ended?

She could accept but suggest conditions of her own. But what would she demand?

Her breath caught.

No, she couldn't. Could she?

Yet her future as a spinster stretched out endlessly before her. Proposing such an arrangement would be far riskier. The chances of her refraining from becoming even more emotionally involved were slim. None in fact.

"Lettie, dear, is something wrong?" her mother asked as they assisted Rose prepare for the ball that evening.

Her question was tempting and, for a moment, Lettie considered sharing all of her concerns with her. But a glance at her face made her decide against it. Somehow, Lettie was certain the concern marking her expression wasn't truly for her. Oh, she knew well enough that her mother loved her in her own way, but the days when she might've confessed her dilemma had long since passed. Unless the issue pertained to Rose and her duke, nothing Lettie said would truly interest her mother.

"I have a bit of a headache is all," she lied.

"Very well," her mother said with some relief. "Will you find the hairpin with the blue stones? I think that will match Rose's gown perfectly."

"Of course." Lettie turned to leave.

"Lettie?" Rose called out. "Do sit and rest. I am perfectly capable of finding the pin myself." Rose squeezed Lettie's shoulder as she hurried past her out of the room before their mother could protest.

"Whatever is wrong with Rose?" her mother asked.

Lettie couldn't stop her smile at the warmth that filled her at Rose's concern. "If you'll excuse me, Mother, I believe I'll follow Rose's suggestion and rest in my room."

She'd only been resting in her room for a short while before she decided she would've been better off staying busy. Indecision continued to plague her. At the knock at her door, she said, "Come in."

Dalia opened the door, balancing a tray in her hand.

"What are you doing?" Lettie asked at the odd sight.

Her sister scowled at her. "I would think it obvious. I'm bringing you tea."

Lettie could only stare at her.

"What?" Dalia asked.

"I'm thoroughly confused by your behavior."

Dalia sat the tray on the bedside table and poured a cup, adding a bit of sugar, just as Lettie preferred it. "You seemed out of sorts earlier, and Rose told me you had a headache. I thought you might like some tea."

Lettie sat up on her bed to take the cup and saucer Dalia held. "That was very thoughtful of you." She couldn't keep the incredulous note out of her voice. Dalia had never done such a thing before.

Dalia sighed. "Rose and I were speaking earlier. We both agreed that we take you for granted. You are always so generous with your time and never ask anything in return. The least we could do is show some concern when you're not feeling well."

"That is kind of you." Lettie hardly knew what to say.

"Is everything all right?" Dalia asked, studying her.

Lettie took a sip while she considered her answer. Though the idea of talking over the situation was tempting, she didn't think either of her sisters would understand. This was a decision she needed to make by herself. For herself.

"Merely a bit of a headache. Nothing some tea and rest

won't cure."

Dalia smiled. "I'm glad to hear it." Her sister sat on the edge of the bed.

"What is it?" Lettie could tell by the look on Dalia's face that something was on her mind.

"Mr. Brover is attending the ball this evening. Which gown do you think I should wear?"

Lettie sighed. "Are you certain he captures your interest?"

"Why do you ask?"

"In all honesty I don't think he's good enough for you." Lettie hoped that by stating it that way, her sister wouldn't take offense but would consider her words.

Dalia opened her mouth as though to protest only to close it once more. Several seconds passed before at last she nodded. "You're probably right."

"Then it doesn't matter what you wear." Lettie held her breath, hoping her sister agreed. She hadn't cared for Mr. Brover.

"On the contrary. His interest might spur the interest of others." She glanced apologetically at Lettie. "That sounds mercenary of me, doesn't it?"

Lettie understood her logic but even more she was relieved Dalia's heart wasn't at risk with Mr. Brover. "I believe Rose is wearing a pale blue gown this evening. What about the yellow one? That color is very becoming on you."

"Do you think so?"

"If you have Cora braid your hair so it sits along the side of your neck, we could place those little yellow satin roses in the braid."

"Oh, that's an excellent idea." Dalia rose. "Perhaps when you finish your tea, you might help me find those roses?"

"Certainly." Lettie sighed, aware her rest was at end. While it was nice to be needed, she'd grown weary of the demands of her family.

She could say no, but it seemed petty of her to refuse.

Perhaps she should accept Nathaniel's business arrangement if only for the shock it would give her family.

CHAPTER SEVENTEEN

"Haggard, weary-eyed infants, who never could have been babies; little slips of things, whose heads are scarcely above the belt of the burly policeman lounging out his hours of duty on the bridge, but who have a brow on which, in lines indelible, are scored a dreary account of the world's hard dealings with them."

~ *The Seven Curses of London*

Nathaniel perused the crowded ballroom that evening, hoping Lettie was there, and hoping she'd decided to agree to his suggestion. Perhaps she needed more than a few hours to consider it. It was a big decision. But if she looked at it logically, surely she'd see an engagement was the best option.

Never mind the voice in his head that desperately wanted her to agree. The idea of saying goodbye to her was unappealing to say the least. He told himself it would be easier to do so now than after spending several more weeks in her company.

But that didn't change his hope that she'd say yes.

He'd deal with saying goodbye when the time came. He wanted Lettie—needed her in more ways than he cared to admit.

The internal battle continued until he was scowling, no longer certain what he wanted.

"You're going to frighten the other guests."

Lettie's voice at his side startled him. Normally he found her first. That showed him just how much this whole matter had unsettled him. Somehow, he needed to regain control. And as soon as he had her answer, he could.

He turned to face her, hoping her answer would be clear in her expression. But her eyes were guarded with worry lurking in their depths.

"Good evening," she said.

"And to you."

The small smile she gave him provided no clues. When had his wallflower become such an enigma?

"I'm certain this evening finds you well," Tristan said as he joined them.

Nathaniel could've throttled his brother. Though he probably thought his presence would allay any gossip, it had the opposite effect. Nathaniel could already feel stares from half of the ballroom, which he would've preferred to avoid.

Lettie looked from Nathaniel to his brother and back again, that small smile still in place.

Nathaniel made the introductions as quickly as possible, hoping his brother would be satisfied and take his leave.

"It's a delight to meet you, Miss Fairchild. I believe I've seen my brother at your side several times of late."

"We have found that we share a common interest," Lettie said as she glanced at Nathaniel before returning her attention to Tristan. "Do you share your brother's hobbies as well?"

"Which ones would those be?" Tristan asked.

Nathaniel cleared his throat. He didn't appreciate their conversation excluding him while he stood between them. "Nothing that would capture your attention," he said to

Tristan.

"Ah. You must be referring to that curses book."

Letitia's smile widened and a familiar light filled her eyes—the light he'd always considered his and his alone. The tightness in his chest was as unwelcome as Tristan's presence.

"Are you familiar with the book?" Letitia asked.

"Indeed. Quite enlightening," Tristan said. He offered her one of his rare, charming smiles.

Nathaniel braced himself, waiting for the expected results he'd seen in the past. His brother had charisma, and he so rarely used it that when he did, the affect was stunning. Their father had possessed the same ability. In their father's case, it had hidden the beast within, deceiving those around him. Nathaniel hoped that wasn't the case with Tristan.

With reluctance, he looked at Letitia, expecting to see a besotted glaze in her eyes.

To his surprise, her expression held the same skepticism she often had, as though completely unaffected by Tristan's charm. "Which curse caught your interest the most?"

Nathaniel tried to hide his smile. She was testing his brother to see if he spoke the truth, ignoring the fact that he was an earl. For some reason, that lightened his heart.

Tristan's brow rose, as though asking how dare she question him. But Letitia held her ground, her silence speaking volumes as she awaited his answer.

"I found the first one the most intriguing. And you?"

"Difficult to say," she said. "All were equally concerning."

Tristan nodded in agreement, making Nathaniel doubt he'd read any of the book.

"The farming was one of the worst though, don't you think?" she asked.

"Indeed," Tristan agreed. "To think the newspapers permits ads for people willing to farm out their children.

That only worsens the problem."

Letitia's eyes widened in respect. "I couldn't agree more."

Nathaniel was impressed. Tristan had read the book—at least part of it. He shared a look with Letitia, seeing she'd come to the same realization. The idea of having someone who understood what he was thinking with only a look was a novelty. It only made him like her all the more.

Affection? Was that all this was? In truth, he feared his feelings for her had grown beyond that, but he wasn't willing to label them.

Tristan glanced between them, as though sensing they were sharing a moment. That was far more than their father would've realized.

"Letitia's sisters are in search of husbands. Perhaps you'd like to meet them?" Nathaniel asked, hoping the question would chase away his brother.

"Not this evening. Thank you." He offered Letitia a smile. "It's a pleasure to have made your acquaintance. I look forward to future conversations."

"As do I." Letitia gave him a curtsy.

Tristan glared at Nathaniel, making him smile.

"It was lovely to have met him at last." Letitia watched the dancers swirling along the dance floor with a wistful expression.

"Would you care to dance?" he asked.

She smiled. "That's not necessary."

"I beg to differ." He reached for her hand as the musicians began a waltz. A pang of guilt struck him as he realized he wasn't above trying to convince her to agree to his proposal. But dancing with her when he had no intention of doing so with anyone else would cause more gossip.

As he looked into Letitia's eyes, none of that mattered. He wanted to give her everything she longed for. Instead, he had to settle for giving her this dance, as awkward as it would be with him as her partner.

He held out his hand, hoping his leg would cooperate.

With a smile, she took his hand, and he tucked hers under his elbow. A feeling of completeness came over him, one he refused to question.

He kept to the edge of the dance floor as no matter how much he wished otherwise, his steps did not match the other dancers.

Letitia didn't seem to mind in the least. She took his hand, placing her other one on his shoulder. Her small steps mirrored his, and they moved with perfect rhythm. Her obvious delight was his reward for the twinge in his thigh.

She tipped her head back slightly, her laugh one of pure joy as they moved.

As he watched, he knew without a doubt he'd give anything to hear that joy again. If only he was more than who he was. He reined back the longing that filled him. He was used to doing so. After all, he'd done it his entire life.

He set aside the question he'd wanted to ask and focused on the feel of her moving to the music. Even more delightful was the happiness on her face. He wanted these few minutes to last forever.

Then he wanted to kiss her senseless.

He shook his head slightly, annoyed the thought had crept into his mind. Kisses were not part of the agenda, regardless of whether she agreed to his proposal or not.

When the music ended, he continued to hold her a moment longer. Her smile lit his entire being, and he didn't want the feeling to end. Her gaze met his and for now, they were in complete accordance.

But as the other dancers left the floor, Nathaniel realized they needed to as well. He escorted her toward an alcove, hoping they might have a moment to speak in private. Even if she hadn't yet decided, he wanted to speak with her. The idea that this could be one of the last times he did so did not please him in the least.

"Have you thought further on my suggestion?" It was unfair of him to press her, but he couldn't help himself.

"Yes."

His heartbeat sped as he held his breath. Had she meant yes, she accepted, or merely yes, she'd thought on it?

"After careful consideration..."

He couldn't take his eyes off her. Couldn't breathe.

"I believe your suggestion is a practical one."

Though he waited several moments, she said nothing more. Was an answer hidden in her words? If so, he couldn't decipher it.

"And?" He knew he sounded far too eager. After all, it shouldn't matter what she decided. But it did.

She blinked. "And yes."

His knees went weak with relief, making him wish he had his cane. "Good." He frowned, not quite certain what his response should be in this particular instance. While Letitia had said this was the first time she'd been proposed to, it was also the first one he'd offered. "Very well." He tried to grasp a thought but his mind was blank. "We'll need to act as though it's a normal engagement."

"Of course. I'll do my best to pretend as though it's quite exciting." She glanced away as she spoke, as though her attention had already moved on to something else.

The oddest urge to take her into his arms and kiss her until her focus centered on nothing but him came over him. That would never do. He had to remember this was only temporary. While he'd gotten what he wanted, it didn't feel like it. Something was amiss.

"Within a fortnight or so, you should be able to terminate it for whatever reason you'd prefer."

"That sounds agreeable." Yet she still didn't look at him.

"I'll move forward with the plan and call upon your father on the morrow."

Her head turned sharply as her worried gaze sought his.

"My father?"

"I must ask for your hand."

"Surely I'm old enough to disregard that tradition."

"Doing so will only cause people to wonder if we are truly engaged."

Dismay fell over her features. "I suppose you're right. But I dislike deceiving him."

Nathaniel couldn't help but notice she didn't mention her mother. Or her sisters for that matter. He nodded. "I understand, but if we want to be convincing..."

"Yes, I know." She sighed. "Very well. There isn't any way to avoid it."

He took her gloved hand, his gazed locked on her. With a slow, deliberate movement, he lifted it to his lips to kiss her arm just above where the glove ended. "Until the morrow." He bowed his head and took his leave, wishing he knew where this had gone wrong.

The next morning, Mr. Fairchild stared at Nathaniel as though he'd lost his mind. "You're asking for what?"

"For Letitia's hand in marriage."

The older man continued to look at him without saying a word, his expression one of puzzlement.

Nathaniel felt compelled to offer more of an explanation. "I've come to know her over the last few weeks and found we have much in common." He gritted his teeth, disliking having to say more. "She is a wonderful lady, intelligent, attractive, and I care deeply for her." He swallowed hard at the words, feeling an odd pressure in his chest.

Slowly, much like the sun coming out from behind a cloud, Mr. Fairchild's lips turned into a grin. His eyes lit, reminding Nathaniel of the way Letitia's often did. To his surprise, the older man chuckled. "I can't believe it. My Lettie?"

Nathaniel was quite sure the question was rhetorical so he held his tongue.

Mr. Fairchild ran his finger back and forth over his upper lip as though still processing Nathaniel's request.

"My dear, Lettie." He shook his head, once again meeting Nathaniel's gaze. "I've never understood why no one sees the same amazing young woman that I do. She is bright and beautiful. She cares deeply for others and is loyal to a fault." His smile broadened again. "At last, someone understands who she really is. I confess that I am thrilled. Surprised, but thrilled all the same."

Nathaniel held a few of those same thoughts and so felt a connection with the man. He didn't understand why Letitia was still unmarried either. But he was grateful for it, and for this chance to know her.

As they worked out the details of the betrothal, guilt flooded Nathaniel. He wished he were the man Letitia truly deserved, one that would make her father proud. In truth, he was rather surprised her father was so enthusiastic about the suggested union, considering he was a second son. Yet Mr. Fairchild didn't comment on that.

What Mr. Fairchild didn't realize was how damaged Nathaniel was, inside and out. And Nathaniel didn't think it was possible to put the pieces together and make him whole.

Lettie was a bundle of nerves. She hardly knew what to do with herself. For a brief moment the previous evening, she thought she'd had the upper hand, acting as though the betrothal was of little concern to her.

Then Nathaniel had stared into her eyes as though he could see through her meager defense and had asked her to dance. Darn him. He already knew how to melt her resistance. When he'd made that ridiculous gesture of kissing her arm before he'd left, her heart had squeezed in her chest, just as it did each time she relived the moment.

It had been such a sweet, romantic gesture. Time and again she had to reminder herself it had only been a sham. A ploy. If only her family knew that. If only she could tell them.

Her mother had acted outraged at the gesture, though Lettie was fairly certain she hadn't witnessed it for herself, which was probably the reason for her upset. Rose and Dalia had been all atwitter during the carriage ride home and so delighted for her.

When Lettie's eyes had filled with tears, her sisters had been so understanding and helped her hide her upset from their mother. Of course her mother had given her another lecture on how she needed to take more care with her behavior as the duke had once again danced with Rose.

Luckily, they hadn't asked why she was so emotional. She had no idea what she would've told them. Certainly not the truth. That she longed for it to be real. That she feared she was losing her heart to the handsome captain.

Now she paced the length of her bedroom, wishing she would've thought to ask Nathaniel what time he might be calling on her father. Waiting was making her crazed.

What would her father say? And the rest of her family? She couldn't imagine their shock. She held a hand to her jumping stomach. She hadn't been able to eat breakfast that morning so great were her nerves.

Despite the fact that she'd been waiting for it, the knock on her door startled her. "Yes?" Perhaps it was only Holly come to see what she was doing.

Howard, the footman opened the door. "Your father wishes to see you, miss."

"Thank you. I'll be down directly."

As soon as he closed the door, Lettie sank to her bed, trying to catch her breath. Why was she allowing herself to become so overwrought? This was a temporary business arrangement. Nothing more. While she was sorry to deceive her family, it wasn't truly harming them in any way. Right?

She slowly rose. Her thoughts needed to stay on the girls. That was the end goal for this arrangement and it justified the means. Those reasons didn't help to settle her nerves as she descended the stairs and entered her father's library.

Her nerves worsened when she caught sight of her mother in the room as well. Somehow, that made it all the more real.

Movement from the corner caught her attention, and she glanced over to see Nathaniel standing there. His presence was incredibly reassuring. Her nerves eased as his gaze held hers.

"Letitia, I'm sure you know why Captain Hawke is here," her father said.

"Yes, I believe I do."

"The captain and I have come to an agreement, assuming you wish to marry him."

Lettie's breath hitched at the word. No, she reminded herself. This is only a temporary business arrangement. She rephrased her *father's words in her mind, repeating them over and over. And wish to enter into a temporary business arrangement with him.*

Her father's eyes narrowed at her hesitation. She'd taken too long before answering. She gathered herself with a stern reminder that she needed to pretend this was real. With effort, she smiled. "I'd be honored to marry the captain."

Nathaniel came forward and took her hand in his. By the look in his eyes, she could tell she was being less than convincing.

"Are you quite certain this is what you want, Lettie?" her mother asked. She eyed Nathaniel with what could be called suspicion.

From the expression on Nathaniel's face, he'd noted it as well.

That straightened Lettie's spine and firmed her

determination. "Yes, I have become quite fond of Nathaniel."

Nathaniel's eyes widened ever so slightly as though startled at her admission. Or perhaps it was the honesty in her words that had struck him. She couldn't help but wonder why. Surely he knew she cared for him.

A muscle bulged in his jaw before he spoke. "And I have grown to care for you as well."

Temporary business arrangement. She said the words in her mind once again, but it didn't halt the butterflies fluttering about in her stomach. She swallowed hard, trying to rein back the longing attempting to spring forth.

What she needed to remember were Alice and other girls like her.

With as much strength as she could muster, she looked back to her father and smiled. "I'm delighted with his...proposal."

Her father frowned for a moment, worry crossing his features before he returned her smile. "Very well then. It's settled." He rose and crossed to the two of them, clasping Nathaniel's hand firmly before drawing Lettie into his embrace. "Congratulations to you both."

"Thank you, sir," Nathaniel said.

Her mother rose and smoothed her skirts before drawing near. "Well then, we have much to do, don't we?" She glanced back and forth between them. "Oh, Rose needs the crystal necklace to wear with her gown this evening. Do you know where that is?"

Lettie's heart twisted. Some things would never change. She needed to remember that. "I'll find it for her."

"I'm sure you'd like to wish us well," Nathaniel said to her mother, surprising Lettie by standing up for her.

"She does," Lettie defended her mother, uncomfortable as she stood between the two. No one had ever attempted to do that before. She had no idea how to react.

"Of course." Her mother smiled, but it didn't reach her

eyes. "I'm certain we'll be seeing more of you," she said with a nod at Nathaniel.

Lettie felt the weight of Nathaniel's gaze as he said his goodbyes, but she didn't met his eyes, too afraid he'd see the secret she held deep inside—that her place in her family was also more of a business arrangement. It seemed that was what she was fated to do in her life, to serve in the capacity that most assisted others.

Why did that hurt so much?

CHAPTER EIGHTEEN

"Some are dogged and sullen-looking, and appear as though steeped to numbness in the comfortless doctrine, "What can't be cured must be endured;" as if they had acquired a certain sort of surly relish for the sours of existence, and partook of them as a matter of course, without even a wry face."

~ The Seven Curses of London

Nathaniel's anger had not cooled by the time he returned home.

"Did it not go as planned?" Dibbles asked as he followed him into the library. Nathaniel had told him of his suggestion to Letitia that they pretend to be betrothed to better pursue the group of men engaged in the selling of young girls.

"Yes, it went as planned. Her father seemed pleased, at least. Shocked, but pleased."

Dibbles waited, his hands folded before him, a sure sign he expected more information.

"The mother treats Letitia more like hired help than a daughter. She didn't offer her congratulations or any well wishes. She only wanted to know where some necklace was for Letitia's younger sister. Obviously, the *possibility* of the sister receiving an offer from a duke far outweighs an *actual* offer from a captain who is merely a second son."

"Or it's the daughter, not the suitor, who makes the difference to Miss Fairchild's mother."

Nathaniel sat heavily in his desk chair as he pondered Dibbles' point. He'd assumed Mrs. Fairchild's behavior had to do with him, not Letitia. "How so?"

"I do not know her well, but it seems to me that Miss Fairchild has a giving soul. She genuinely enjoys helping people, just as she helped Miss Alice. Her mother probably enjoys that same level of help from Miss Fairchild. Why would she want to give that up when she has four other daughters who all need something?"

"Perhaps you're right. But I would think any mother would treat a daughter as a treasure rather than the hired help."

"Indeed. Just as any father should treat a son as a treasure."

Nathaniel could only stare at the man who'd been with him for so many years.

"But the temporary betrothal is in place?" Dibbles asked. At Nathaniel's nod, he added, "You might wish to call upon your brother to share the news before he hears of it from someone else."

Nathaniel groaned. "If you think it's necessary."

"It is. The question is, do you intend to tell him the truth?"

He pondered Dibbles' question. "I don't believe so. He would only insist on knowing the details. Besides, my supposed engagement might urge him to marry as well."

A strange look crossed Dibbles' face.

"What is it?" Nathaniel asked, wondering what the butler knew that he didn't.

"There may be more to the earl's avoidance of marriage than we suspect."

"Such as?" What could it be other than not having found the right woman to both catch his interest and keep the bloodline strong, which was something their father had always harped on?

Dibbles shook his head. "I do not know. Your brother holds his secrets closely."

Nathaniel had only recently realized his brother had secrets, though in truth, he'd thought Tristan didn't care enough for Nathaniel to share them. It was certainly something to consider.

Lettie was amazed at how quickly word spread about the engagement over the next two days. People that she didn't realize knew of her existence congratulated her everywhere she went. She even ran into someone at a bookstore where she was making inquiries who wished her well.

The niggle of guilt that came with each well wish was growing, especially when they came from people she genuinely cared for.

Julia had called upon her and been so kind, suggesting they celebrate by going shopping. Explaining the entire situation was out of the question, yet guilt plagued her at Julia's excitement for her. She'd picked up Lettie in her carriage, and they'd driven to Bond Street to see Julia's modiste.

Lettie watched with interest at how Julia once again managed to convince others to do what she wanted with kindness and smiles from her footman to the bookstore owner and now to the modiste.

"Miss Fairchild has just become engaged," she told the woman enthusiastically. "I couldn't think of a better way to celebrate than to request one of your beautiful gowns for her."

Flattery was an amazing motivator, Lettie decided. She needed to remember that next time she wanted one of her sisters to do something.

"I'm so envious. Now you can move away from all

these silly pastels." Julia glanced down at another of Lettie's fawn-colored dresses as well as her own primrose gown then turned to the modiste. "What color do you think would best suit her?"

"I would suggest an emerald green," the woman said, after studying Lettie closely, much to her discomfort. "That would bring out her eyes and complement her alabaster skin."

Lettie frowned. "My eyes are hazel." She knew it was rude to argue, but what was this woman thinking? How could her eyes look good with green? And her skin was pale compared to her sisters' peaches and cream complexions. No one had ever suggested her skin was alabaster.

"No, they have a lovely green ring around the pupil," Julia argued as she looked at Lettie.

Confused, Lettie stared into the mirror in the shop. What did the two women see that she didn't?

"Please step into the back where we can take your measurements," the modiste, Mrs. Channing, directed.

Before Lettie knew what was happening, the woman had stripped away her gown, declaring the fawn-colored dress ugly, had her assistant take her measurements, then hold up a partially completed gown of deep green to Lettie.

"Yes," Julia declared as she clapped her hands in delight. "That is perfect. Can we see a blue one as well?"

Lettie continued to hold up the gown as the assistant left the room, staring into the mirror at the stranger looking back at her. The green was indeed a flattering color. But it was so different from what she normally wore that it just didn't seem like *her*.

"Julia," she whispered when the modiste and her assistant stepped away. "I couldn't possibly wear a gown like this." She trailed her finger along the silk, amazed at the way the fabric shone from the light of the window.

"Why not?" Julia asked, drawing nearer.

"I—It would draw far too much attention. I would look like an ugly duckling dressed in swan's feathers. It's not me."

Julia turned Lettie toward the mirror again, looking over Lettie's shoulder, motioning her to hold up the gown again. "Don't you see? This is you. You've been hiding all along. I think love has transformed you, inside and out."

Lettie's heart turned over in her chest as tears filled her eyes. Love. It was true. She did indeed love Nathaniel. How ironic that she'd at last found a man to care for but he didn't love her in return. She had to find a way to rein in these feelings.

This was a temporary business arrangement. She'd forgotten to say that to herself today.

But how could she possibly explain all that to Julia? The last thing she wanted to do was draw attention to herself by changing her clothing, only to break off the engagement in two weeks time. How terribly embarrassing would that be? The thought of everyone staring at her with pity made her palms damp.

"Julia—"

"What better way to make certain the captain's attention remains on you than to transform yourself? I can't wait to hear about his reaction when he sees you in this. We all need a change sometimes. Your time is now."

Your time is now.

She found repeating that phrase much more enjoyable than the other one.

Julia's excitement was contagious. Despite a nagging voice of doubt that told her all of this was nonsense since the engagement would soon be at end, she found herself nodding when Mrs. Channing returned with several other fabrics she thought would complement Lettie's coloring. It had been some time since she'd had any new gowns. When Nathaniel exited her life, perhaps these new gowns would be a good way to enter spinsterhood.

Mrs. Channing also suggested a variation to Lettie's

normal chignon, leaving the knot looser with wispy strands on either side of her face.

"Oh, that makes your eyes look even bigger," Julia exclaimed.

By the time they left the shop, Lettie's head was spinning. Would she be brave enough to wear the gown and change her hair for the next event?

Nathaniel lingered on Blackfriars Bridge as the factories closed for the day and workers started filing across to return home, hoping to catch sight of Rutter.

Langston had lost him the previous day, and the man had yet to resurface. To Nathaniel, that meant trouble. Rutter had been the key to signaling the group's movements in the past. Langston had managed to identify one or two other men involved, but had yet to map their movements. Without more information, coming across them would be pure chance.

Once again, Nathaniel acknowledged the need for more men in order to be effective at any attempt to stop those involved. Between the brothels that took the girls, the workhouses and areas such as this bridge that provided a supply of them, there were too many variables to find patterns to the movements of the group.

As far as Nathaniel knew, others ships might be taking the girls to Brussels besides Warenton's. His frustration was building as he knew girls were being taken each day. Soon the new brothel would open that was rumored to specialize in virgins. Christ only knew what that meant.

Their best hope would be to determine a way to land a bigger blow to the organization. That meant either capturing one of the leaders or severing their financial means. At this point, Nathaniel didn't have the capacity to do either. If only he could trust the authorities with this, but since Rutter had already escaped jail twice, they knew more than one person on the police force was involved.

Langston had asked around at a few of the pubs to see if anyone knew Jasper Smithby. Those he'd spoken with had denied it, but based on the uncomfortable reaction he'd received from a few, Langston had surmised the man was known but no one was willing to talk about him. He'd also tried his remaining contacts on the police department but thus far, that hadn't resulted in any assistance.

If they couldn't find Smithby, they couldn't stop him.

Nathaniel realized one other option existed that he hadn't considered until now. If he was enough of a thorn in Smithby's side, perhaps the man would come to him. That potential solution was problematic as it meant drawing the man's attention. Doing so would draw greater risk to himself, Langston, and Letitia.

Normally, he didn't mind taking risks, but not when Letitia was one of those who might be in danger. He refused to consider the chance. While becoming betrothed had offered her protection from gossip, it may have put her in more danger. He hadn't realized that until now.

"Damn." Since when was he willing to sacrifice a mission to protect one individual? Unease settled low in his belly. Since he'd grown to care for Letitia, he realized. That shifted his priorities.

Surely she'd be safe in her family's home, which was filled with people and servants. But Smithby was bold. He'd had Teddy's body dumped on Nathaniel's step in broad daylight. That was an act of a man who considered himself above the law.

Until a more obvious solution appeared, Nathaniel could only continue to watch for men who might be working for Smithby. They would be obvious by their presence in places such as this one, especially if they approached girls leaving the factory.

And if he could cause a few problems when he found some of those men, that would be all the better. He'd take a cautious approach and hope additional information surfaced.

More and more workers crossed the bridge, most of them young girls. This time, he'd selected a new spot from which to watch. He didn't want to be too predictable.

His attire had also changed with a different color jacket and hat from the last time he'd been on the street. He hoped it would make him less noticeable. Of course, there was little he could do to disguise his limp.

The hour was growing late when a man emerged from one of the nearby buildings and walked toward the bridge. Nathaniel's attention was immediately caught. He waited where he was, trying to determine what was happening from a distance. He'd promised to attend the ball where Letitia would be tonight and didn't want to risk ending up in a physical altercation with the large man. She would not be pleased if he was delayed.

Just the thought of her was a distraction. He continually reminded himself their betrothal was not real. If only his body would remember that. Some part of him seemed to believe she was now his. An odd possessiveness had come over him as the hours had passed, the knowledge that she was his—however false—growing.

Telling his brother had been more difficult than he'd expected. After all, Tristan was the one who'd brought it to his attention that people were talking. But his brother had questioned his motive for offering for Letitia. He'd pushed and prodded for the truth, despite Nathaniel's attempt to try to make it a casual announcement.

His attention returned to the man, who now spoke with a young girl. Not too far away, two other girls stopped to talk to a young street urchin. But when the lad looked over his shoulder and pointed at the other man, Nathaniel knew the two were connected. Now they were involving young boys in the scheme as well? Damn. What would they devise next?

The organization had to be stopped before it gained more ground. But how? He strode forward to see what minor problem he could create to disrupt their conversations with the girls.

Lettie descended the stairs of her home that evening, nerves fluttering. She'd been the last to prepare for the ball, as was always the case. But tonight, she'd done so deliberately. She knew her mother would be unhappy at her new appearance. The time had arrived to leave, so there was little she could do about it. Changing would delay their arrival too long.

This evening, she wore the emerald green gown the modiste had quickly finished and sent over. The design was deceptively simple—no ruffles or bows in sight. It complemented Lettie's curves without being vulgar. The neckline was lower than what she was accustomed to, but still well within the realm of modest.

Her hair was swept to the side with a soft wave along her forehead and several curled strands loose to frame her face. The only jewelry she wore was a diamond comb in her hair that her aunt had presented her with on her twenty-first birthday.

Julia had told her the secret to wearing something different was to act as though she wore such clothes each and every day, as though it were nothing unusual. But Lettie feared she didn't have the confidence to manage it, especially not in front of her family. Still, she attempted a mask of confidence along with a small smile.

Violet and Dalia's mouths dropped open as she entered the room. Their mother turned to see what had caught her daughters' attention and her jaw joined theirs. None of them said a word as they looked her up and down.

Lettie felt her mask begin to slip, prepared to return to her room and not attend the ball after all. That sounded far more appealing than listening to what her family might say.

"Oh, my," Holly exclaimed. She often saw them off as

she liked to see how everyone looked. Her eyes grew round and she came forward to walk around Lettie. "You look—"

"Where did you get that gown?" her mother asked as she continued to stare at her.

Lettie lifted her chin. "Julia and I went shopping today, remember? She helped me select it. You've always appreciated her taste. Isn't it lovely?"

"It's very...bright." Her mother frowned. "That's hardly an appropriate color for an unmarried woman."

"But Mother, she's engaged now," Violet reminded her. "This is the perfect color for a woman soon to be married."

Heat coursed through Lettie's cheeks at the lie she'd perpetrated.

"Wait until your captain sees you," Dalia whispered as she, too, circled around Lettie with a grin. "You look so beautiful."

"Thank you." The support of her sisters bolstered her courage. She hadn't expected support from anyone, especially not her mother as she didn't adjust well to change.

"I'm sorry to have kept everyone waiting," Rose said as she entered the room. She looked up from having adjusted her glove to see Lettie. "Oh."

Lettie waited, knowing that if Rose showed her even the smallest support, her mother would hold her tongue. But if Rose declared the gown wrong, her mother would join in the fray.

"Oh, Lettie." Rose stepped to one side and then the other until at last her gaze met Lettie's. "You look beautiful."

Tears of relief filled Lettie's eyes. "Thank you."

"I had no idea that color would be so becoming on you," Rose continued. "Between the glow of happiness your betrothal has brought and this gown, you are stunning."

Lettie laughed. She knew she was far from stunning. But in truth, she felt different in this gown. Or perhaps it did have something to do with being engaged, even if it was only a temporary business arrangement. She swallowed hard. For tonight, this one night, she would put away that secret. This might be one of only a handful of balls she would attend as an engaged woman rather than a wallflower. Why not enjoy it?

"Will Captain Hawke be in attendance this evening?" her mother asked.

"I believe so."

"Well..." She continued to study Lettie with a critical eye. "I suppose we shall see what he thinks of your attire."

"I know what he will think," Dalia said with a giggle. "He'll want to take you out to the garden for a private moment or two."

Violet and Rose joined in the laughter but their mother did not.

"I would take this moment to remind all of you that our behavior must be above reproach if Rose is to keep the duke's interest. Now let us be off. Your father is arriving separately."

With that, they bid Holly farewell and made their way to the carriage. As they drew closer to the Galvert's home only a few blocks away, Lettie's nerves returned. What if Nathaniel didn't like her new appearance? What if he wasn't even there?

Dalia elbowed her in the ribs. "Stop worrying," she whispered. "All will be well."

The footman assisted them out of the carriage one by one. As was her habit, Lettie lingered in the rear. Rose looked beautiful in a new soft pink silk gown, the ruffles and lace making her look like a princess. But when her sister was nearly at the door, she turned and waited for Lettie so they might walk in together.

"I will give you the same advice you so cleverly gave me," Rose whispered. "Be yourself. That is what attracted him to you in the first place." With a smile, she looped her arm through Lettie's as they made their way inside.

After greeting their hosts, they entered the ballroom. Lettie was certain Nathaniel would arrive later as he normally did. But as she approached the few steps that descended into the ballroom, Nathaniel stood waiting.

He glanced up at their approach, staring at her as though he didn't know her at first, then as though he was puzzled by the changes.

Lettie's heart sank to her knees.

Nathaniel couldn't believe his eyes. The stunning woman before him looked like Letitia, yet she didn't. The vivid emerald gown made her skin glow and turned her hair to gold. She was beautiful as she'd always been, but the differences in her clothing and hair enhanced her beauty, causing him to catch his breath.

Pride swirled with desire as he reached out his hand to take hers and escort her down the stairs. He felt the tremor in her gloved hand and reached with both hands to hold it. "You look so beautiful, Letitia."

She smiled at him, squeezing his hand in return. "Thank you."

"I am amazed. You've always been beautiful but..." He couldn't put words to his thoughts.

"You are very kind."

"No. Actually, I am not. But being with you makes it easy to be."

"Good evening, Captain Hawke," a woman's voice interrupted him.

He turned to see the woman who had been so cruel to Letitia at the first ball he'd attended this Season. He watched with pleasure as she glanced at Letitia, her eyes widening as she realized who stood next to him. "You remember Miss Fairchild, my betrothed."

The woman's mouth gaped even wider. "Betrothed? Lettie?"

"Lady Samantha," Letitia said with a cool tone.

Why Letitia even bothered to be kind to the woman was beyond him. But it gave him no small measure of satisfaction to see how astounded the woman was by Letitia's appearance.

He leaned closer to the woman. "Haven't you heard? You should never judge a book by its cover." Without a second glance, he turned back to Letitia. "Will you dance with me, my sweet?"

She smiled warmly, holding his gaze. "I would love to." She looked at the woman still standing near them as though she'd almost forgotten she was there. "Excuse us, won't you?"

Lettie couldn't have been more pleased with Nathaniel's reaction. His was the one who mattered. Leaving Samantha on the edge of the dance floor while she went to dance was a nice plus. She'd nearly reminded her to close her mouth, that it was unattractive when agape.

But she'd decided it best to hold her tongue. After all, in another month, she would return to her place standing on the edge of the dancers.

"What is it?" Nathaniel asked as he turned her slowly to begin their dance.

"What?"

"Your glow dimmed ever so slightly. I want to know the cause. Would you prefer not to dance? I realize I am not the most nimble partner."

"Oh, no. I enjoy dancing with you," she reassured him. "It is nothing of consequence." Or rather, it was only of consequence to her. But she reminded herself this was her night, and she intended to enjoy every moment of it. "Are you certain this isn't too much for your leg?"

"Not at all." He nodded at another man on the dance

floor. "Word of our engagement seems to have spread quickly." He sounded quite proud of the fact.

"Indeed. Everywhere I've gone, someone congratulates me." Her gaze narrowed ever so slightly. "How did your brother take the news?"

"Well enough."

"Did you tell him the full truth? Perhaps that would smooth things over."

"How do you mean?"

"Only that it would surely ease his worries if he knew ours was a temporary partnership."

When he stared at her in confusion, she had to wait until the movements of the dance allowed them to speak again. "You can't tell me he was pleased that you'd offered marriage to a wallflower who's seen her fifth Season with no offers. After all, you're a captain."

"I'm not the heir."

She frowned, not understanding his point. "I'm well aware of that. What difference does that make?"

"It matters a great deal."

"To who?" she asked.

"Everyone."

The emphasis he put in the word caused her to study him more closely. She knew she'd struck some sort of nerve, but for the life of her, she couldn't understand what.

The music ended, and they moved to the outskirts of the dancers. She gestured toward an alcove, hoping they could speak privately for a moment.

Nathaniel reluctantly complied.

"I believe you're confused," Lettie began. "I'm the one who was on the shelf until you—" She caught herself before she said 'proposed'. This was only pretend. And that made all the difference in the world. She couldn't allow herself to forget for even a moment. "Suggested this arrangement."

"A proposal from the likes of me is hardly worthy of

celebration. Nor does it do anything to improve your status, I'm sorry to say." His self-deprecating smile saddened her. "I'm a second son."

Anger filled Lettie at his words. "You are an amazing man. Your birth order doesn't change that. Nor does a title or lack thereof."

Nathaniel appeared taken aback at her vehemence. But she couldn't help it. How could he question for even a moment how valuable his existence was?

"How many lives did you save while earning that drawer full of medals?"

He shook his head, once again dismissing her point.

She continued on anyway. "I can only imagine the risks you took and the number of lives you saved. And you continue to do the same thing here." The pain in the depth of his eyes twisted her heart.

What had caused this doubt? She reached out to place her hand on his chest, wishing for the privacy to do more.

"You are an amazing man, Nathaniel. Not because of your name or title, but because of who you are. You prove it in your actions each and every day." The words to tell him how she truly felt were on the tip of her tongue, but she closed her mouth firmly. Those words would not aid him. More likely, they would add one more obligation to the many he already shouldered.

She hated the idea of adding to his burden when he had so many. But she wanted him to truly understand what a difference he was making in the world. In her world. For that, she would always be grateful.

"Thank you, Nathaniel, for all you've done and continue to do. You are a blessing in so many ways."

His gaze held hers for a long moment before dropping to her mouth. To her surprise, he leaned forward and kissed her. "As are you, Letitia."

Shock held her to the spot—both at his gesture and his words. How could she possibly guard her heart against this man?

CHAPTER NINETEEN

"In a recent report made to the Commissioners of Sewers for London, Dr. Letheby says: "I have been at much pains during the last three months to ascertain the precise conditions of the dwellings, the habits, and the diseases of the poor. ...where from three to five adults, men and women, besides a train or two of children, are accustomed to herd together like brute beasts or savages; and where every human instinct of propriety and decency is smothered."

~ The Seven Curses of London

"Thank you for seeing me home," Lettie said as she settled in Nathaniel's carriage. Though she feared it was a mistake, she hadn't been able to decline when he offered.

Not after the evening had been nearly perfect. She and Nathaniel had danced three times, much to her delight though she knew it was no small feat for him. Several people had visited with them, offering their congratulations. He'd spent much of the evening by her side. It had been a new experience for her.

Never mind that it was all a lie.

But she was determined to ignore that for this one night along with the danger in which she was placing her heart. Each considerate, attentive gesture he performed softened the few defenses that remained, leaving her vulnerable. Did he realize the power he now had over her?

"My pleasure. Having a few moments of privacy will allow us to update each other on our progress."

Disappointment speared through Lettie. She'd hoped he wanted to spend time together, yet since they'd entered the carriage, he was keeping her at a distance. Perhaps his only purpose in offering her a ride home was to discuss their work.

"Is your leg hurting?" she asked, wondering if it could be the cause for his sudden reserve.

"Not terribly."

Then what could be wrong?

A part of her had hoped her improved appearance would convince him to dismiss the temporary part of their agreement, that it might make him desire her.

Now she had to wonder if she'd imagined his earlier affection.

Unable to resist testing the waters, she patted his thigh with her gloved hand, lingering along the muscled length. "I hope it doesn't bother you later this evening after dancing several times."

He jolted at her touch, sending a tingle of awareness through her. Maybe he did feel something for her after all. This attempt to explore passion was new to her, and she had yet to determine how to tell if he was truly attracted to her or what she might do to make him so.

She left her hand on his thigh, waiting to see if he'd remove it. Where her sudden bravery came from, she didn't know. Perhaps it was a side effect of her new appearance or their betrothal. Surely being engaged had advantages, even if the arrangement was temporary. A certain intimacy was one of those, wasn't it?

Her heartbeat raced at the thought.

Nathaniel shifted in his seat as though uncomfortable. Before she could decide if she should remove her hand, he placed his own on top of hers, molding her fingers over his thigh. Though several layers of cloth separated them, she could feel the heat of him, and it stirred something deep inside her.

"Letitia?" he whispered as his gaze caught hers in the soft glow of the carriage light, his expression unreadable.

"Yes?"

"Would you care to come home with me so we might discuss matters in a more...comfortable setting?"

Heat pulsed through her entire body. Though she hoped his question meant what she thought it might, she was equally terrified it did.

Yet what if this was her one and only chance to have more time with him? "That is an excellent notion."

He tapped twice on the roof of the carriage, apparently signaling the driver to deliver them to his home instead of hers. He kept his hand on top of hers as they changed course but made no attempt to take her into his arms.

Confusion reigned as she tried to quell her hope. Maybe he only wanted to discuss what she'd learned about *The Book of Secrets*. Unfortunately her efforts to discover anything had been less than successful. Should she tell him so now?

But when Nathaniel moved his hand to rest on her thigh, all such thoughts flew out the window. The intimacy was unmistakable though what he intended was still uncertain. Did she dare hope he'd make her his in full? She told herself she could barely feel the warmth of his fingers through the silk gown and the layers beneath it, but that didn't matter. Heat spread upwards from the single point of contact.

She drew a long, slow breath, reminding herself that she need only enjoy the moment.

Before long, the carriage drew to a halt, and they exited the conveyance and entered his home.

"Good evening, Miss Fairchild." Dibbles greeted her with a warm smile as he opened the door.

"How are you this fine evening?" she asked.

"Well, thank you. May I say you look lovely?" he asked as he took her cloak.

"Why thank you, Dibbles."

Nathaniel escorted her into the drawing room. Dibbles followed, lighting the fire previously laid before taking his leave, closing the door behind him.

Nathaniel poured her a glass of sherry and himself some brandy before joining her on the long settee before the fire. Despite it being June, the fire's warmth was welcome, as were the flickering flames, which created a cozy glow in the room.

"I believe our engagement has been a success thus far," Nathaniel said as he settled beside her but not touching her.

That he'd used the word 'engagement' didn't escape her notice. "It seems so. My mother is still adjusting to the news."

"Her eldest daughter becoming betrothed is a significant event."

"Perhaps." She knew there was more to it than that, but she didn't care to discuss it. Not tonight. Moments like these were not to be wasted on such things.

She took a sip of sherry as the silence grew long. Uncertain what other topic she could raise, she said, "Unfortunately, I have discovered little about the book. The bookstores I checked with that specialize in such things don't have it and couldn't offer any information on it."

"I appreciate you trying."

"I'm not giving up yet. There are more shops I intend to visit as time permits."

He smiled. "I wouldn't expect anything less." His gaze shifted to her hair, and he reached out to finger a loose strand alongside her face. "You truly do look lovely tonight."

"Thank you. I went shopping with Julia today. Her modiste suggested a few changes. Now that my mother believes me to be engaged, she can no longer insist I wear pastels." She bit her lip before she shared any other ridiculous details. Her nerves were getting the better of her.

"That makes me even more grateful we're...betrothed." He leaned closer and captured her lips.

The kiss seeped through Lettie, the taste of brandy swirling through her, the heat of his mouth sinking into her very bones.

Nathaniel paused, taking her glass from her and setting it with his on the side table. Then he drew her into his embrace, his intense gaze sweeping over her. "I've been wanting to do this since you walked into the ballroom."

"Truly?" she whispered breathlessly.

"Truly. I wanted to kiss you." He pressed his lips to hers, making her long for more. "To touch you." He drew a finger along the neckline of her gown, sending a shiver of desire through her. "To taste you." He bent low to kiss the bare skin just below her throat, causing her to gasp.

She leaned her head back, reveling in both his words and the feelings his touch evoked. "That is lovely."

"You are lovely. I would like to make you feel the same." His heated gaze tangled with hers before he kissed her once more, his mouth even hungrier than before. His tongue swirled with hers as his hands rested on her waist, squeezing gently. He raised them to where the curve of her breasts began, and she caught her breath. The tip of her breasts tightened, making her wish he'd touch her there.

"You do," she whispered, wanting to give as much as she received and kissed him once more. She had no intention of being the only one to experience passion this time.

She raised her hand to his whisker-rough cheek, loving how different it felt from her own. Then she ran her hands along the breadth of his shoulders, marveling at his strength. She slid a hand inside his jacket, anything to get closer to his heat.

He unfastened the buttons of his jacket and shrugged it off, then did the same with his cravat and vest, leaving him in his shirtsleeves.

"Letitia, you drive me mad." He breathed in near her ear, sending a shiver of longing down her spine. "You smell of orchids. I can't get it out of my mind."

"Oh." She had no idea a scent might be so engaging, but then as she drew in his woodsy fragrance, she knew it to be true. "I like how you smell as well. It reminds me of the woods, but with a slightly foreign layer to it."

He smiled down at her before kissing her again, his tongue seeking hers, building her passion even more.

"I want you so badly," he murmured.

Relief mingled with the desire flooding her body. She'd wondered, worried even, whether any man would ever feel that way about her. For so long, she'd thought something was lacking in her that made her unattractive to men. Now she realized she simply hadn't met the right one. She couldn't imagine feeling like this with anyone except Nathaniel. The idea of another man touching her like this was unimaginable.

She eased back to look into his eyes, her heart expanding with love. But she held back the words, certain this wasn't the time for them. "I want you as well. So very much."

He studied her closely. "Do you know what you're saying?" The heat in his gaze curled her toes. The lines of his face had sharpened, becoming more defined. Did her desire change the way she looked as well?

Then his question sunk into her passion-fogged brain. "Yes." And she did. There was no doubt in her mind. Right or wrong, she wanted Nathaniel. And somehow their being betrothed, even though it wasn't real, helped to make it right. That, along with the way she felt here, in his arms. "Yes," she said again, her heartbeat speeding at the thought of what was to come.

"Letitia." He said her name with such reverence that it

brought tears to her eyes. As she tried to blink them away, he touched her face. "Tears?" he asked, worry clouding his tone.

"Of joy," she reassured him, offering a smile to prove it. "I feel so much when I'm with you. I'm overwhelmed in such a lovely way."

"There is more to come," he promised. He rose, gesturing for her to remain where she was while he went to lock the door. When he returned, he held out his hand to draw her to her feet. As she stood, he turned her so she faced the fire, her back to him. He wrapped his arms around her tight, nuzzling the sensitive area of her neck. "May I remove your gown?"

The question melted her inside. That he'd ask rather than assumed was one more gesture that swept away her last defense. "Please."

How odd to feel a man's fingers at the laces of her bodice. There was no mistaking how different they were from Cora's. He soon lifted the loosened bodice over her head then pressed kisses along the bare skin of her shoulder. Layer by layer, he disrobed her, kissing and touching as he went until she was trembling with desire.

At last he turned her so she stood facing him in only her thin chemise and pantaloons. The look of reverence on his face swept away her nerves. With one finger, he reached out to touch the tip of her breast through the thin fabric, and she jerked in reaction. How could his touch there pluck a string that led to her very center?

Unable to bear it, she wrapped arms around him, kissing him as though she never intended to let him go. He returned the kiss, matching her bold passion with his own.

His hands spanned her waist and caressed her curves. They moved down to the flare of her hips, back to her bottom, then returned to cup her breasts, leaving heat in their path. Desire shot through her, weakening her knees, building layer upon layer as he touched her everywhere.

He eased her down to the settee where his mouth

shifted to her neck, then lower still to the top of her chemise. He tugged down the chemise to reveal her breast, lifting it free, the pink tip startling to see in his masculine hand. Even more startling was his kiss there, licking and suckling until her head fell back. Her body filled with liquid heat.

She gathered herself, wanting to give him the same pleasure, anxious to feel his bare skin against hers. With clumsy fingers, she unbuttoned his shirt, parting the linen to reveal his muscled chest and the slight covering of hair that trailed down his abdomen. Fascinated at the sight, she ran her hands along his torso, loving the feel of him beneath her hands. Eager now, she eased off the shirt, loving how his shoulders bulged with corded muscles. He moved his arms to shed his shirt, and she couldn't help but trace the shifting muscles.

"You are so different than me," she whispered in amazement.

He laughed. "I am very glad for that."

"As am I," she said with a smile. "You're so strong."

"Then why do you make me feel so weak?" he whispered, as he drew her once more into his arms. "I can't get enough of you."

"That is lovely to hear." She felt his smile against her skin and thought she'd never experienced anything as wonderful.

"So beautiful," he murmured as he caressed the length of her curves.

"You understand my body far better than I," she whispered. "What do you feel when I touch you?" She touched his chest, lingering at his male nipple.

His abdomen rippled inward, giving her a thrill.

"Letitia, your touch is nearly more than I can bear. I want you so much."

She loved knowing that he felt that way, loved the power it gave her to touch him even more. But when it came time to remove the rest of her clothing, she hesitated, all her insecurities coming forth. She wriggled out of her pantaloons then slowly reached for the hem of her chemise, unable to find the courage to take it off as well. What if—

Nathaniel placed his hands over hers, helping her remove this last barrier. His moan as his reverent gaze swept along her bare body was all the reassurance she needed.

"Perfect," he declared and drew her into his arms.

She blinked back tears once again, amazed at how he knew exactly what to say and do to make her feel so good. Love swelled through her, giving her the power to reach for him, to move her bare skin against his. His chest felt marvelous, the coarse hair adding another layer of sensation. His kisses made her head spin, and she was barely aware of him laying her back against the cushion of the settee. His body partially covered hers, his pants an unwelcome obstruction between them.

Her hands roamed across his broad back and explored every hill and valley. His weight on top of her felt wonderful. His hands lingered here and there, alternately making her sigh and catch her breath. He explored her curves, seeming to enjoy every inch of her and, for the first time, she was grateful for her figure.

When his fingers grazed the top of her thighs, she couldn't help but moan in response. Heat pooled low in her belly as he touched the juncture of her thighs, moving to her center, working magic as he went. As he caressed her intimately, her hips bucked in response, his fingers lingering until she could stand it no more.

"Nathaniel?" she whispered, needing him desperately.

He rose and took off his pants, his manhood springing free. She knew her eyes went wide at the sight, but he was so large.

Her gaze shifted to the jagged scar on his thigh, still red and puckered. She ran her hand along it, wondering at the terrible pain he must've endured. He sucked in a breath as his body moved in response. Curious, she shifted her fingers to touch the hot length of his manhood, amazed at its velvety softness.

"Letitia," he ground out as he grabbed her hand. "Your touch undoes me."

When she looked up at his face, she could see the desire etched there, echoing her own.

Releasing her hand, he lay down, his body once again on hers. He kissed her long and hard, his hands trailing a path along her heated flesh that had her writhing beneath him. He nudged her legs to settle between them. Then the tip of his manhood brushed against her, and all thoughts fled at the foreign sensation.

As though reading her thoughts, he eased back to look into her eyes. "Trust me?"

"Yes." That much she knew beyond doubt.

Before her nerves could return, he kissed her again, his tongue dancing with hers as his manhood pressed against her, demanding entrance. With a growl, he lifted her knee slightly and eased inside.

Letitia froze at the pain of the invasion. This was nothing like she'd imagined. But desire swelled once more as the pain faded, and she couldn't help but tilt her hips.

He dropped his forehead to hers as he stilled. He seemed to be fighting for control, but over what? With an oath, he sheathed himself, filling her completely. The sensation was remarkable, to have part of him inside her, to be joined in this way. She couldn't help but move again, trying to understand how they fit.

"Oh, Christ. Letitia," Nathaniel groaned. He drew back only to enter her again, the feeling more amazing than before. He repeated the movement, her body finding the remarkable rhythm he set.

And it was glorious. The movements layered on top of each other, overwhelming her senses. From his kisses, to his breath against her neck, to the weight of him, to the feeling of him inside her. Tightness coiled deep within her as her world shifted. Her hips thrust beneath his as though racing toward a common goal.

"My sweet," he murmured as he reached down to touch her intimately, caressing her until that coil sprung free.

Her bottom lifted off the settee and he thrust deep inside her, his body shuddering with hers. She'd never felt such a shattering of her soul, only to have it gather above her, stronger than before, then floating down inside her once again, bringing with it a completeness she'd never experienced.

Nathaniel made her complete, she realized. Words of love came to her lips, but she held them back, uncertain of their welcome.

She could feel the strong beat of his heart slowly easing along with his breath. He shifted onto his elbows to look down at her, the concern in those blue eyes touching her heart. "Are you...well?"

"I am amazing." She shook her head. "I had no idea."

"Nor did I," he whispered.

"What?" Confused at his response, she studied him.

"Nothing," he said and closed his eyes for a moment before moving to her side to take her into his arms, his hands still caressing her.

He held her tight, as though he cherished her, but she knew something was on his mind. She could feel it. Her heart ached as she said a little prayer.

Please, please don't let this be our one and only night together.

CHAPTER TWENTY

"...I found [the room] occupied by one man, two women, and two children; and in it was the dead body of a poor girl who had died in childbirth a few days before. The body was stretched out on the bare floor, without shroud or coffin. There it lay in the midst of the living, and we may well ask how it can be otherwise than that the human heart should be dead to all the gentler feelings of our nature, when such sights as these are of common occurrence."

~ *The Seven Curses of London*

Nathaniel's mind whirled as he walked toward the site of the new brothel the next morning. He wanted to study the place, take measure of its size, and with luck, see if anyone walked in or out of it. Unfortunately, his mind was not on the task before him.

Something significant had shifted last night when he'd taken Letitia as his own. Something he wasn't certain he could name.

He'd never felt as he had with her. Their union hadn't been only physical. It almost felt as though she'd taken a piece of him when they'd made...

Christ. He didn't even know what to call it. But as crazy as it sounded, he now held a piece of her inside his heart.

He had the ridiculous notion that from this point forward, nothing would ever be the same.

He couldn't afford to permit such a sentiment. If he allowed himself to care for Letitia, to grow fond of her, then he had to wonder if she might feel the same, which meant he *mattered* to her.

Nothing in his previous existence made such a notion possible.

Nothing.

Yet even as he tried to call a halt to these bizarre concepts and feelings now holding him captive, part of him feared it was impossible. It was too late. The damage had already been done and there was no going back.

Nor did he want to.

Because there was nothing to go back to. His world had been empty before Letitia.

His steps slowed as he realized exactly what was bothering him. Fear.

In all his years of service, it was an emotion he'd rarely experienced, at least not for himself. He'd feared for the lives of his men, for the civilians that were often caught in the crossfire, but never for himself. Never for his own feelings or his life. He'd always understood he was expendable. His father had drilled that into his head as far back as he could remember.

He felt completely unworthy of any affection Letitia might have for him. He was afraid he didn't deserve it, and he would fail her in some way, causing her to turn her back on him. He feared that once she truly knew him, without the mask he presented to the world, she would no longer care about him.

Wouldn't it be wiser to walk away now before that happened?

In all honesty, he wasn't certain he had the strength of will to do so. Where did that leave him?

With no true options.

Unable to solve the problem, he tried to put aside his

roiling emotions and focus on the task before him.

He settled in a spot across the street from the two-story building. If this was truly the brothel, it was smaller than the one he'd rescued the other girls from. The exterior of the house was in far better shape. A fresh coat of paint had recently been applied. The front garden was well tended. It looked much like the other houses on this street. Perhaps that was the point.

He studied the front door. At first glance it appeared to have a wrought-iron front common in the neighborhood. But as he studied it closer, he realized it was far thicker than normal. The windows had decorative ironwork as well but painted white to be less noticeable. It seemed they were taking precautions to guard what they kept inside.

That meant he needed to do all he could to prevent the girls from arriving. But unless he knew where they were coming from or when, it was a difficult task.

Which brought him back to Jasper Smithby.

He was the true target. Finding Rutter or any of the other men involved in the operation would be helpful, but not nearly as effective as finding Smithby.

After spending some time watching the front door, he made his way around to the back, taking the long way around, hoping his presence had escaped notice.

The rear garden was equally well enforced. The fence was in good repair from what he could tell at this distance. The plants offered few places to hide. What he'd accomplished at the other brothel would be far more difficult here.

He pondered drawing nearer, wondering if the reward would be worthy of the risk. He could do no good for anyone if he was caught.

He sensed a presence behind him but turned too late. A sharp jab in his ribs stopped him.

"What have we here?" a man's voice asked.

Nathaniel didn't bother to answer. He bent low and spun on the ball of his good foot in the opposite direction of where he'd felt the jab. He raised his forearm to shove away the man's hand holding the knife.

Surprise was on his side as he drove his fist into his assailant's middle. He gripped the man's wrist tightly, forcing him to release the knife and it fell to the ground. Keeping a tight hold on his wrist, he spun again to twist the man's arm behind him. With a hard shove, he wrenched the man's arm up his back.

"Ack! Damn ye," the man muttered.

"Next time, be careful who you disturb," Nathaniel warned. "Just because you hold a weapon doesn't mean you have the advantage."

The man only groaned in response.

"Who sent you out here to confront me?" Nathaniel demanded.

"No one."

He wrenched the man's hand up farther, causing the man to squawk with pain.

"Who?"

"Rutter."

Nathaniel sighed in disappointment and eased back on his hold. He'd hoped Smithby was inside so he could confront the man. But perhaps this was for the best. He didn't want to underestimate Smithby, so he needed to be prepared when he confronted him. "Perhaps you'd be so kind as to give Rutter a message."

"What would that be?" The man glanced over his shoulder warily at Nathaniel.

"Tell him I'm coming for him and all of his other associates." Nathaniel lifted the man's arm one more time, causing him to grunt, but he wanted to make certain his message was heard. "If I were you, I'd make myself scarce after I gave him that message. Otherwise you and all of your cohorts will find yourself in prison or worse. Do I make myself clear?"

The man nodded, sweat beading his brow from the pain.

"Off with you." Nathaniel released him, giving him a shove in the process.

The man sent a fearful glance over his shoulder. His gaze dropped to his knife.

Nathaniel moved to stand on the blade. The man shot him a disgruntled look but hurried toward the rear entrance of the house.

Nathaniel glanced around to make certain no one else waited in the shadows to pounce. Seeing no one, he picked up the knife and ambled away. He chose not to hurry. If anyone was watching, he wanted to make it clear he wasn't frightened. He hoped he'd made an impression on the other man.

He couldn't help but berate himself as he walked. Letitia was even more of a distraction than he'd realized. Under normal circumstances, he'd have noted the man's approach and avoided being threatened with a knife.

Somehow he needed to keep his thoughts on the task at hand and not on his pretend betrothed.

Lettie waited at the party that evening, beginning to worry as Nathaniel had not yet arrived. She'd known he was going to investigate the new brothel that morning. In all honesty, she wasn't certain what that meant. Surely he didn't intend to go inside, did he? She realized now that she should've asked more detailed questions.

Something about Nathaniel's confidence tended to put her fears at rest when she was with him. It was only when she'd had more time to think about what he'd told her that she considered the danger he'd truly encounter.

Last night had been amazing, something she thought she'd never experience. Nathaniel had been so considerate. His desire had fueled her own.

Though she was well aware of the risk they took, it was difficult to believe that they'd be caught or that she might end up expecting a babe. Becoming pregnant seemed to be something that often took many months to accomplish based on what little she knew from acquaintances who'd been married a year or more and had yet to produce a child. Perhaps it was naïve of her, but she wanted one more night with Nathaniel before they parted.

The modiste had sent another gown, this one in a unique turquoise blue she absolutely adored. Oddly enough, she found wearing these brighter colors lifted both her mood and her confidence. Cora had swept her hair back in a loose chignon once again, leaving curls tumbling from the back knot.

She'd wanted to look her best but only for Nathaniel. Had her changed appearance pushed him to make love with her or would it have happened anyway because of their betrothal? In truth, it didn't matter. She was grateful for whatever the cause.

"Miss Fairchild," Nathaniel's brother greeted her as he came to stand beside her, much to her surprise. "I trust you are well this evening."

"I am, thank you. And you?" she inquired after curtsying.

He nodded, his gaze skimming the crowd as though little there caught his interest.

Lettie considered him more closely. She hadn't yet decided if she cared for him or not. There was a cold reserve about him that made it difficult to decide if he was anything like Nathaniel. From what little she could tell, the brothers were not especially close. She wondered why.

"Have you seen my brother?" he asked.

"I'm hoping he arrives soon."

The earl's gaze narrowed as he studied Lettie. "Do you happen to know where he spent the day?"

Lettie shifted her gaze to the crowd, unwilling to look him in the eye when she lied. "I'm not certain." It was true in part as she didn't know the address of where he'd been.

"I confess I'm becoming concerned with his secretive

life."

"Oh?" She nearly winced, hoping he wouldn't ask her for details. What could she possibly say?

"I called by his home this afternoon, but he wasn't there. Dibbles seemed uncertain where he was."

"Does your butler always know where you are?" Lettie couldn't help but defend Nathaniel.

The earl stared at her, obviously astounded she'd question him in such a manner. She frowned as doubt assailed her. Perhaps that wasn't proper behavior when addressing an earl. In truth, she wasn't quite certain as she hadn't spoken with any before.

As the silence grew overlong, Lettie wondered if she should apologize.

"No, I suppose he doesn't."

She gave a little sigh of relief that his tone didn't sound angry. Before she could respond, her mother arrived at her side with Rose in tow. Lettie could've groaned but that wasn't proper behavior either.

"Lettie, dear, I hope I'm not interrupting," her mother said as she looked up at the earl.

As Lettie made the introductions, she could nearly see the earl stepping back and his defenses going up. For a moment, she almost felt sorry for him.

Her mother handled the introduction to Rose, who looked equally uncomfortable. Lettie could only guess this was some attempt on her mother's part to show the duke he wasn't the only man with a title interested in Rose.

Nathaniel's brother made his excuses as quickly as possible and departed. Lettie couldn't blame him. How annoying it must be to be hunted like a fox the way matchmaking mothers hunted potential husbands for their daughters.

Soon after his departure, her mother dragged Rose to some other person she wanted her to meet. Lettie was glad not for the first time that their mother had never pursued a husband for her the way she did with Rose. Her poor sister looked quite miserable as well as embarrassed.

Her mother hadn't said anything more about Lettie's betrothal, much to her surprise. Maybe somehow, she sensed an actual marriage would never happen. The thought disquieted Lettie.

"Another lovely gown," Julia exclaimed as she came to join her. "That color is amazing on you."

"Thank you." Lettie smoothed the simple lines of the fitted gown. "Not a ruffle or bow in sight. I am quite beside myself."

Julia beamed. "Nothing pleases me more than seeing others happy. I'm so glad you like the gowns. Your hair is lovely as well."

"You are too kind."

"Oh," Julia said, "before I forget, I meant to tell you I spoke with my father about the book you mentioned."

Lettie's interest perked up immediately. She felt as though she was letting Nathaniel down by her lack of progress on her part of the investigation thus far. "Had he heard of it?"

"Unfortunately no, but he said if anyone in London knows of it, it would be Oliver Bartley, Viscount Frost. Father says he specializes in ancient texts and lives in London. I can obtain his address if you need it."

"That is very helpful. I can't thank you enough," Lettie said with a smile. Now if only Nathaniel would make an appearance so she might share it with him.

She'd nearly given up hope as the evening progressed, but at last he arrived. One glance at his face told her something was amiss.

"What's happened?" she asked as soon as he was close enough to hear her.

He frowned as though puzzled by her question. "Good evening."

"Yes, yes. I do think we're beyond normal pleasantries. I can see by your expression that something has occurred."

He studied her as though curious at her comment.

"Truly?"

"Of course." She couldn't help but look him up and down. "Are you well?"

"I thought you said we were beyond normal pleasantries."

Lettie had the sudden urge to throttle him. "I believe you know what I am asking."

A small smile ticked up the corner of his mouth. "Remarkable."

"What is?"

"You seem to have developed the same awareness Dibbles has when it comes to events in my life."

"Then something did happen." Lettie stared at him, heart pounding at the idea that he'd had a near miss. "What was it?"

"All is well, I can assure you. I had a minor skirmish with one of Rutter's men outside the new brothel."

"Did you go inside?" She was appalled at the thought of him putting himself in such danger again.

"Nothing of the sort. Merely observing, I assure you. But they didn't seem to care for me loitering."

When he stopped as though he'd reached the end of the story, Lettie held her patience by a thread. "And?"

He glanced at her as though he'd forgotten what they were discussing.

"Nathaniel." She hoped he'd heed the warning in her voice.

He shook his head. "Nothing untoward. The man made threats. I removed the knife he held and made threats of my own. End of conversation."

Lettie closed her eyes for a moment. Then she drew a deep breath and moved to stand before Nathaniel, taking both his hands in hers. Surely such bold behavior was permitted when one was betrothed. She stared deep into his blue eyes. "You are not to take such risks. What if that man had succeeded? I wouldn't even know where to search for you." The fear the thought gave her sent cold shivers chasing down her spine. "If you won't take care for me, please do so for those girls. Without you, no others will be saved."

An emotion Lettie couldn't name shifted in Nathaniel's eyes. She couldn't read his expression, couldn't tell if he was taking her words to heart.

She did the only other thing she could think of. "Please?" she added as she squeezed his hands.

It was as though all the other people in the room fell away. The intensity of his stare made her desperately want to wrap her arms around his neck and kiss him. To try to show him what he meant to her since her words didn't seem to have any effect on him.

At last, he gave the barest of nods. "I will try."

"Thank you." She drew a deep breath, feeling as though she'd won a small battle. Perhaps next time he considered doing something dangerous, he'd remember her plea. "Your brother asked after you earlier."

"Oh?" Nathaniel appeared surprised at the thought.

"I also learned from Lady Julia that a man named Oliver Bartley, Viscount Frost, might be our best hope to learn more about the book."

"Frost?" Nathaniel's surprise turned to shock.

"Do you know him?"

"Yes, he was in the Navy with me." He shook his head. "I had no idea he was a scholar."

"According to what Lady Julia learned from her father, he is quite an expert on ancient texts."

"Shall we call upon him on the morrow?"

Lettie's heart lifted. "I would like that very much." She'd been afraid he'd insist on pursuing this information without her.

"Excellent." He reached out to tuck her hand in the crook of his arm. "I look forward to it." With a glance around, he added, "I wish there was more privacy at these events." Then he looked into her eyes, and the hidden meaning there stole her breath.

"As do I, Nathaniel. As do I." She couldn't help her smile anymore than she could help the love spilling out of her heart.

CHAPTER TWENTY-ONE

"Great social grievances are not to be taken by storm. They merely bow their vile heads while the wrathful blast passes, and regain their original position immediately afterwards."
~ The Seven Curses of London

Late the next morning, Nathaniel made his way to the Fairchild's home to pick up Letitia so they could venture to Frost's residence. He couldn't have been more surprised when she'd told him the name of the man who might have information on the book.

Frost had been a good friend during their years in the service. He'd chosen to retire well over a year before Nathaniel had been injured. Frost had been involved in a terrible skirmish in India and, from that time on, hadn't been quite the same. Nathaniel didn't know what had occurred, but it had changed Frost. Despite that, Nathaniel knew he was intelligent, clever, and an honorable man. That was all that truly mattered.

Last he'd heard, Frost's parents still lived. The man was quite wealthy but with only a minor holding awaiting him, he'd followed his desire to serve his country, wanting the chance to make a difference. He and Nathaniel had had much in common.

As he handed Letitia into the carriage and sat beside her, he couldn't resist settling close to her. Hadn't he told himself that he needed to maintain some distance? Yet he was like a moth to flame when it came to her. Staying away was impossible. Now that he was with her, the voice in his head questioned why it had seemed imperative that he keep her at arm's length.

And when he looked into those hazel-green eyes of hers, he had no answer. Certainly she was a distraction, but she also made his life worth living. Her gaze dropped to his lips, and she leaned forward the tiniest bit, a nearly imperceptible movement that stirred him to no end.

What could he do but comply? He met her halfway, her lips soft under his. He kept a firm hold on his desire or rather tried to. Now was not the time to allow it free rein.

"Thank you," he whispered.

"For what," she whispered back, a small smile playing about her lips.

"For the kiss. I do not think I will ever grow weary of them."

"Nor will I." Her smile bloomed, right alongside something in the recesses of his heart. He nearly lifted his hand to rub at the unfamiliar sensation.

Soon they neared the neighborhood where Frost lived, and the carriage drew to a halt.

The large, three-story, stately mansion was in excellent repair. Nathaniel could only think that it was a large house for one man to rattle around in.

He gave his card to the footman who answered the door with Lettie at his side, hoping Oliver was home and would see them.

After a brief wait, the footman returned to show Nathaniel and Letitia into the massive library. The room was more than twice the size of a normal library for such a house. Both he and Letitia stared at the numerous, floor-to-ceiling shelves of books as they walked into the richly appointed room.

"Hawke. What an unexpected surprise," Frost said as he came around his massive mahogany desk piled high with more books, a wary look in his eyes. "To what do I owe the honor?"

"Good to see you," Nathaniel replied, clasping his friend's hand with both of his own, truly pleased to see him looking well. He decided to ignore his wary expression for now. "We heard from an acquaintance that you are quite knowledgeable on ancient texts, so we've come to request your expertise."

"Oh?" Frost frowned as though less than pleased. He was a bit taller than Nathaniel with straight dark hair that swept to the side. His piercing green eyes had always given Nathaniel the impression he saw far more than the average man. His dark suit was modest but still showed he was in fine shape.

Frost's gaze shifted to Letitia, and Nathaniel made the introductions.

At the mention of their betrothal, Frost's brows raised. "Congratulations to both of you. I heard you were injured," he said as he gestured toward the chairs before his desk. "I trust it wasn't too serious."

"A bullet struck my leg, shattering the bone. Unfortunately, the doctor could do little to knit the bone," Nathaniel said, well aware of Letitia's curious regard. "I was discharged once they determined I wouldn't make a complete recovery."

"I'm sorry to hear that but pleased you've returned to London. I must also apologize for not seeking you out upon your return." Frost looked away as he said it as though uncomfortable. "I don't leave home often."

"I can see why," Letitia offered. "You have a beautiful residence."

"Thank you." Her words seemed to put him at ease once again. "May I ask you how two met?"

Nathaniel shared a look with Letitia. "The first

occurrence was at Blackfriars Bridge."

"That's an odd place," Frost commented, obviously curious at the idea.

"It's a rather long story we will share if you have a few minutes. But it so happens that we met again that evening at a ball."

"*You* attended a ball?" Nathaniel could only smile at Frost's skepticism. "I remember you swearing off such events."

"My mother badgered me into going for my brother, but who did I see?" He touched Letitia's gloved hand briefly. "Miss Fairchild. We've since joined forces to fight a terrible problem."

Nathaniel could only hope he'd caught Frost's interest. The man seemed to have become a recluse since leaving the service and didn't appear overly pleased to see him.

"What problem would that be?" Frost asked, a hint of caution in his expression.

While information on the book would be helpful, Nathaniel needed more help than that. Having another military man he knew he could trust with his life would be an incredible advantage. But he no longer knew if Frost was interested in fighting battles or saving lives. Not after all he'd seen and done. Perhaps his return to civilian life had put him firmly on the side of peace. And firmly inside his house.

Nathaniel waved his hand in dismissal. "I'm not here to worry you with such things." He hoped that by building Frost's curiosity, he'd be more likely to aid him. It was a bit like fishing. Offer a little morsel and jiggle it to see if he took the bait and hook. "Our true purpose here is to inquire as to whether you have any knowledge of *The Book of Secrets*?"

"*The Book of Secrets*," he repeated as he glanced about the room as though running the name through his mental files. "That sounds vaguely familiar." He picked up a pen from the desk and jotted the title down on a piece of paper. "Do you happen to know the author?"

Nathaniel shook his head. "We only know it is an old text supposedly giving the owner fantastic powers."

"A book that gives power?" Frost chuckled. "Sounds more like something to be found in one of those romantic novels that have become so popular of late."

"Don't you believe in romance, my lord?" Letitia asked.

Frost smiled politely. "I believe in knowledge, first and foremost." He glanced back at the title he'd written on the paper. "I know I've seen the name referenced somewhere. If you could give me time to conduct some research, I should be able to offer more. It might help if I knew to what it was in reference."

Nathaniel weighed his options, wondering if he'd built up the man's curiosity enough to draw him into joining their forces. He glanced at Letitia to see if she'd give her opinion. At her nod, he looked back to Frost. "Have you read a recent book called *The Seven Curses of London*?"

"I tend to avoid anything published in this century."

Nathaniel bit back his disappointment. Obviously he had no interest in the problems currently plaguing London. Nathaniel didn't blame him. He'd served enough time on behalf of his country. Such a cause would more than likely not interest him. "Never mind then." He glanced to Letitia. "We should be on our way. We've obviously interrupted your work." He gestured toward the numerous books and papers littering the desk.

"What sort of curses?" Frost asked.

"The sort that plague our city," Letitia offered even as she rose to leave. "Neglected children, professional thieves. That sort. But as Nathaniel said, we should leave you to your work."

Nathaniel hid a smile as he realized his clever fiancé had understood what he'd been attempting to do. She'd given a little more information to wet Frost's interest.

"How are the two of you involved in such a thing?"

"We are attempting to stop a very small part of it,"

Nathaniel said as he stood as well.

"The neglected children curse specifically," Letitia added. "But this goes even further. These men are tricking young girls—" She covered her mouth. "I'm terribly sorry. I'm certain you aren't interested in such crimes."

"Crimes? That involve tricking young girls? To do what?" he asked.

Nathaniel only smiled. "We've taken far too much of your valuable time." He turned toward the door, taking Letitia's hand to tuck it under his arm.

"You're going to leave without sharing the details?" Frost asked.

Nathaniel turned back, feigning surprised. "Well, as Letitia said, it doesn't seem as though it's anything that would interest you. But these men offer young girls fraudulent positions, only to take them to brothels."

Letitia faced Frost as well. "Some of the girls are only eight years of age. The men must be stopped."

Frost shook his head. "While one hears of such terrible crimes, it is far easier to continue on to read the next article in the newspaper rather than dwelling on how something like that could happen in our own city."

"I stumbled upon the situation by accident. Otherwise, I might not have investigated it any further myself," Nathaniel admitted.

"What does *The Book of Secrets* have to do with the young girls?"

"Supposedly, one of the leaders of this nasty group claims to have gained powers through the book. I hope that by learning more about it, we might find some way to counter it."

"That seems highly unlikely."

"True," Nathaniel said with a nod, "but sometimes it's not the true power an object contains, but the belief others have in it that creates the power."

Frost seemed to consider his words. "Give me a day or two, and I will see what I can discover."

"Excellent," Nathaniel said, hiding his disappointment. He'd hoped Frost would insist on joining them. But all was not yet lost. Perhaps the information he uncovered would stir his outrage enough that he'd assist them.

Letitia gave Frost a curtsy. "It was a pleasure meeting you, my lord."

"The pleasure is all mine." As Letitia moved into the foyer, Frost caught Nathaniel's gaze. "She is special, is she not?" he whispered.

Nathaniel glanced to see Letitia had left the room. "Indeed she is. I fear I don't deserve her." He couldn't help the note of honesty that slipped out. It was the truth.

"After all you've been through, you deserve happiness. Have no doubt of that."

"What of you, Frost?" Nathaniel asked as he studied his friend. "How have you adjusted to civilian life?"

"What's to adjust to?" He gave the cocky grin Nathaniel had seen so often over the years. But somewhere in the depth of his eyes, a darkness told of something more.

"In all honesty, it's been a hell of an adjustment for me," Nathaniel admitted. "Far more difficult than I expected."

Frost lost his smile. "It has?"

Nathaniel nodded. He couldn't help but run his hand along his injured thigh. "Still can't sleep. Hearing loud noises makes me—" He paused with a shrug. "You know."

"I do," Frost admitted.

"Well, if you ever want to speak of it, I'm here. And I look forward to hearing what you learn about the book. The sooner the better as the men involved are nasty and have big plans."

"I'll see what I can do."

Nathaniel clasped his shoulder. "Good to see you. Thank you for your time."

As Nathaniel walked out with Letitia, he had to wonder

how Frost had adjusted—or if he truly had. He knew his friend didn't move about in social circles. He hadn't married. It didn't sound as if ever left his house. That left only those piles of books to keep him company. What kind of a life was that?

In truth, it wasn't so different from the empty life he'd led prior to meeting Letitia. She'd dragged him reluctantly amongst the living. He couldn't imagine life without her now. That was a frightening revelation. The only thing he could do was draw Letitia closer to his side, determined to enjoy the short time they had together.

CHAPTER TWENTY-TWO

"I trust and hope that what is here set down will not be regarded as mere tinsel and wordy extravagance designed to produce a "sensation" in the mind of the reader. There is no telling into whose hands this book may fall."

~ The Seven Curses of London

Lettie returned home to find chaos had ensued. Several servants rushed back and forth through the foyer as she removed her gloves. She raised a brow at the footman who'd opened the door for her, but he shook his head, apparently not privy to the cause of the commotion.

"Holly," Lettie called out as her sister hurried down the stairs. "Whatever is going on?"

"Didn't you hear?" Holly asked, her eyes wide with excitement. "The duke proposed."

"He spoke with Father?" Lettie clarified. While Holly made it her business to find out what was going on in their household, she didn't always have her facts correct.

"Yes. Rose is over the moon. I'd best hurry or Mother will be calling for me again." Holly dashed through the foyer toward the rear of the house on some errand.

Excitement filled Lettie as she hurried up the stairs to

find Rose. Her sister had been waiting for this day all Season long. As she neared Rose's bedroom, she could hear the voices of her mother and sister.

"But why wouldn't we have a celebration for Lettie as well?" Rose asked.

Lettie's steps slowed at the sound of her name.

"Her engagement to the captain is hardly on the same level as yours to a duke. Besides, your sister is nearly on the shelf. Who knows if they will actually marry. In fact, I have to wonder what the captain's intentions truly are."

"What do you mean?"

"Yes, Mother. What do you mean?" Lettie asked from the doorway. While her expectations of her family's reaction to her engagement compared to Rose's were realistic, that didn't mean this conversation didn't shock her.

"Lettie, dear," her mother exclaimed. "Where have you been? Your sister has the most exciting news."

Lettie's gaze shifted from her mother to Rose. The look of sympathy on Rose's face was nearly more than she could bear.

She didn't know what to say. Nothing she said or did would change her mother's opinion. She decided to do what she'd always done—ignore her mother's comments.

Lettie kept her gaze on Rose as she moved forward to give her sister a hug. "You must be so happy. I wish you the very best, Rose."

"Thank you." Rose's eyes filled with tears, and she blinked rapidly.

"I hope you and the duke have a long and happy life together." Before her mother could say any other hurtful words, Lettie walked out.

Once she'd shut the door behind her, she leaned back against it, trying to catch her breath. What could she say when her mother had spoken the truth? Lettie would have to deal with all the "I told you so" comments once she broke off the engagement with Nathaniel. She hadn't considered the details of exactly what would occur when it ended. There would be more pain than she'd anticipated.

No longer having Nathaniel in her life would be nearly unbearable, but she'd also have to listen to her mother continually say such things. Somehow, Lettie was certain her mother would never let her live this down. Then there would be the pitying glances from those who'd so recently congratulated her.

Maybe it was time to make plans for her future. She'd write a letter to her aunt to see if it would be possible to join her. At the very least, some time away would be welcome once she'd said goodbye to Nathaniel.

She swallowed hard, trying to keep the lump in her throat from becoming a sob. After all, she'd agreed to the temporary business arrangement. It would never do to start believing it was real, even if Nathaniel had briefly made her think it meant something.

"Greetings, Langston," Nathaniel said as the older man entered the library after being announced by Dibbles the next day.

"Good evening, Captain." He took a seat before Nathaniel's desk, his expression somber. "I fear I bring bad news."

"Oh?" Nathaniel braced himself.

"Six girls have gone missing from the Whitechapel Workhouse off Charles Street. All between the ages of eight and ten."

Nathaniel shoved back from his desk. "Damn."

"Indeed. I just returned from there and came directly to tell you. I thought you'd want to know."

"Any additional information as to their whereabouts?"

"Only that a man of medium build and dark hair, wearing a bowler hat was seen lurking about of late."

"Which describes half the men in London," Nathaniel

bit out with frustration.

Langston shook his head, obviously discouraged. "Some days it feels as though we take one step forward and three steps back." He rubbed his hands over his face. "Those poor girls," he muttered.

"Indeed. We need more men," Nathaniel said, trying to think of how they could gain additional help. "Can you try your contacts on the police force with this latest development to see if they'll now take a greater interest in the problem?"

"It's certainly worth a try. I'll advise them we have a witness who can attest to the missing girls."

"We'll do all we can to rescue them. We have an excellent idea of where they are taking them."

"Yes, you're right. This battle is not yet over," Langston agreed, seeming to regain some hope.

"Far from it." Nathaniel felt obligated to do all he could to improve the man's spirits though he knew exactly how he felt. "I am awaiting word from someone who might be able to give us more information on *The Book of Secrets*."

"That would be helpful. If Smithby thinks he has some power over the others, or at the very least, has convinced them of such, knowing more would give us an advantage."

"Exactly. Have you found out when the brothel opens?"

"In two days' time. More men are guarding the place now."

"So they're expecting something or someone? Interesting. We must think of something we could do that would be unexpected."

Langston frowned. "What might that be?"

"I don't know yet. But I will see what I can put together."

"Shall I continue to have the woman at the workhouse report any unusual activity?"

At Nathaniel's nod, Langston added, " If only we had

others like her who were willing to share information."

"For a fee," Nathaniel said dryly. Nobody was willing to do something for nothing. That seemed to be part of what was wrong with the world. But wishing it were different didn't make it so.

Langston sighed. "I, for one, appreciate your efforts and the money you put towards the cause."

"And I appreciate yours. We wouldn't have gained this much ground if not for your assistance." Nathaniel paused but felt compelled to offer a warning. "The more we threaten Smithby's existence as well as his men's, the more dangerous this will become."

"I realize that," Langston reassured him. "I am aware of the risks we take and face them willingly."

"Don't take any unnecessary ones," Nathaniel warned. "Your life is just as important as that of each girl."

Langston raised a brow. "I would suggest you remember the same. Especially now that you're betrothed."

Nathaniel nodded. "I will keep that in mind." The image of Letitia came to the forefront of his thoughts. Not that she was ever far from it. He still worried about how much of a distraction she was. That he wasn't thinking clearly because part of his thoughts were focused on her.

Yet how could he not do so? He was engaged to her, whether it was temporary or not. She was in danger as well, simply by her association with him. He had to assume Smithby and his cohorts, including Rutter knew who he was. They certainly knew where he lived since they'd dumped Teddy's body on his back door. His staff was still fearful after that discovery.

Langston rose to his feet. "I'll ask the woman to remain extra vigilant. I'll send word if I can gain assistance with the police force. And if I can discover anything more about the brothel, I will advise you."

"Perhaps instead of going directly to the brothel, you might find a pub in the area. The men guarding it will be thirsty after their shifts are over." Nathaniel handed Langston some money. "Buy them a pint or two and see if it loosens their tongues. That might be more beneficial to us at this point than watching the brothel."

"Excellent idea." Langston stuffed the coins in his pocket. "I'll send word when I learn more."

"I'll do the same." Nathaniel hoped they had some sort of break soon. Otherwise it would be too late for those poor girls.

Nathaniel waited at Blackfriars Bridge for Frost just before luncheon the next day. His friend had sent a message telling him he'd uncovered some information he thought worth sharing.

Nathaniel had requested they meet here, partly to see if Frost would venture out of his house and partly to show him some of the young girls who crossed this bridge each day as they shuffled to and from work. Perhaps seeing them would prompt Frost to become more involved. He could only hope so.

He'd advised Frost to wear his oldest suit. No doubt his friend would think his request odd. With the brothel opening soon and more girls missing each day, Nathaniel was getting desperate to find some way to stop Smithby.

At this hour, little traffic clogged the area, so he anticipated easily seeing Frost's arrival. Sure enough, Frost strolled down the street directly toward him as though he knew precisely where Nathaniel waited near the end of the bridge.

"I assume you have a reason for wanting to meet here," Frost said as he glanced around.

"Have you ventured to the bridge before?"

"Can't say that I have."

"It provides an excellent view of St. Paul's," Nathaniel said as he gestured toward the cathedral in the distance.

"I doubt that's why you wanted to meet here."

Frost's timing couldn't have been better. The noon hour had arrived, and the masses of girls who worked in the factories on the other side of the bridge started their trek home for a quick bite to eat. Nathaniel hoped that by Frost actually seeing the girls, he'd be more inclined to aid them with more than information on the book.

Nathaniel kept his gaze on the young girls as he spoke. "Smithby and his crew are taking girls anywhere from ages eight to twelve, occasionally older girls as well, depending on their condition. The girls who work in the artificial flower factories don't seem to be in danger."

"Why is that?"

Nathaniel pointed toward a group of girls just exiting the bridge. "See how gaunt they look? Their teeth are discolored, their noses chafed. That comes from using arsenite of copper for the green parts of the flowers they make."

"Isn't that poisonous?" Frost asked, obviously taken aback at the thought.

"Indeed." Nathaniel continued to watch as people of all shapes and sizes, mainly girls, passed by.

"Have you considered going after the other end of their operation?"

"What do you mean?" Nathaniel asked.

"The men who frequent brothels are numerous, but surely those who request children are fewer. Exposing them or merely threatening to would surely slow Smithby's business. Nothing like striking them at the source of their money."

"That is an excellent idea," Nathaniel agreed. "But I don't have enough men to attempt such a feat. There is only Langston and myself."

"And Miss Fairchild."

"Yes, but I am doing my best to keep her at a distance from the worst of this. It's far too dangerous."

"How is that working for you?" Frost asked with a

smile as he studied Nathaniel.

"Not well. She insists on remaining involved despite the danger."

"She must be a special lady." Frost glanced away, leaving Nathaniel to wonder at his thoughts. "As to the book about which you inquired, I can advise you that it is indeed an ancient text thought to be written in the thirteenth century by Albertus Magnus. Some would argue whether he is truly the author of the entire text or only a portion of it."

"Should I have heard of Magnus?" Nathaniel asked. The name sounded vaguely familiar but he couldn't place it.

"He was a member of the Dominicans and an admirer of Aristotle. He served briefly as a bishop and was well-known for his negotiating skills and his knowledge of physical science. Some purport him to have been an alchemist and magician. He had much to say on the power of certain stones. He discovered arsenic and other chemicals."

"Do you have any indication as to what *The Book of Secrets* contains?"

"Information on those stones as well as certain herbs. Beyond that, I cannot say."

Nathaniel shook his head in frustration. "We need a copy of the book to truly understand how Smithby might be using it."

"I have reached out to a few private collectors I know to see if they have it or any knowledge of it." Frost shrugged. "I'm sorry I'm not more help."

"You have been. A random piece of information could prove to be vital. I appreciate your efforts more than I can say." Nathaniel studied his friend. "I had no idea you were such the scholar."

"I have always had a great affection for books. They're far more reliable than people. Something my grandfather passed down to me, I suppose. He left me his collection, and I've enjoyed expanding it."

By now, the river of people crossing the bridge had slowed to a trickle. Nathaniel was relieved he hadn't seen Rutter or any other men speaking to the girls walking by. He motioned for he and Frost to return the way they'd come.

"Let me know if your search uncovers anything more," he suggested. A glance ahead revealed a familiar man escorting two young girls toward a hackney. "Damn."

"What?" Frost asked.

"That man ahead of us. He's one of Rutter's men, and he's taking those two girls." Nathaniel didn't bother to say goodbye. Instead, he rushed forward as best he could with his injured leg. But in his hurry, he failed to see another man approaching from his left until it was nearly too late.

"Leave off," the approaching man demanded with a snarl.

A quick elbow to the gut took away the man's breath and stopped him in his tracks. Nathaniel continued to limp forward, reaching his original target just as he and the girls arrived at the hackney.

"Release them," he demanded.

The man turned in surprise then glared at Nathaniel. "This ain't none of yer affair." He gestured for the girls to step into the hackney, but both girls stopped to stare at the arguing men with wide eyes.

"If he told you he has a high-paying job for you, he's lying," Nathaniel informed them. "The only position he has is one in a brothel. Isn't that right?"

He saw the fist coming out of the corner of his eye and dodged it, nearly losing his balance when his thigh protested at taking his full weight.

The man he'd struck earlier grabbed Nathaniel's arms from behind in an attempt to subdue him. Before Nathaniel could do more than twist to escape his grasp, Frost joined the fray, landing a perfectly placed blow to his face. The man dropped like a rock to the ground.

Nathaniel gave Frost a quick nod to thank him for his assistance before turning back to the man with the girls. Except the girls were hurrying away.

"Tell Rutter he needs to find a new line of work," Nathaniel ordered. "I'd suggest you do the same. Inform him that each girl he attempts to take will cost one of the lives of his men. Do I make myself clear?"

The man scowled, glancing back and forth between Nathaniel and Frost. At last he nodded then backed up slowly before pivoting to hurry away.

Nathaniel drew closer to the hackney driver. "Next time a man is attempting to take young girls with him, make sure they're his daughters. I wouldn't want you to be accused of providing transport for girls being abducted."

The grizzled old driver sputtered a denial.

With a shake of his head, Nathaniel added, "If I receive word of you hauling girls from this area, your life will be the forfeit."

He nodded and slapped the reins, jerking the hackney forward.

"What an exciting life you lead," Frost said, sarcasm edging his tone as he brushed off his clothes and flexed his hand. "I had no idea."

Nathaniel scoffed, straightening his hat. "Books sound like a much safer hobby. Thank you for your assistance."

"Do you encounter this sort of violence often?"

"More of late, unfortunately."

Frost held Nathaniel's gaze for a long moment. "Feel free to call upon me if you need assistance. Meanwhile, I'll see if I can discover who among the *ton* might have an appetite for such a thing."

A spark of hope lit inside Nathaniel at having more assistance fighting this battle. He reached out to clasp Frost's shoulder. "I truly appreciate that."

"I'll be in touch."

Nathaniel nodded then watched Frost walk down the street. Perhaps they'd be able to stop that damned brothel from opening after all. He would call upon Lettie and tell her the good news.

Lettie had hoped to hear from Nathaniel by now. At the very least, she'd expected him to update her on how Alice fared.

Wondering if she might learn something more that could aid them, she decided to consult the Seven Curses book again only to realize her father must still have it in his library.

With a sigh, she ventured downstairs to retrieve it, hoping to avoid her family if possible. She'd kept to her room for the past two days with the excuse that she didn't feel well. It wasn't a complete lie, but it had more to do with her roiling emotions than her physical wellbeing.

The hallway was quiet, and she peeked into the library, only to find her father at his desk. She quickly backed away, not wanting to disturb him.

"Lettie?"

Reluctantly, she returned to the doorway, attempting a smile. "Yes?"

"Come in. Your mother said you haven't been feeling well." He rose and came around the desk, his brow creased with concern. "How are you faring?"

A lump filled her throat at his genuine concern. The urge to tell him everything, from her attempts to help neglected children to her temporary business arrangement with Nathaniel to what her mother had said all came to the tip of her tongue. Still, she hesitated.

"What is it, dear?" he asked, putting his arm around her shoulders. It had been a long time since he'd held her thusly. The familiar, comforting scent of his bay rum cologne mixed with the faint scent of cigars tugged at her, bringing to mind similar times from her childhood.

He leaned back to study her. "Is it the excitement over

Rose's engagement? Takes a bit of the attention away from yours, eh?"

"Well..." She bit her lip, wondering how best to explain it without sounding as if she resented Rose's good fortune, because she didn't.

"Pay the rest of our family no mind." He whispered in her ear, "Especially your mother."

That admission loosened her tongue. "Why does she dismiss me so easily?"

"She doesn't," he said with a shake of his head. "Quite the opposite. I think it's only that she can't imagine managing your sisters without you. You've been her rock since Rose was born. She has never been quite sure what to do with all your sisters, especially since they've needed her far more than you ever did."

Lettie considered his words, wondering if they might be true.

He released her to cup her face with his hands, holding her gaze. "Please know that I couldn't be more pleased with your young man. Though Rose seems to care a great deal for her duke, he's a bit of a cold fish if you ask me." His eyes lit with a smile. "But your captain has passion. The look on his face when he spoke of you told me just how much he truly cares for you. I believe the two of you have something special. That is incredibly rare."

Lettie's eyes filled with tears as her heart wrenched. Oh, if only that were true. She didn't know what her father had seen in Nathaniel's expression, but she knew the truth.

Her father smiled all the broader, obviously assuming his words had pleased her. "Ignore your mother, Lettie, for I know your union is going to make you happy. Nothing could please me more."

"Please you more than what?" her mother asked as she entered the room.

"To see our Lettie feeling better." He winked at Lettie.

"Oh?" Her mother studied her closely. "Well, I'm sure the captain would rather wait to see you until you're fully recovered."

Lettie frowned, uncertain to what her mother referred.

She waved her hand in dismissal. "I told the footman to tell him you weren't receiving visitors."

"Mother, why wouldn't you ask me before doing so?" Lettie couldn't hide her frustration.

"I think I know what's best for my daughter," she protested.

"And I know I'm old enough to make such decisions on my own." The idea of Nathaniel calling upon her only to be sent away was terrible.

She hurried out of the room, determined to pay him a visit. , putting her father's misguided notions out of her mind.

Perhaps Nathaniel had new information to report. After all, they had a business arrangement, and she needed to fulfill her end of the bargain.

And perhaps her father's notions weren't so misguided after all. Maybe he had seen something in Nathaniel's expression she'd missed. If there was anything she could do to convince him that their arrangement be more than temporary, she would do it.

A future with him was worth fighting for.

CHAPTER TWENTY-THREE

"The law takes account of but two phases of human existence, the child irresponsible, and the adult responsible, and overlooks as beneath its dignity the important and well-marked steps that lead from the former state to the latter."

~ *The Seven Curses of London*

Lettie glanced out the carriage window as Nathaniel's home came into view. They drew to a halt, and the footman appeared at the door.

"Miss, I believe I saw the captain step into his carriage with another man. What would you like to do?"

"Follow him, please," Lettie requested. "Perhaps I can speak with him at his next stop."

The footman did as she bid, and they were soon on their way once again. Lettie watched curiously, wondering where Nathaniel might be going and with whom he traveled. Soon she realized they were headed for the docks. The only reason for him to venture here was because of the investigation. Had he discovered something? The idea made her all the angrier at her mother for sending him away.

When the carriage stopped again, she opened the door

to alight before the footman could assist her.

"You may proceed home, Howard," Lettie advised him as she watched Nathaniel leave his carriage a short distance away and start down the street. Unfortunately, he hadn't yet seen her. "I'll have the captain take me home."

"But, miss—"

Lettie waved him away. "Have no worries. I'll be fine." She hurried after Nathaniel, not wanting to lose him in the crowded street.

She'd never before visited the dock and couldn't help but look about at the unfamiliar sites. People walked with purpose here as though intent on their business. Men with dirt-smeared faces hauled goods on their shoulders. Carts piled high with crates and barrels passed. More men came in and out of stores she hadn't realized existed, such as biscuit bakers and sail makers. Smoke lingered in the air, no doubt a result of the factories near the docks. Between the smoke, the sea air, and the biscuit maker, her nose twitched.

She glanced ahead, looking for Nathaniel, only to realize she'd lost sight of him. Concerned, she hurried forward, searching the throng for his dark bowler hat. The limping rhythm of his step should've made him easier to find, but still there was no sign of him.

Nerves dancing down her spine, she slowed, wondering if he'd entered one of the many stores or warehouses. People brushed by her, staring rudely, making her all too aware that she looked and felt completely out of place here. She should've kept a closer watch on him. Swallowing back the fear in her throat, she turned slowly, still searching but to no avail. Her carriage had departed, which made retreat impossible.

She breathed deep, trying to slow the trickle of panic chilling her. Now what should she do?

Nathaniel studied the door of the warehouse a short distance from where he and Langston stood. "Are you certain this is the one?"

Langston consulted a piece of paper he withdrew from his pocket that contained the address of Smithby's warehouse. "Indeed. How shall we proceed?" He'd finally roused the interest of his former superior at the police department when he'd provided proof of the girls recently missing from the workhouse.

The police had already been following Smithby's movements and knew of his warehouse but had not uncovered the information Nathaniel and Langston shared with them. Based on all Langston told them, they'd decided to raid both the brothel and the warehouse—the former for underage girls and the latter for illegal goods.

Nathaniel had doubts as to whether they'd actually do as they said, but he kept that information to himself.

"We'll wait for the police to arrive," he told Langston. "If we have a chance to go inside along with them, we'll take it. I don't want Smithby to slip away or all will be lost."

"I hope Chief Inspector Calver honors his agreement to send men to the brothel as well," Langston said as they eased into a doorway two buildings away to wait.

Nathaniel smiled. "I have a contingency plan in case they don't." He'd already learned not to rely on the police based on their lack of action the past few weeks as well as their failed attempts to keep Rutter in prison.

"What would that be?"

"I stopped by Arlington Street Church earlier. They were holding their weekly women's meeting. I spoke with the leader, a Mrs. Bellany, and advised her of the situation at the brothel and how innocent girls were being held there. She and the other women were outraged. They are gathering women's groups from two other churches and going to the brothel in large numbers to demand the girls' freedom by whatever means necessary."

He only wished he'd thought of it before. There would be well over thirty women standing outside the brothel united in the cause of gaining the girls' freedom. That was the sort of interest the brothel madam would not appreciate.

"Brilliant." The look of appreciation on Langston's face made Nathaniel's smile broaden.

Until he saw Rutter moving toward the warehouse door. His heart stopped as he realized who was at the tall man's side. "Letitia."

"What?" Langston followed Nathaniel's gaze. "Isn't that—"

Before he could utter another word, Nathaniel rushed forward only to pause and turn back to Langston. "Stay here. Wait for the police. Tell them I'm inside with Miss Fairchild so they don't use unnecessary force."

"But, Captain—"

Nathaniel didn't wait to hear his protest but ran as best he could, using his cane, toward where they'd disappeared into Smithby's warehouse. All he could think about was Letitia. How had she come to be in Rutter's clutches? It made no sense.

No. That wasn't true. He knew it was his fault. He should've told her more of what was happening. His efforts to protect her had only put her in more danger. He'd stopped by her house earlier, but when her mother had said she wasn't feeling well, he hadn't taken any other action. He should've left a message, informing her of his whereabouts. Or insisted on seeing her, however briefly. He should've done *something*.

Instead he'd continued home. Langston's arrival advising him of the upcoming police raid had changed his plans for the day. But if he'd warned her before of Smithby and Rutter—told her what they were truly capable of—perhaps she would've kept her distance instead of following him to the docks.

He drew a deep breath, forcing back the hot ball of

panic in his gut. He wouldn't—couldn't—allow anything to happen to her.

The door was unlocked, much to his relief. He strode in as if he owned the place, trying to determine a plan as he went. The wide-open room contained piles of goods, some draped in canvas, some heaped in crates. His gazed skimmed the room, not perceiving any immediate threat. Several men lingered in the corner near where a man sat at a large desk, along with Letitia and Rutter.

She stood facing the desk with her back to him alongside Rutter, who held her arm.

"Release me at once." The anger in her voice reassured him that she was well. At least for now.

He need only keep her that way.

"Ain't you a fiesty one," the man at the desk said with a grin. "Where did you find her, Rutter?"

"She's with me," Nathaniel said as he limped toward them, relying heavily on his cane in part because his damned leg hurt but mainly hoping to convince the men he wasn't a threat.

Two of the men rushed toward him, knives drawn, as Rutter spun to face him.

"You," Rutter said, eyes narrowed. He gestured for the two men to hold their positions. "I knew you had to be around here somewhere if this one was." He jerked on Letitia's arm.

Her eyes met his, wide with worry. The sight of her unharmed allowed him to breathe again. He drew as close as he dared until Rutter pointed at him.

"Stay back," the man demanded.

"Who are these people, Rutter?" the man at the desk asked, gesturing for Rutter to move aside so that he could see Nathaniel. "What the hell are they doing here?"

"That one," Rutter said as he gestured toward Nathaniel, "is the man who's been causin' us so many problems." He glanced at Letitia. "And I've seen this one with him."

Nathaniel cursed under his breath. How could he not have taken greater care? He'd known they might be watching him and therefore see Letitia in his company.

"Let her go," he demanded. "Your quarrel is with me."

Rutter glanced at the man behind the desk then shook his head. "Neither of you are goin' anywhere."

"Jasper Smithby, I presume?" Nathaniel asked, easing closer.

The man's brows rose. "The one and only." He glanced between Nathaniel and Letitia. "You must really care for her if you're risking coming in here."

Nathaniel held Letitia's gaze, hoping she knew it was true. Why hadn't he told her before? He had to determine a way to free them both so could tell her.

Drawing his resolve, he turned to study the contents of the warehouse more closely, realizing many of the goods must be stolen based on Smithby's other business pursuits. "Your interests are quite diversified. Virgins and silk. Tea and opium."

"You're a ballsy one, aren't you?" Smithby asked as he rose from his chair to stand before his desk, his cold blue eyes studying Nathaniel.

"Let's kill him while we have the chance," Rutter suggested. "He ain't nothing but trouble."

"I've come to make you an offer," Nathaniel continued as though Rutter hadn't spoken. As though two armed men weren't standing guard directly behind him.

"Oh? What would that be? Doesn't seem like you're in a position to offer much."

Nathaniel could only hope the police would arrive at any moment. If he could stall a few minutes more, he and Letitia might make it out of here alive. "If you release the girls and stop abducting them, I'll walk out of here and leave you alone. But if you insist on continuing to deliver them to brothels, I'll see you dead."

Smithby laughed. "I'll have to refuse your offer. Those girls make me a lot of money." He pointed at the men behind Nathaniel with their knives at the ready. "Besides,l you're not much of a threat at the moment. There's only one of you."

Letita stomped on Rutter's toe, evading his grasp as he cursed, and rushed to Nathaniel. "No, there's two of us," she boldly informed Smithby.

Yet before Nathaniel could take her hand, the men behind him took hold of each of them, one wresting the cane from his hand.

Nathaniel's stomach tightened. As grateful as he was to have her at his side, he wished she weren't.

"Enough of this," Smithby said. "You're costing me money. Get rid of them." He nodded at Rutter who stepped toward Nathaniel and Letitia, a snarl on his face.

Before he could draw closer, Nathaniel jerked his arm free from the man behind him and struck Rutter, sending him stumbling back. Then Nathaniel spun on his good leg to punch the man behind him and shoved him sprawling into his companion.

As the man caught his balance and rushed forward, a loud commotion sounded at the door. He turned at the sound to see the cause.

"Coppers!" the man exclaimed and ran toward the rear of the building.

Rutter glared at Smithby. "I told ye we should've killed them."

"Then do it," Smithby snarled back. He grabbed some papers off the desk and ran toward the back, leaving Rutter standing there in surprise, hesitating.

That was the moment of delay Nathaniel needed. He moved in front of Letitia to protect her then struck Rutter again, this time in the jaw.

"Nathaniel," she cried out as Rutter regained his balance.

A policeman caught Rutter before he could take action while several more policemen arrested the other men who hadn't yet escaped.

"Are you all right?" Nathaniel drew a trembling Letitia into his arms, torn between the need to hold her and the need to give chase after Smithby. But he was no longer the best man to catch the villain, not with his injured leg. The need to reassure himself that Letitia was safe took precedence over catching Smithby.

Langston emerged from the group of officers entering the warehouse and hurried toward them. "Are you both well?"

"Yes, but Smithby escaped out the back."

Langston called for several policemen to accompany him as he rushed toward the rear of the warehouse.

Letitia laid her head on Nathaniel's shoulder, returning his focus to her. "Oh, my goodness," she muttered.

"Letitia." Words failed him at the relief he felt. "I'm so glad you are unharmed. I should've warned you, told you about—"

She leaned back to look into his eyes as she put her finger to his lips. "Shh. This was not your fault. And I am glad I was here. I couldn't bear it if anything happened to you."

When tears filled her eyes, his heart filled as well, overflowing with his love for her. He couldn't deny it any more than he could deny her. The chaos in the warehouse fell away as he held her gaze.

"Letitia, I love you so very much. I cannot imagine my life without you."

"I love you too, Nathaniel." Her tears spilled over. "You are an amazing man."

"We are amazing together. But I am far from perfect. You should know that more than my leg is damaged." He paused, uncertain how to explain it to her.

She lifted up on her toes to kiss him. "Nothing is wrong that we can't make stronger together."

"I couldn't have said it better." He gently wiped a tear from her cheek. "I know I asked you once already, but this time I am suggesting a permanent arrangement. And it would have nothing to do with business. Will you marry me?"

"Yes." Her smile rivaled the sun as she beamed up at him. "I'd be honored to."

He drew a shaky breath, hardly able to believe his good fortune. "The honor would be all mine." The curses and shouts around him brought him back to reality. "Let us step outside while the police do their job."

"Does that mean you'll be retiring from this endeavor since the police are involved?" she asked as he retrieved his cane then drew her through the warehouse and out the door.

"One can hope, though I have doubts they are capable of stopping Smithby."

Once they'd stepped outside, she turned to face him, her expression serious. "You must take care. I cannot imagine a life without you, Nathaniel. I refuse to consider it."

He smiled. "Good as I feel the same. Believe me, I will proceed with the utmost caution." He drew her into his arms. "Your family will have to manage on their own. Do you think that's possible?"

"They'll learn."

"Then how soon can we marry?"

She laughed. "Not nearly soon enough." She rested her hand along his cheek. "I love you, Captain Hawke."

"And I love you, soon-to-be Mrs. Hawke. I would very much like to bring you home so that I may show you just how much you mean to me."

"An excellent idea." Heat darkened her eyes and fanned the flame that burned deep within him, all for her. "Let us be on our way."

That was a request Nathaniel was eager to fill. How quickly his life had changed in a few short weeks. The woman at his side had made him whole, inside and out. He intended to spend the rest of his life showing her how grateful he was. Somehow he'd find a way to prove to her and himself that he deserved her love.

The next evening, Letitia waited impatiently at the Taft's ball for Nathaniel's arrival. Each moment they spent apart felt like an eternity. As far as she was concerned, they couldn't be married soon enough. Nathaniel was doing all he could to speed the process.

A familiar prickle of awareness ran down the back of her neck. Before she could turn, Nathaniel arrived at her side.

"Where did you come from?" she asked. "I've been watching the entrance for you."

He smiled, his gaze sweeping over her face in that thorough manner that told her he cared. "I entered through the garden to avoid the crush."

"Any news?" she asked, anxious for an update.

"Still no sign of Smithby. Rutter remains in custody, though I expect somehow that will change." The look of frustration on his face came as no surprise. "The madam of the brothel has been arrested as well."

"And the girls?"

His expression eased. "They've been returned home. I fear that for some of them, the police arrived too late. Their lives have already been changed, and not for the better."

"That's terrible. But Mrs. Bellany from the Arlington Street Church and the other ladies have promised further assistance to all of the girls, right?"

"Yes, thanks to your suggestion. They were picking out a name for their new organization when I spoke briefly with Mrs. Bellany this afternoon. Something about the Society of Women Assisting Young Women in Need." His pleased smile warmed her heart.

"She was thrilled at my suggestion to have them offer help on a more permanent basis." Lettie couldn't help but grin. When she'd set out to make a difference, she'd never dreamed she'd have so much reach. Over thirty women had volunteered thus far, and together, they could truly change lives for the better.

"Alice has been reunited with her family as well. They're moving to my brother's estate as her father is now employed there."

"Excellent. I suppose that means there is an opening at Madam Daphne's for a new apprentice. Perhaps we can find someone together to fill it."

"Have I mentioned how proud I am of you?" Nathaniel asked as he held her gaze.

"Once or twice."

"How about how much I love you. Did I tell you that?" His heated gaze along with the words made her tingle.

"Several times but feel free to repeat yourself. I promise not to complain." She took his hands in hers, facing him. "Have I mentioned how much you matter to me?"

Nathaniel blinked at her. "You have. I am still adjusting to that. After all those years of hearing I didn't, it may take several reminders."

"Lucky for you, I am available to remind you each and every day for the rest of our lives." She lifted his hand and kissed the back of it. More than anything, she wanted to show him how much it was true.

"I believe it is beginning to sink in," he whispered, his cobalt eyes full of promise.

"Lettie. Whatever is wrong with you?" Her mother's stern reprimand had Lettie's cheeks heating.

"Mother—"

"Displays of affection are completely inappropriate, especially in public. Now please go and tell Dalia that she may not speak with that terrible Mr. Brover any longer. The man has no prospects."

"Good evening, Mrs. Fairchild," Nathaniel said, the stern note of his voice warning Lettie how he felt about her mother speaking to her thusly.

"Captain," her mother responded coolly before glaring at Lettie who had yet to release Nathaniel's hands.

As Nathaniel started to say something more, Lettie squeezed his fingers. "Mother, I'm speaking with my fiancé at the moment. Why don't *you* speak with Dalia?"

"But—" she sputtered.

"I believe this dance is ours, Letitia." Nathaniel nodded at her mother. "Excuse us."

Lettie could only smile up at him as they walked away. "Thank you."

"For what?"

"For giving me the heart to stand up for myself."

"If I matter, that means you do as well," he said. "It's only fair."

"Indeed. I never realized that loving the Hawke would be so easy. I love you, Nathaniel. Always and forever."

"Always and forever," he repeated solemnly as he drew her into his embrace.

THE END

OTHER BOOKS BY THE AUTHOR

Victorian Romances:

Trusting the Wolfe, a Novella
Book .5 of The Seven Curses of London

Unraveling Secrets, Book I of The Secret Trilogy

Passionate Secrets, Book II of The Secret Trilogy

Shattered Secrets, Book III of The Secret Trilogy

Medieval Romances:

A Knight's Christmas Wish
Falling for A Knight Novella, Book .5

A Knight's Quest, Falling for A Knight, Book 1

A Vow To Keep, Book I of The Vengeance Trilogy

A Knight's Kiss, Book 1.5 of The Vengeance Trilogy

Trust In Me, Book II of The Vengeance Trilogy

Believe In Me, Book III of The Vengeance Trilogy

If you'd like to know when a new book is released, I invite you to sign up to my newsletter to find out when the next one is released: http://www.lanawilliams.net

If you enjoyed this story, please consider writing a review!

29694026R10184

Made in the USA
San Bernardino, CA
26 January 2016